Hungry River
A Yangtze Novel
Third Edition
Millie Nelson Samuelson

In the midst of the 1900 Boxer Rebellion riots in China, Nils and Lizzie Newquist attempt to flee to safety down the treacherous Yangtze River. When rebel troops capture them, a fierce-faced commander takes one look at them and their children, then shouts to his men, "Where are the foreign devils? I see only white Chinese. Release them!"

Hungry River tells the story of this daring family struggling to survive in war-tormented China – a story highlighted by their granddaughter Abbie's modern-day journal entries. Adventure, romance, danger and tragedy are all part of their story. But so are faith, hope, love and triumph. The sequels are *Dragon Wall* and *Jade Cross*.

Cover photo: A Yangtze River gorge in pre-1950s China, taken by A. Fred Nelson, author Millie's father. A special thanks to missionary "Uncle" Ernie Boehr (in his nineties) for enhancing this "old" photo and making it usable.

Hungry River:
A Yangtze Novel
Third Edition
Millie Nelson Samuelson
Yesterday's Stories for Today's Inspiration

"Watching *Hungry River* grow from a memoir to a fascinating novel has given me a special interest in it. My favorite parts are the journal entries."
~ Linda Wells, memoirist, novelist, artist, and *Hungry River's* greatest fan, and named Da-Lin/*Great Jade* in this novel by Millie in gratitude

"What a treat to be reading your trilogy! The books are fascinating, heartbreaking, inspiring and challenging. Thank you! I am reading, reading, then passing them on."
~ Janet (Holsinger) Friesen, Taiwan Morrison Academy friend

"The story of Lizzie transcends culture. I'm already reading it again, and am eager for the sequels."
~ Melissa Rees, murder mystery novelist and writing buddy

"A phenomenal novel! I missed the characters as soon as I read the final page and closed the book. I can't wait to walk with them again when the adventure continues in *Dragon Wall*."
~ Katie Rizer, Chesterton-Porter Rotary Club member

"*Hungry River* was challenging and uplifting at the same time. Without exception, the book club members said they couldn't put it down once they started reading, and they are expectantly waiting for the sequel."
~ Sandi Andrews, book club leader in Virginia

Author Millie (above) was born in China, where she spent her childhood amidst the horrifying devastations of World War II and China's civil war. This historical novel is inspired by her family's century of extraordinary China experiences. The "fictional" narrator Abbie IS Millie.

Hungry River:
A Yangtze Novel
Third Edition

Book One
Yangtze Dragon Trilogy

Millie Nelson Samuelson
Yesterday's Stories for Today's Inspiration

True story
blessings!
Millie

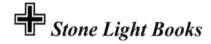

Stone Light Books

Hungry River:
A Yangtze Novel
Third Edition
Book One
Yangtze Dragon Trilogy

Millie Nelson Samuelson
Yesterday's Stories for Today's Inspiration

All photos in the trilogy belong to
the Nelson/Samuelson family collection.

For information or more copies:
millie@milliesbooks.org
www.milliesbooks.org
Amazon.com

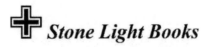 **Stone Light Books**

ISBN-13: 978-1511734738
ISBN-10: 1511734736

for my Nelson grandparents
whose China journals and memoirs
inspired this novel
and for all courageous multiculturalists
of faith like them
and their families
who sometimes adventure,
sometimes suffer

1895 wedding photo
of author Millie's grandparents,
Lizzie and Nils Newquist in the trilogy.

Contents

Author's Historical Preface

. . . if you're wondering whether or not to read this preface before skipping ahead to the novel, ask yourself a question – Who led the revolution in China that established the Republic, and in what year? Don't know? Even if you do, try this one – True or False: The new democratic governments in Afghanistan and Iraq struggle to control warlords and bandits in their countries not unlike those that devastated China a century ago. Or how about this one – During the Boxer Rebellion of 1900, how many Chinese were massacred compared to Westerners? Unless you know the answers, maybe you should keep reading. . .

It's generally acknowledged that China has the longest history of any country in existence today – more than 6000 years. And for many centuries, it was the greatest civilization. In fact, China or *Zhong Kuo* or Middle Kingdom means "central country," referring both to importance and geographical centrality.

It's also fairly well known that gunpowder, silk, tea and spices came to the West from China a long time ago. Not so well known is the fact that Chinese ships reached the Americas centuries before the Vikings, Columbus, and other Western claimants.

Nor do most of us know much about the great literary works of ancient China. Maybe we know names like Confucius and Lao-tze, but do we know why their writings are classics or who the other great writers are? And how about the names of even a few artists or artisans from thousands of years of amazing artworks?

This lack of knowledge, and perhaps interest, is not surprising. Until the 1800s, China was essentially closed to the Western world – to those barbarians with monstrous noses, owlish eyes, ghostly complexions, and atrocious manners. There were exceptions, of course, such as the Nestorian missionaries in the ninth century and Marco Polo in the thirteenth century, along with various other intruders who were allowed to live and tell about it.

As was true for most civilizations until modern times, China was ruled by an imperial class. These emperors and empresses and their families paralleled the royal kings and queens of the West in power and wealth. Like the West, their riches were made possible by the subjugation of millions and millions of slaves and peasants.

In between the Imperials and the wretched workers were the magistrates and the warlords with their fighting men. These magistrates and warlords controlled the workers for the Imperials in return for land and other benefits – in much the same way Western nobility and church leaders were rewarded for similar services by their royalty. Also similar were the ongoing bloody battles among warlords, between emperors, and occasionally against invaders, both Eastern and Western.

In addition to centuries of ruler-inflicted bloodshed, rebel soldiers and peasants often formed bandit packs that terrorized and plundered anyone they could, especially travelers. Historians have estimated that in any given year, tens of thousands of bandits roamed the mountains and rivers of China. For every bandit caught and gruesomely executed, it seemed two took his place.

What you have just read is certainly an oversimplification of a complicated and corrupt sovereignty system. Even though it leaves out the gracious aspects of Chinese culture, it presents an adequate enough sketch of China at the end of the 1700s – a time when the Industrial Revolution had swept through Europe, but not over to China.

Suddenly, China was vulnerable to invasion. After thousands of years, it was no longer the center of world progress. The Great Wall was a useless defense against attacks from the sea, and China's wooden junks with their cloth sails were no match for metal ships with steam engines. Nor could the bows and arrows and swords of Chinese armies defeat armies that had learned to manufacture and use gunpowder weapons.

The same countries that conquered and colonized the Americas and other parts of the world for trade, now attempted to do the same with China. The inevitable defeat of China by Great Britain in the Opium War of 1842 was a bitter blow to a great land. As a consequence, not only were the Chinese forced to open their country to "foreign devils," they were forced to accept opium – an evil that nearly destroyed the Chinese.

However, submission to the West resulted in more than evil. Along with the traders came missionaries and others to China. They brought with them inspiring and equalizing ideals for all people, including peasants and females.

Before long, scores of Chinese were clamoring to visit the countries of these intriguing Westerners. Thousands of young men were soon attending institutions of education in the West. Those that returned to China, brought back appealing concepts like democracy, and wonders in transportation like railroads. Even peasants who went to the West as laborers discovered life could be free of oppression and dire poverty.

By the end of the 1800s, all over China secret societies were forming to overthrow the Imperials and warlords. So the bloodshed of centuries continued. Only now the peasants and those in disfavor with the Imperials were suffering for a better life for themselves, not for someone in power over them.

One of the young men who studied abroad with intense longings to improve his homeland was Sun Yat-sen. His studies led him to become a surgeon of Western medicine, and also to embrace Christianity. What radical steps for someone from a traditional Chinese family!

About this time in 1889, the story of **Hungry River,** *Yangtze Dragon Trilogy Book One, begins.*

With Japan's attack on China in 1894, Dr. Sun took another radical step. He became a powerful revolutionist against the Imperial Manchus who had resisted China's becoming a modern power. Thousands of Chinese overseas and in China responded to Sun's dynamic orations and joined his patriotic Prosper China Society.

However, not all secret societies in China were against the Imperials. Some of them were against Westerners who were seen as invaders and evil doers. One of these societies was nicknamed the Boxers. When they told the aging Empress Dowager they had magical powers against foreign devils, she believed them. Through the Boxers, she thought she saw a way to free China from foreign encroachment.

In 1900, the Empress issued a proclamation ordering the Boxers to massacre all white people throughout the land. She hoped this would restore China to its lost glory. The Boxers followed her orders, and massacred hundreds of Westerners, as well as thousands of Chinese who befriended them.

The Boxer Rebellion was quelled in several months by combined troops from Western powers. This defeat also signaled the end to the Imperial stronghold over China, and opened the door even further for revolution – as well as invasion, especially from neighboring Japan.

Sun Yat-sen's revolution finally succeeded in 1911 after years of fighting and setbacks. In 1913, China became a Republic. The next year, Sun became the Republic's first president. But when he died in 1925, peace and democracy were not yet established in his beloved country. Warlords still fought, and bandits roamed the countryside. Millions of peasants still lived desperate lives. Innocent people continued to die by the thousands, including missionaries and other foreigners.

After Sun's death, two of his revolutionary leaders (both educated for a time in mision-affiliated schools) fought for control of China. These two were Chiang Kai-shek and Mao Tse-tung. Before either won, the two called a truce between their armies and fought together against Japanese invaders for more than a decade.

*About this time, the story of **Hungry River** ends in 1931, followed by the sequels **Dragon Wall** and **Jade Cross**, Books Two and Three of the Yangtze Dragon Trilogy.*

After Japan's World War II defeat in 1945, General Chiang and General Mao resumed fighting against each other. For a time, America backed Chiang in his fight to establish a free and democratic China, then withdrew its support. Mao, in his effort to establish a Communist government throughout China, was backed by Russia. And Russia did not withdraw its support.

In 1949, General Chiang was defeated enough to flee to the Island of Taiwan (still called by its better-known Portuguese name of Formosa at the time) with what survived of his army and supporters. There he established the Republic of China, today's Taiwan.

Back in Mainland China, General Mao established the Peoples Republic of China. He eventually unified China for the first time in its long history – but at a terrible, terrible price in human lives and freedoms.

Today both Taiwan and China honor Sun Yat-sen as the Father of the Republic of China. However, the two republics face unknown future political ties. For while

China claims sovereignty over Taiwan, that island country maintains its independence. Taiwan has achieved democracy and prosperity; China has yet to do so – though after decades of isolation and repression under Communism, China is an increasingly open country, gaining in power and prosperity.

. . . with its vast untapped resources and immense population, some historians predict by the next century China will once again become the central power of the world. Should that happen, we can only hope this colossal land will also become the world's center of peace and human rights. . .

~ Millie Nelson Samuelson
2005, 2011, 2015

The sequel, Book Two **Dragon Wall** begins in 1933 and ends in 1959. Book Three **Jade Cross** begins in 1962, and the trilogy ends in 2008, the year of the spectacular Olympics in Beijing, China.

PART ONE

Rivers . . . Vows
Storyline 1889 to 1891
Journal Excerpts from 1999 and 2000

A wise one is always good at helping people,
so that none is cast away.
~ Sage Lao Tzu (6th century b.c.)

God is our refuge and strength,
a very present help in trouble.
~ Psalm 46:1

Prolog

Abbie's Journal
July 4, 1999
. . . *it's hard to believe – today I've seen it again at last –
the Great Long River of my family's memories and stories!
This afternoon Dan and I walked along its banks. We'll fly
upriver tomorrow to cruise its magnificent gorges. But we
won't get all the way up to Fengshan where Gramma and
Grampa built Great House. That'll have to wait for another
trip, maybe with our kids. I can't get over how wonderful
everything in China seems these days – everything, that is,
except the river's same smelly murkiness. . .*

*. . . I've always been haunted by my childhood recollections
of escaping down the Yangtze, one of China's many dragon
rivers, its head in Cheungking and its tail in Shanghai.
Back then, I was stunned to silence by grotesque bodies
swirling around in the dark turbulent waters, by terrible
sounds and stench of war everywhere. . .*

*. . . little Philly and I survived years of fleeing, but our
brothers didn't. When Mom and Dad talked about losing
Donny and Kilby, I imagined them actually lost somewhere
in China. I made sure Philly and I stayed close so we
weren't lost too. Standing beside the river a few hours ago,
I felt again the terror of the day Dad rushed us to the dock
in Cheungking. . .*

    *That day Communist soldiers armed with American
guns grudgingly protected us from crowds taunting:* Zou
bah! *Go away, foreign devils, you with ugly eyes and noses.*
Hai! *Go away! Return to your own country. Mom covered
my mouth with her hand to keep me from shouting back,*

What do you mean? We're not foreign devils! My father was born here. I was born here. We've always lived here. This IS our country.

When we reached the river, we could barely see the ship because hundreds of desperate Chinese war refugees were jammed alongside. Miraculously, our traveling permits were authorized by a sober-faced official. Then Dad, with his permit in his teeth, forced his way into the mob and struggled with his suitcases up the makeshift stairs of piled barrels and onto the crowded deck to save us a place.

As Philly and I clutched Mom's skirt, she frantically tucked our permits into her bosom, opened her suitcase and took out some precious photos. She shoved them into my little case and kicked her suitcase aside. She grabbed our hands and said, Hold tight to your suitcases, but if you drop them, just let them go so we don't fall. Somehow, she dragged us up the barrels and onto the ship's deck to Dad.

As the ship pulled away, dozens of Chinese trying to climb on board fell and sank into the river. I wondered, was it because they had the weight of gold or silver hidden in their clothes like we did? As the old steamer chugged along, we were far too miserable to notice the splendor of the ancient gorges. Every day, we prayed we wouldn't sink or be shot. We quoted Scripture verses we had memorized to strengthen us.

Days, maybe weeks later, we clambered down from a train. Dirty, ragged war survivors, we staggered past the border guards and over Liberty Bridge into free Hongkong. Mom kept crying, Oh God, oh dear God, oh God. One guard said, Just listen to that crazy white woman. Angry and defensive, I rudely looked him straight in the eyes and struck my forefinger twice against my cheek in the Chinese manner to shame him. He laughed at me and spit on the ground.

. . . at the time of our escape, I didn't know Dad was an informer for the U.S. military. I was too young to be aware of such dangers, or of Dad's earlier Marine Corps service. Had the Communists found out, I might have been another Anne Frank. Except there's not a chance Dad would have survived to publish my journal like Anne's father did. . .

. . . after fifty years, how wonderful to make new Yangtze River memories – memories peaceful and friendly. I know I'm not really Chinese, though my heart feels a warm comfort being back in my motherland. Maybe now the nightmares Dan awakens me from will cease. Maybe now when we get home to Windridge, I'll at last be able to look through my China boxes and read my family's old journals and letters. Maybe now I'll see beyond the anguish of my parents' and grandparents' experiences. . .

Chapter 1

Abbie's Journal
Feb 17, 2000
. . . compulsive journaling must be in my genes. For years our basement storeroom has housed my family's China boxes, filled with a century of journals and letters and such. After the folks died, I vowed to sort through them all and read everything. But I kept procrastinating. Sure I loved reminders of our extraordinary lives in China. It was the haunting memories of suffering I couldn't bear to recall. Since our wonderful visit to China last year, at last I'm sorting and reading and remembering. As the Chinese say, it's an auspicious year to do so – it's their astrological Year of Dragon. . .

Fengshan, China
1889, Year of Ox

Beneath the sleeping village of Fengshan rushed the Great Long River, its dark waters glowing like oiled mahogany. Here and there among turbulent swirls, huge foam shapes appeared for a moment, then disappeared.

They look like ghostly temple gods, Mei-lee thought, peering down at the River as she staggered along on painful bound feet. She clutched the infant asleep in one arm and her walking stick with the other and crept on along the steep river bank.

Once past the village, the River flowed with swiftness to a bend in its course. There it briefly became a lake, encircled by shadowy mountain peaks jutting majestically upwards. Because it was night, no junks swept by, no boatmen shouted. Only stillness and moonlight kept the River company through the gorge.

Ai! If only I had been a male, I might have gone to school. Mei-lee paused to gaze and ease her gasps. *I might have learned to brush on scrolls this scene that soothes my despair.*

Soon she reached the sacred old weeping willow standing guard between the dwellings of her village and the River. She longed to sit on the smooth earth but ached from giving birth – and from her husband's beating. Instead, she leaned on her walking stick to rest beneath the tree that had been her friend since childhood.

The tree had become her confidant the day her husband first beat her, when she first displeased him by asking to spend her fifteenth birthday at her ancestral home. She leaned painfully against her friend's familiar trunk, its strength and calm soothing her.

"See," she said softly to its leafy branches, "here is my precious second baby, born this afternoon. You are happy for me and for her, are you not? *Ai!* Thank you for your *gung-shi* wishes – though we are undeserving of your congratulations, though we are but worthless females and her birth has angered my husband."

For a long time, tears dripped from her cheeks onto the tiny black head tucked between her swelling breasts.

When at last she obeyed the River's call from beyond the tree's gnarled roots, the moon hung low among a few fading stars. Tottering on the stumps of her bound feet, she slowly made her way down the ancient stone steps to the River's edge.

"Honorable River gods," she sobbed, "I offer you my second precious daughter. Since you received my first one, my village has had only a little hunger, and few hardships at the hands of bandits and warlords. And only a few children and old ones have been dragged off by wolves. Thank you, Honorable River gods. Thank you. Tonight I ask, please favor us again."

Moaning and swaying, she waited for a response. It came quickly. In the River's spray she saw the arms of a goddess reaching out to her.

Suddenly she gasped, "*Ai yah!*" For she saw a second pair of ghostly arms rising out of the water and beckoning to her. But she was ready, was she not? She was dressed in her best blue cotton jacket and pants. Her newborn she had tenderly swaddled in a piece of flowered cloth.

Then for the first time since stealing away from her husband's home, she turned around and gazed up towards the village wall behind the tree. There in the shadows, just as she expected, was a dark, familiar shape leaning over a cane. Next to it was a similar shape, only smaller.

Holding her precious bundle before her, Mei-lee bowed low in the direction of the shapes. She waited a moment, then turned to the River and staggered forward with bent head to meet the waiting arms.

Up at the wall, Mei-lee's mother struck her breasts in anguish as she watched her older daughter and tiny grandbaby disappear into the churning water. Groaning, she fell to her knees beside her shivering younger daughter. Soon both began to cry out and wail aloud. Before long, women from the village surrounded them, also wailing. As the two were escorted home, no one asked why they mourned. Everyone knew.

Later that morning, Mei-lee's mother and younger sister were again joined by the village women. Together they dutifully burned spirit money and incense and offered meat pastry *bao-tzes* beneath the sacred tree at the River's edge. Chanting and moaning, the women shuddered as they sought to appease the hunger of the river gods. They begged for favor for their families, and for protection from roaming evil spirits.

All that long, sorrowful day, Mei-lee's mother waited for her husband's words. But he did not speak. Nor did he go to Mei-lee's husband to apologize for his daughter's worthless womb. His evening meal of rice and stir-fried peanut greens he ate bravely in the family's front courtyard as usual. Then he cleared his throat, spit several times into his spittoon, and spoke loudly enough to be heard by the listening neighbors.

"Wife, some say we have lost face today. Why should we care? For even worse, we have lost our pretty elder daughter because of her husband's foul temper. He is the one who should feel ashamed. He should have been patient with Mei-lee or returned her to us."

He gulped and coughed. "*Tai-tai,* we will miss our kind, obedient daughter – even though the gods have favored us with sons and another daughter. *Hai!* Let us never speak to that man or his family again. May demons plague them all."

Mei-lee's weeping mother urged her husband to be seated in his favorite bamboo chair, then poured them both some tea.

"Drink, Honorable Husband," she said between sobs. "Surely, your words have defended our family and pleased our ancestors. Probably our daughter's next child would have been a grandson for us. With you I curse, her husband who has caused us loss and grief. And I curse any male descendants he may have."

That night, Mei-lee's mother lay sleepless on the family's fire-heated brick and mud *kang* bed. When muffled sobs from under the quilted *pugai* by the wall broke the painful silence, she crawled out from under her husband's *pugai* and over to her younger daughter. She lay close to Hui-ching, gently stroking the young girl's cheeks and hands.

"Be comforted, Second Daughter," she whispered under her daughter's *pugai*. "What happened to Mei-lee will not happen to you, I promise. Listen carefully now. I will unbind your feet as you have been pleading. I will persuade Ba to allow you to attend one of those schools for girls run by the fearsome foreigners."

She paused to breathe deeply several times, then continued in a low shaky voice. "If you learn to read and stroke the brush with excellence, perhaps we will not need to arrange marriage for you for many years. In time, you may even find your own husband like others are doing in these days of new ideas."

She felt her younger daughter's trembling body slowly calm, and the soft touch of Hui-ching's hands on her cheeks and soft voice in her ear.

"In truth, Ma, in truth? *Ai*! I vow not to disappoint you or Ba. I will learn for all of us – but especially for Mei-lee. If the gods favor me, one day I vow to paint the gorge as she longed to do. Ma, I vow to live brave and restore honor to the memory of Older Sister."

*   *   *

Abbie's Journal
Feb 24, 2000
. . . this week I've been reading one of Dad's journals I've not read before. Dad cleverly disguised it for some reason, so Phil and I overlooked it when we packed up his China things. In a 1936 entry, Dad mentions an art scroll by his family's "dear artist friend," but later Dad blacked out the name. He describes the painting as a classical one of a Great Long River gorge near Fengshan, with a "lovely calligraphy inscription." He thought it was probably valuable. Makes me very curious – who was the artist Dad was protecting? And the scroll – did he get it out of China

before we escaped down the River that last dreadful time? Or did he hide or destroy it? It's not a scroll I remember. Maybe a cousin has it, or maybe it's still in Dad's China boxes. There's so much more to sort. . .

Chapter 2

Abbie's Journal
Mar 20, 2000
. . . Gramma Lizzie's journals are difficult to read – she wrote in small notebooks with pencil, now faded. All my life I longed to know her in person. Now as I'm reading her journals, I feel like her spirit is visiting mine – it's inspiring to discover how strong and independent she was, especially for her time. Today I read about her frightening experience in the Des Moines River. She doesn't exactly say so, but I sense that's when she first became aware of the preciousness of life, and that her own life would somehow be used by God in extraordinary ways. . .

Des Moines River, Iowa, 1889
Same Year of Ox

High above the jagged river, Lizzie crouched in the crevice of an enormous boulder. She drew her legs close to her body, and snugly wrapped herself in her long skirts and shawl. Sheltered and safe, she watched the rain stream down from rumbling clouds into the turbulent waters below. As the river surged by her hideout on the bluff, the words *I'm an adult, today I'm of age* sang over and over in her mind.

"It's my most important birthday," she called to the racing river. "You must help me decide. What answer shall I give Oliver tonight *– ja* or *nay?*" She stretched her arms towards the water, then quickly withdrew them when the icy rain sent chill bumps over her body.

Oh min min! She shuddered and pressed her crossed hands over her heart. *Was that her answer?*

Lizzie never tired of the river. Ever since her family had arrived in America and settled beside it, she loved to hike among the huge rocks and trees clustered on its banks. When rain and snow turned the smooth blue water into flashing silver like today, she liked to sit on her hidden stone shelf and look down unafraid.

In summer, she swam with her brothers and friends in the river's pool that edged their farmland. Like many who grow up near a river, she was a skilled boater. But the Des Moines River provided more than fun and travel. It supplied tasty fish for men and boys to catch – and a place for women and girls to wash rugs and heavy bedding. To those who knew its secrets, the river gave logs and firewood – and sometimes other treasures.

Years ago, Lizzie thought, *it was firewood that nearly drowned me right here in this spot. If not for Oliver and his father, I might not be alive and of age today.*

In her mind's eye, she went back to that frightening scene as she had so many times in the years since.

*   *   *

Her brothers had been busy with farm chores, so she had volunteered to go with Papa to the river for firewood. The task took two people, and Mama couldn't leave her Sunday baking.

"Do you think she's strong enough?" Mama asked in Swedish.

"*Ja*, but of course," Papa said. "An eleven-year old is big enough to be the helper. After all, the horse and me do the heavy work, don't we?"

He had smiled and winked at her.

Lizzie would do anything for Papa when he smiled like that. His smiles made her feel so special and capable. She quickly dressed in one of her older brother's warm coats, and put on wool stockings inside her winter boots. When they reached the river, Oliver and his father were there too, and greeted them from downstream. "Lots of logs coming today, my friend Thor," Mr. Bergstrom shouted, waving to them along with Oliver. "So soon we have all we need. Must be new workers at the mill."

Papa and Lizzie called and waved back. Then Papa guided the horse and sledge into a good loading spot. Next Papa handed her the long, rake-like pole.

"Here, Lizzie, be very careful when you pull in the branches. You don't want to lose your balance. Better practice a little first."

For a while, she had fun pulling driftwood to shore. But when her mittened hands became wet and cold, she wanted to quit. She saw several good-sized logs beside Papa, and hoped he was soon finished.

This will be my last one. She eyed a branch speeding into reach. *Won't Papa smile when he sees my big pile.*

The branch was larger and heavier than it looked, and Lizzie's cold fingers had lost their strength. When she tightened her grip, suddenly she found herself dragged into the water by the branch. She tried hard not to lose Papa's pole. That was a mistake. The next thing she knew, she was being swept downstream by the rushing river.

"Help, Papa, help me! Papa help!" she screamed.

At eleven, Lizzie swam like a young champion. But in her heavy clothes and boots, she was no match for the river's winter current.

"Save me, Papa! Save me, Jesus!" She choked on the waves pulling her under.

Weak and numb from the cold, she struggled to the water's surface again and again, trying to swim towards shore. All at once, a strong arm locked around her neck and held her firmly. She heard men's voices and felt herself being pulled from the river.

Slipping and stumbling, someone carried her to a large boulder and laid her face down over it. Hands pressed up and down on her back. She coughed. Water streamed from her mouth and nose.

"Lizzie, Lizzie, open your eyes. Lizzie, can you breathe?" she heard Papa's worried voice, muffled by the warm coats thrown over her.

With difficulty, she raised her head and opened her eyes. "Help me up, Papa."

He did, hugging the coats tightly around her. Beside him stood Mr. Bergstrom staring at her, also Oliver wet and shivering.

"Thanks be to God," Mr. Bergstrom said. "Oliver was given strength to save you."

"Amen," Papa said. "Edvard, let's get them to my house. We must hurry."

Lizzie liked how Mama fussed over her and Oliver, turning that awful experience of near death into a special celebration of life. While her mother served them sweetened hot chocolate and buttered cinnamon rusks, they sat close together by the warmth of the kitchen stove, telling over and over what had happened.

Finally, long past the supper hour, they bowed their heads and held hands as the fathers thanked God for sparing their youth.

On Saturday when Lizzie and her family went to town, she was surprised everyone seemed to know what had happened. Store owners and friends called her a brave girl and gave her treats and hugs. She didn't know what to say except she was glad Jesus helped Oliver save her.

The words she never forgot were the ones spoken by her friend with the long, black braid – the little brown man in the laundry who did Papa's Sunday shirt and collars. He told her how lucky she was to be rescued. Back in China beside the Great Long River where he was from, no one saved girls from drowning. Even worse, girls were often drowned on purpose, especially infant girls.

Young Lizzie listened with eyes wide as he leaned over the counter and said to her, "Maybe you special, young friend. Maybe gods want you be somebody. Maybe eh? You think about reason and you better honor river gods."

Squeezed between her parents on the bumpy wagon ride home late that Saturday afternoon, she had asked, "Is it really true baby girls in China get drowned by their families?"

*   *   *

After all these years, remembering Mama's soft "*ja, min dotter*" still brought tears to Lizzie's eyes, and renewed the urgency of her longing to rescue those poor little girls in China.

Oh min min! What if no one had rescued me? she thought, and not for the first time.

Realizing she had lost track of time and the rain had stopped, she quickly climbed down from her river refuge. She paused for a few moments to touch what she had secretly chipped onto a bluff boulder years before, then hurried home.

Some experiences change you forever. She ran up the back porch steps. *And some people become special friends forever. But does that mean you should marry?*

When she entered the kitchen, her mother asked what she wanted for a birthday treat.

"Hot chocolate and buttered cinnamon rusks, *tack sa mycket.*"

"So then, Elizabeth, you go to the river?"

Lizzie nodded.

"*Ja*, how I remember that day too," Mama said. "I suppose Oliver comes soon for your birthday supper?"

"Probably." Lizzie sighed. "I wish now he wasn't. I still don't have my answer."

*   *   *

Abbie's Journal
Apr 13, 2000

. . . Gramma Lizzie wrote in her journals about her lifelong fascination with rivers – a fascination I share! In one entry she writes about studying China's great Yangtze River in geography class. From then on she read everything she could about it – probably never dreaming she would one day travel on the river from its Shanghai head to its Cheungking tail and even beyond to Fengshan. Or that she would experience personally why river people feared and worshiped it as a great dragon god. . .

Chapter 3

Abbie's Journal
Apr 20, 2000
. . . seems all I do these days is sort through my China boxes, and wipe tears from my cheeks. This week I've spent hours looking at old photos. There are hundreds – and even more negatives, with many stuck together, ruined probably. I can't decide what to do with them, so I'm just packing them away again, still unorganized. Phil says whatever I do with them is fine with him. I've kept out a few prints to frame and display. One is of Gramma Lizzie as a young woman. Dressed in her uniform, she looks at me so earnestly. . .

Des Moines, Iowa
1890, Year of Tiger

Lizzie looked in the dresser mirror as she fastened the metal buttons on the tunic of her new uniform. After a bit, she tilted the mirror so she could check the skirt's hemline. *Ja*, it came right to the top of her laced boots. Her measurements were correct.

"I have my uniform on," she called to her mother through the partially open bedroom door. "Come see."

Mama hurried to Lizzie's room, patting her hands on her apron.

"My, you look so fine, Elizabeth. The dark color suits you. So proud I am of you to be wearing the uniform tonight for the Salvation Army meeting! Dear Papa will be proud too when he sees you. But of course, he won't say the words, you know."

"*Ja*, I know."

She put her smooth cheek next to Mama's wrinkled one, her brown wavy hair next to Mama's soft grey hair.

"This uniform is the most difficult dress we've sewn, don't you think?"

Her mother nodded, touching the brass "S" pin on Lizzie's collar.

"*Ja*, but so nice it is. And next time will be more easy. I'm just thinking, would you like a matching bag? A nice, strong handbag for the many books and papers you carry? Tomorrow, shall I sew a handbag?"

But the handbag was never sewn. That evening, while Lizzie in her new uniform played her accordion and sang with the Salvation Army choir, Papa fell from his horse. About twilight, Charlie and Johann heard his dog barking and found him in the field near the river.

The brothers carried their unconscious father home. They laid him on Lizzie's bed in the downstairs bedroom. Then Charlie headed to town for the doctor.

"*Oh min min!* Get Lizzie too," Mama called with urgency, "at Bergstroms, after the meeting."

All that long, long night, Lizzie helped Mama and the doctor. By morning, exhaustion and anxiety showed on their faces. But dear Papa was alive, and they knew he had fallen because of his heart.

As the doctor ate breakfast with them, he said, "There's nothing to do now except wait and see what happens. Strong men sometimes survive these attacks, even when they're past sixty like Thor. He's a fortunate man to be in the care of a wife and daughter who have healing skills, and to have grown sons working the farm."

The doctor rose from the table, patted Lizzie on her shoulder, then headed to his horse.

"I'll be back tomorrow," he said to Mama, who had walked outside with him. He touched his hat and was soon out of sight.

Word of Thor's heart condition spread quickly. Neighbors and friends took turns visiting and bringing food. The whole community admired the hardworking, generous Swede who had done well at the mill and in farming. Afraid he was dying, they came to make sure he knew how they felt. To encourage him, they sang hymns and read Psalms aloud from his Swedish Bible. Sometimes they prayed with the whole family.

Every evening while her mother rested, Lizzie sat by Papa. She tried to lighten his spirit by telling the stories he had so often told his family.

"What story shall I tell tonight, Papa Dear?" she liked to ask.

"Any story is fine, but how about a church one from the old country?" was often his reply. If he was too tired, he just smiled and nodded. Then she told whatever story came first to her mind.

A story none of them ever tired of hearing was the one about the visiting preacher who lost his voice when he came to their church in Smaland for a special Sunday service. Because Papa was the head deacon, the preacher was staying at their house.

"What should be done?" the adults worried as Lizzie and her brothers listened. People were coming from long distances for the service, and Papa didn't want them to be disappointed. No one could think of another preacher to come on such short notice.

Then Mama had an idea. "Papa, why don't you speak for the preacher?"

"That won't keep the congregation from being disappointed," he answered. "Besides, they already hear me too often when we don't have a preacher."

Mama laughed. "*Ja*, but of course, this time they won't know it's you speaking. They'll think the visiting preacher is."

This was the place in the story when everyone started grinning because they knew what was coming next. Papa would mimic the preacher trying to ask Mama what she meant. Papa exaggerated the preacher's croaks and gestures, and watching him pretend to be a voiceless preacher was indeed comical.

"I can't do it as funny as you, Papa," Lizzie said.

She didn't need to. They were all laughing anyway and kept laughing to the end of the story – to the part where Papa hid in the pulpit. Secreted there, he disguised his voice and read aloud the preacher's sermon through a carefully made hole. Standing behind him at the pulpit, the preacher mouthed the sermon and gestured to match Papa's reading.

"And if anybody in the congregation figured it out," Lizzie finished the story, "they never said anything, at least not to our family. But Papa always tells about the puzzled glances he got from some of his friends during the church picnic that afternoon and the next Sunday."

*   *   *

Sometimes in the evenings, Oliver joined Lizzie at her father's bedside. Lizzie could tell Papa liked that. She knew he was hoping she would soon agree to marry Oliver and give up the Salvation Army. Papa called it her obsession.

Not that he was against the Army. He was pleased about her promotion from soldier to officer. He said he just didn't like to think of his only daughter leaving home to work with rough, ungodly people – at the same time, he agreed he wanted her to obey God, and he knew many people needed help.

One evening as she and Oliver sat by his bedside, it

dawned on Lizzie that now her parents were unlikely to return to Sweden for their much talked about visit. Such a trip to the old home and relatives would be too strenuous for Papa with his weakened heart. Without thinking, she blurted out her thoughts.

"Oh Lizzie," Papa said. "I guess I never really expected to take that trip. Fun it was to plan, and a way to keep us remembering the old country. You children must go instead of us old folks. *Ja,* traveling like that is more easy for the young. Sometime you and the boys must visit where you were born."

Then he turned his head away from her and Oliver. A few minutes later, they saw tears seeping from his closed eyes. Lizzie reached over and took one of Papa's hands in hers. Oliver put his hand on her knee and they softly hummed hymns until Papa went to sleep.

* * *

Six months after her father's invaliding heart spasms – months that seemed more like years – Lizzie gazed at her reflection in the darkening window of the train speeding her home. In spite of Papa's condition, she had completed her Salvation Army officer's training on schedule.

At first, she had wanted to postpone the last part of the training. But her mother had encouraged her otherwise.

"Elizabeth, I think you should finish officer's training if that's what you really want to do, and if you're not going to marry Oliver soon," Mama said one afternoon as they walked arm in arm beside the river.

"When I pray about you, God gives me peace for this. It's a wonderful opportunity from God before marriage ties you down. So go on to the training place, since Papa gets better."

"But what about you?" Lizzie asked. "Don't you want me to stay home to help you?"

"*Ja*. But of course, neither Papa nor I wants you to stay here if God wants you somewhere else. And we have your brothers and our good neighbors."

Tears came then to both their eyes, and they had hugged each other tightly.

Now months later, Lizzie was officially Captain Beckman – an officer prepared to fight in God's Army against evil. Did she look different? Certainly not in the train window. But she felt different. She felt courageous and daring.

The Army does that for us women, she thought. *It makes us feel on the same level as men.*

She liked that affirmation. Just then she needed it. She needed courage for the months ahead. She had been selected as one of an advance corps being sent soon to China to see about establishing the Army in Shanghai. *Ja,* she would need extra strength to say "goodbye" to her family and friends for years, maybe even forever.

China, China, China, her brain chanted along with the rhythmic clanking of the traincar wheels beneath her.

She wondered why she was so eager instead of afraid. She was pretty sure she knew what her parents would say. But what about Oliver? Whatever would he say? She thought about those times he had begged her to marry him, and she kept saying "wait."

Lizzie sighed and her shoulders slowly slumped.

Ja, going to China probably meant saying a final *nay* to Oliver. He had been part of her life for so long, she could scarcely imagine life without him. But he steadfastly refused to join the Army, and she was sure the Army and now China were right for her.

Lizzie stared again at her reflection in the window, as if the familiar person there could advise her. Maybe she would never marry. What about that? Some women didn't. Or maybe she would marry a Chinese or someone else in China. She just didn't want to marry right now. The things she first wanted to do tugged so hard at her. Besides, Oliver had written only two letters this time she was away, so maybe he wouldn't take her final *nay* too hard. She knew several of her friends would love to be Oliver's girl. Not one of them wanted to leave America and go to China for God like she did.

Ja, Mama's advice had been good. Finishing Army training was the right decision. Lizzie felt it so in her heart. Nor could she forget the words of her childhood laundry friend. She was needed in China to help rescue girls. Sighing again, she picked up her book.

Shanghai is situated, she read, *in the lush delta at the mouth of the Yangtze River. Often called the Great Long River by the Chinese, the Yangtze brings both life and death to the millions who live along its banks. The river's source is unknown.*

Before the end of the chapter, Lizzie was asleep. The rhythmic rocking of the train took the book slowly from her grasp and onto the empty seat beside her.

*   *   *

Abbie's Journal
May 6, 2000
. . . this afternoon one of Dan's clients who often travels overseas brought his recent China photos to show us. We had fun comparing trips. When I mentioned my family's old China photos I've been sorting, he told about being in Shanghai with the Navy in 1947. We agreed that much along the Yangzi is the same, but desperate poverty is no longer so obvious. He shared one of his most lasting memories from his Navy days was seeing greenish corpses

tied together with a rope and bobbing down the river. He didn't see any bodies this time, nor did we. But not long ago some broker friends told us how shocked they were to see bodies floating in the river during a Yangzi cruise they were on last year. . .

PART TWO

Promises . . . Choices
Storyline 1892 to 1895
Journal Excerpts from 2000

To see what is right and not do it, that is cowardice.
~ Sage Confucius (5th century b.c.)

You shall do what is right and good
in the sight of the Lord,
that it may be well with you.
~ Deuteronomy 6:18

Chapter 4

Abbie's Journal
May 20, 2000
*. . . because I so enjoy her Chinese-ness, I'm rereading
some of Pearl Buck's books, something I do every few
years. Right now I'm reading* Dragon Seed. *She begins the
novel with a note explaining "dragon seed" – To the
Chinese, she says, the dragon is not an evil creature, but is
a god and the friend of those who worship him. He holds in
his power prosperity and peace – I'm sure that's why
millions of Chinese put the religious and superstitious
symbolism of dragon-power into various aspects of their
daily lives, something not even decades of brutal
Communism were able to eradicate. . .
. . . what a terrible shame that the older Pearl Buck
became, the more she lost her faith in the power and hope
of Christianity. It's like she succumbed to dragon-power
more and more each year. My family, who knew her family
well, mourned her loss of faith. Just think of the witness she
might had. In spite of the many parallels between her life
and mine, I thank God I have never, ever, to the slightest
degree, shared her God doubts. I also thank my parents
who in many ways were not like hers, at least not as
portrayed in her biographies of them. . .*

Shanghai, 1892
Year of Dragon

Moments after the 16:00 o'clock whistle, Nils dashed from
the freighter's engine room and up three flights of stairs.
Joining other off-duty seamen on deck, he squinted in the

bright sunlight at the view before him with disbelief. Several men retched at the rails. The docking crew performed their tasks with difficulty.

"Steady men, heed the junks and gunboats!" the captain shouted in Swedish. "Bring her in safely! Then you can gawk!"

Descendants of Vikings they were, yet these seafarers found themselves with a foreboding that churned in their stomachs and throats. Their first glimpse of Shanghai's notorious Bund was shattering all sense of adventure. The extra wages promised for this voyage now seemed a traitor's trick. Swearing and praying, each wondered how he had been so easily fooled.

Rarely had the crew of the *Sverige Ericsson* encountered such strangeness or threat of danger. Nils and the others stared at the masses of small, dark-skinned Chinese men thronging the wharf and river barges. Long, black braids snaked down scarred backs. Baggy pants belted with coarse rope hung below bony chests. Crude straw sandals encased some feet. Most were bare, blackened and misshapen.

Nor did the cannons mounted in front of fort-like buildings or the gunboats headed straight towards the *Ericsson* signal safety.

"What if they open fire?" Nils said in alarm to the seaman beside him. "We're a merchant ship and not prepared for battle. What if they attack instead of protect?"

But worst of all was the river water connecting them to the ocean. Accustomed to the clear, clean waters of home, Nils never had imagined such water as now swirled viciously around their ship. No wonder it was called Dragon River, and the cause of many superstitions.

"Almighty God!" he choked, struggling against panic and nausea. He leaned over the railing and stared down in horror at the putrid, murky water carrying two bloated corpses past the ship. "Please Almighty God, don't let me die here and I will keep my promise to Pa!"

That evening with difficulty, Nils persuaded four bunkmates to go ashore with him the next day to the nearby Salvation Army Good News Hall. Ever since seeing a sign with those words above a cross earlier on deck, he felt compelled to go but hadn't told anyone why.

Because the captain wasn't allowing anyone shore leave alone, Nils's buddies finally agreed to accompany him. After all, they joked nervously, what could happen on a shore leave within sight of their ship?

Although Captain Johnson refused to go ashore himself, he reluctantly permitted his crew shore leaves in groups – only brief leaves while coolies unloaded his ship's cargo of metal merchandise. When it came time to load the return cargo of carved chests and bolts of silk, then he no longer allowed his men to go ashore.

"For what," he explained when the crewmen protested, "what would I have to bargain with in the event of trouble?"

The next afternoon, Nils and his buddies filed down the gangplank. From the bridge, Captain Johnson called to them, "*God dag!* Good day, men, and God speed. *Gud hastighe!* Be careful, be alert. This is a dark, heathen land."

The sailors strode warily from their ship and along the dockside street of the Bund. Their eyes darted back and forth, not knowing where to look – down at the filth about their boots, around at enticing shops and speeding rickshaws, or behind at the hostile crowd following them and jeering, "*Hai!* Foreign devils! *Hai!*".

Fortunately for the Swedes, scores of armed guards hired by the Western settlements were patrolling. Knowing the guards were quick to fire, the crowd dared not halt Nils and his small band. But that didn't keep them from jeering or begging with outstretched arms, hands and arms blotchy with sores and grime.

Nils and his companions responded by showing empty pockets with one hand, while keeping the other over hidden weapons. They were taking no chances. They knew the reports about Chinese crowds turning violent against foreigners, especially Western ones.

As the men approached the Good News Hall, Nils pointed. "Look, isn't that a European woman standing by the door? And motioning to us?"

In a few more seconds, they could see the woman was young. Her back was towards them, and she was urgently remonstrating and gesturing to someone out of sight. It sounded to Nils like she must be speaking Chinese, for he couldn't understand a word she said.

Just then she turned around. Her face showed instant relief when she saw them.

"Hurry, hurry!" she called in Swedish. "I need your help. Thank Lord God you are here!"

Nils and the others looked at each other questioningly, then quickened their steps and followed her around the buildings. There they came face to face with another noisy crowd. However, this crowd wasn't focused on them, rather on what seemed to be a fight.

A short Chinese man, his face ugly with anger, yelled and struck at a sobbing woman. For a few moments, she staggered about on her stump-like feet, then fell. A cloth-wrapped bundle rolled from her arms. The crowd laughed and jeered. No one stepped forward to help as the man struck her again Her her sobs became moans as she reached out protectively for the bundle.

Simultaneously, the five Swedes lunged forward to help. The instant Nils reached the man, the stout pole meant for the Chinese woman whacked his forehead with tremendous force. With a groan, he collapsed beside her and lay silent. Blood streamed from his forehead.

Nils's buddies grabbed the Chinese man, slugged him, and shoved him face down onto the cobblestone street. Just then, guards came running from around the corner. They scowled at Nils lying bloody and motionless. Several of them seized the man who had struck Nils. They dragged him away, protesting and struggling. The other guards pointed their guns at the onlookers. Waving their weapons and shouting, they forced the crowd to back away from the foreigners.

"*Oh min min!* He will be shot," the European woman said, worry on her face and in her voice. "We must get inside before there's a riot."

She motioned for the Swedes to follow her. Carrying their two limp burdens and pressing a shirt against Nils's bleeding head, they walked swiftly after her. Through an open gate and into a courtyard behind the Good News Hall they hurried. Someone banged the gate shut behind them, and hastily bolted its wooden bar into place.

"*Ja,* he'll be executed," the woman repeated. "Of course, not because of what he was doing to his poor wife and this poor little infant girl, but because he injured a foreign sailor. *Oh min min!* What a terrible situation. I'm so sorry you are involved."

Tenderly, she handed the bundled baby to another European woman who had run out from a building to help.

"Put the woman in this chair, she said to the men. "Ruth here will take care of her and the baby. Come this way with your friend."

*   *   *

Several days later, Captain Johnson of the *Sverige Ericsson* stood beside the bed in the guestroom of the Salvation Army quarters where Nils had lain since his injury.

Shaking his head, his face grave, the Captain placed his hands over Nils's. He liked Nils. Leaving him in this condition was difficult to do. However, time had run out. He agreed with Miss Lizzie and her companions Bertil and Ruth Carlson that Nils would have a better chance of recovering here than on shipboard, especially should the seas turn rough.

As the Captain arranged for Nils's care, he was interested to learn the three Salvation Army officers were Swedes from America.

"We're a pioneer team," they told him, "provisionally stationed here to determine the feasibility of establishing an Army mission at this time."

Pleased to find the three conversant in Swedish, the Captain spent most of the day with them instead of his planned hour or two. Even as they focused intently on Nils's precarious situation, they discussed numerous other topics.

In particular, the Captain asked what Miss Lizzie and the Carlsons thought about the tense political atmosphere throughout China.

With lowered voice, Bertil said, "Serious trouble is ahead for Westerners here unless solutions to the trade problems are worked out soon. And I mean very soon, or more and more terrible things will happen. Paid guards can't keep their countrymen in control indefinitely, especially ruthless rebels like the Boxers. Every day we wonder how long God wants us to stay."

Miss Lizzie added, "The Chinese don't like being exploited by outsiders, and why should they? The forced trade in opium is a dreadful curse. It's not just superstition that makes them call us foreign devils. Unfortunately, those of us with good intentions aren't always separated from the many foreigners who really are devils. I can understand why secret groups like the Boxers have vowed to destroy foreigners and their property until we leave, every single one of us, and it makes me afraid, afraid too for the Chinese who associate with us."

Late in the afternoon the Captain said, "I'm sorry, my friends. I can't delay even one more day. The *Ericsson* must lift anchor for Sweden early tomorrow. The mates insist."

The Carlsons and Miss Lizzie nodded.

"Sir," Miss Lizzie said, "you can rest assured we will give Nils our best care. As you've observed, there are good signs his head wound will heal. Please tell his family we're doing everything possible for him, that we pray for him every day. Tell them we'll send either him or a letter on the next ship to Sweden."

Bending close to Nils's ear, Captain Johnson said, "*Adjo*, son, goodbye. Every crewman sends you a prayer. We'll be looking for you back in Goteborg soon."

Nils opened his eyes. The others watch him as he struggled to smile and say goodbye. He tried to tell the Captain that Miss Lizzie was right. Someone wasn't letting him die. But his words were jumbled and didn't make sense.

The Captain grasped Nils's hand one last time. At that, Nils did manage a weak *adjo,* causing smiles of relief on the faces of those gathered around him.

*   *   *

In a few weeks, Nils was recovered enough to take daily walks around the courtyard behind the Good News Hall. At first he needed someone on each side to support and balance him. Soon he was able to walk well by holding on to another person's arm.

The walks Nils enjoyed most were the ones with Miss Lizzie. He talked easily to her. Repeatedly she told him his progress was a miracle. Not many people survive a cracked skull and brain injury. She helped him in calm ways recall what his injured brain kept forgetting. He could always think better after walking with her.

One afternoon he remembered to ask Lizzie why that was.

"*Ja*, but of course," she said with a smile. "It's because Lord God has given me healing ways, and guides me in the use of remedies. Like the aloe vera treatment I've been using on your injuries. And do you know? Each morning I pray Lord God will touch you with healing and wholeness. Right after your accident, I sensed you wouldn't die, at least not soon. I'm the one who talked the Captain into leaving the crate of merchandise in your room I knew you would need the money it will bring when you recover."

Long into that evening, Nils thought about what Lizzie had said. He was pretty sure this time he would remember and not have to be told again. For the first time, he focused on living in China. He wondered how long that might be and what he should do.

"Thank you, Almighty God," he whispered, nearly asleep. "Thank you for giving me a second chance. Please give me strength to keep my promise."

The next morning, a commotion of voices in the kitchen interrupted their breakfast of rice gruel and toast. Lizzie excused herself. In a few minutes, she returned with the woman whose rescue nearly cost Nils his life.

"Wang Tai-tai hears you are recovering," Lizzie said to Nils. "She is happy for you, and is grateful to be free from the shame of your possible death. She thanks you for rescuing her and her baby, and offers herself to you as wife or concubine. If you say so, she will give away her daughter, though that would be a great bitterness to bear."

Startled, Nils looked at the young woman bowing low before him, a small baby fastened with strips of cloth to her back. Then he looked at the others at the table.

Bertil came to his assistance. Rising and bowing, he said, "Lizzie, please tell Wang Tai-tai she is very generous, and our friend appreciates her kindness. I will be his go-between. Ask her please to return tomorrow to discuss this matter."

Expressing more humble thanks, the woman bowed and backed out of the room, wobbling on her bound feet.

"That's a surprise," Ruth said. "I heard she returned to her family home in one of the river villages. Either she didn't go or she's already come back. What should we do?"

Reaching for the coffee, Lizzie smiled at Nils. "Assuming you aren't planning to marry her, I think we should employ her. We've been talking about another helper. Granted, we don't know anything about her. But because of the circumstances, I think she'll be loyal to us. Perhaps she offered herself to you out of desperation, not just gratitude. Besides, this is an open door to rescue an infant girl and tell her mother about True God."

Nils nodded. Once again he felt overcome with deep gratitude for the care and understanding of these new friends in this strange land. Tears filled his eyes, but the words he longed to say formed too slowly for him to speak them aloud.

In time, he thought, *in time my sentences will come again easily. Everyday Lizzie tells me so. Soon I will tell her how much she means to me, and that I want to spend my life with her.*

*   *   *

Several days later, Wang Sister, as she was now called by her new friends, prepared for night in a small room in a back building of the Salvation Army compound. Never before had she lived in such a fine place or worked for such caring people. She could scarcely believe her good fortune, especially the abundance of food three times a day. She was ready to lie down beside her baby asleep on the quilted *pugais* spread over the strange bed of woven rope and wood. But first she knelt beside the corner of the straw floor mat where she had hidden her paper river goddess image.

"We worship only True God here," she had been told politely after moving in and arranging her few possessions. "Please remove your paper goddess from the wall."

Puzzled, she had complied. Now she worried the river goddess of her village might become angry with her village and yet again stir up the river dragon against them. If she could not burn incense and offer appeasements gifts of food, what should she do?

In a dream that night, her answer came.

She dreamed she saw a beautiful shining light and heard a strange voice – a kind voice that told her not to be afraid. The voice told her to worship the True God of her new employers. That back home in Fengshan, her people longed to hear about True God too. They were weary of trying to please the fearsome river gods.

The next morning, Wang Sister awakened with a new feeling in her heart – peace.

"Little Daughter, Shiao-mei," she said to her suckling baby, "we have a new god whose name is True God."

*   *   *

Abbie's Journal
May 26, 2000
. . . I had a frightening dream last night – and not one of my war nightmares. I was back in China and on trial. I didn't

know for what, but thought it was for being a Christian. As the judge harshly announced my sentence in Chinese, I didn't look at my family, so they wouldn't be in any way incriminated by me. Later I found out it was terrible I hadn't looked at them because – that's when I awakened, not remembering why, and my heart pounding in my ears. Now as I write, I feel great sadness to think of millions of Chinese who really experienced something like that, including many of my family's dear Christian friends. . .

Chapter 5

Abbie's Journal
Aug 1, 2000
. . . Gramma Lizzie wrote her journals in English. Grampa Nils wrote his in Swedish, with occasional phrases in Chinese characters. I have only one memory of visiting him as a child, and how we two Anglos spoke Chinese to each other since I didn't know Swedish. After Dad retired, he translated Grampa's journals and memoirs into English. Dad tried to interest me in his parents' writings, but with minimal success at the time because of my own busy schedule. Hey Dad, I hope you somehow know that now I'm not too busy – now I'm very interested. And I hope Gramma and Grampa know too. . .

Shanghai, 1893
Year of Serpent

Lizzie placed the kerosene lamp carefully on a wooden tray in the center of her bed, then methodically tucked in the mosquito net around her. She took her mother's latest letter from under her pillow, and hoped Ruth wouldn't enter to scold her for reading in bed with the lamp. The mosquitoes were so bad, and this was her only chance to read and think a bit.

The letter, dated nearly a year ago, had taken eight months to reach her. For several weeks now, it had been her nightly bedtime treat. Lizzie unfolded the enclosed front page of the Seattle Times and smoothed it out beside the lamp. She peered closely at the photo of herself and the Carlsons in their uniforms, waving from the rails of the ship departing for Shanghai.

She read again the caption beneath the photo. "Salvationists embark for China to the cheers and prayers of comrades and the tune of *Onward Christian Soldiers* rendered by the Seattle Salvation Army Band. Like Daniel and his friends of old, these brave warriors declare God is able to deliver them from the fiery battles ahead. However, even if God chooses not to keep their bodies from destruction, they still head to a foreign battleground to fight evil, confident of God's sustaining grace."

Back then, Lizzie had felt peace about sacrificing marriage to bring God's love to a country where few followed Christianity. Since Oliver had not shared her call from God, they had parted. As she packed for her journey to the other side of the globe, he had disconsolately helped her.

At the Des Moines train station, his last words were, "I'll be waiting, Lizzie. You'll always be first in my heart. Keep me in yours"

She remembered answersing, "Don't wait for me, dear Oliver. I may not return."

Since arriving in Shanghai, she was no longer so sure about her decision. For the first time in her life, she felt loneliness every day. Living in this land, surrounded by hostile Chinese, she longed to experience intimate companionship like the Carlsons had. Even their bouts of "righteous friction" – their explanation – did not lessen the intensity of her longings.

These days, the constant presence of Nils made her uncomfortably aware of her singleness. Thinking back, Lizzie wondered if her feeling for Oliver had been just a special friendship because he had rescued her. Maybe she had not truly loved him in the man-woman way. Perhaps that's why she had so easily said "no" to his marriage proposals. Maybe it hadn't been a sacrifice after all when she told him not to wait for her.

Nils now – with Nils she felt so different. How devastated she'd be to find out he had someone special back in Sweden. Already she was dreading the thought of telling him "goodbye." And she couldn't bear to think of saying "no" to him should he offer more than friendship. That would be a true sacrifice.

Oh min min! I guess I'd better confide in Ruth, Lizzie thought. She turned down the wick, then placed the lamp and tray on the floor between her bed and her large camphor clothes chest.

The next day, the first opportunity she had, she asked Ruth for advice. She did so with reluctance even though she and Ruth had become close friends. But she had no one else to ask.

"Never before have I felt such a tenseness in my heart and body when a man is near," she disclosed in low, embarrassed tones when the two of them were alone in the kitchen after breakfast.

"Sometimes I can hardly keep from gasping when I'm with Nils."

Ruth looked at her strangely, then said quietly, "Lizzie, that's what passion does to a woman. Why are you allowing yourself to feel passion for Nils? How can you even think of loving him? He's not called to serve God. He's just a seaman."

Lizzie felt her cheeks get hot. "*Ja,* I know that. So what should I do?"

"Well, pray of course. Ask God to cleanse you of unworthy desires."

"Is that what you did when you first had strong feelings for Bertil?"

"No. But our circumstances were different."

"How? Tell me again."

"Well, don't you remember? We were both Salvationists before we became interested in each other. So neither of us had to turn aside from God's work when we married."

"Oh? Didn't you once tell me something about joining the Army because of Bertil?"

Ruth tightened her lips. "Yes, but we weren't actually a couple yet – just acquaintances." She swallowed. "Maybe you'd like me to pray with you?"

"No, not now, not here. Just keep me in your private prayers. And Ruth, I so hope you won't tell Bertil everything I just said."

*   *   *

Several days later, Lizzie took her turn walking with Nils around the courtyard for his exercise – his daily healing time, he called it. After they finished, he invited her to his room. She hesitated briefly, then followed him, leaving the door open.

"I'd like you to help me think about what I should do now," Nils began in Swedish.

"*Fint,* all right then," she tried to sound normal in spite of the feelings swirling inside her.

He sat down on the large wooden bed that nearly filled the small room. She sat close to him in the only chair. Neither said anything.

Thick, comfortable Chinese quilts were arranged over the bed. A mosquito net hanging from the ceiling was tied neatly to the side in its daytime position. Lizzie knew that at night his net covered the entire bed, like hers, a shield from insects – and inquisitive eyes. Glancing down, she noted the earthen floor around the woven mat was smooth and clean.

She said into the strained silence, "I see Wang Sister is tidying your room nicely."

"Yes. She's learned quickly. She's an excellent

servant. I'm glad you hired her, poor young woman."

He cleared his throat, then said, "Brother and Sister Carlson talked to me yesterday, did you know? They suggested I'm well enough to be making plans."

"That's true, thanks be to God." Lizzie hoped the Carlsons hadn't given away her heart's secret in their obvious attempt to remove temptation from her.

Nils continued, "My family are farmers, *ja*, but we are also river traders. Have I told you we are seven sons and two daughters? Because Pa needed to do more than our small farm to support our large family, he became a river trader. Then Mother ran the farm with us children helping. Since Pa's death, all of us still work the farm and carry on the trading. Mother says I'm a born merchant, like Pa. That's why I signed on the *Ericsson* – to learn more from Captain Johnson. Did he tell you he had advanced me to third mate for the voyage home?"

No, Lizzie hadn't known, and she nodded with interest. She liked hearing about Nils's life, and was pleased to note his thinking and speaking no longer seemed affected by his head injury.

"Well, because of all that and the crate of merchandise from Captain Johnson, I think I will try trading here. The Carlsons told me there are many Western traders in Shanghai, too many in fact, but perhaps none on the river. Since I'm a river man, I've been thinking that's where I could start. What do you think?"

For a moment, Lizzie was speechless. "Stay here to live and work? *Oh min min*, Nils, I thought you would use the crate of merchandise to secure your passage home. Besides, you speak only a little English, Chinese not at all, and you're so tall and fair."

You silly woman, she thought, *I guess you won't have to decide whether or not to go back to Sweden with him.*

Nils laughed. "I can't change my looks, but I can dress in Chinese clothes like you and the Carlsons. I can surely learn more English and Chinese. In fact, I already have in spite of my injury, haven't you noticed? Lizzie, that's why I wanted to talk with you. I thought maybe you would help me."

Before she could answer, Nils leaned closer to her. His shoulder touched hers and he asked softly, "Lizzie, have you taken a vow never to marry?"

"Why no! No Nils, it's that. . ."

At that moment, Ruth appeared in the doorway.

"Tea's ready," she announced. "Bertil and I are waiting."

"Oh my," Lizzie said, standing up quickly. "We weren't watching the time. Sorry, we'll come right now."

Nils stood up slowly to avoid blacking out, as she had taught him to do, and followed her into the sitting room.

If Bertil and Ruth noticed signs of increased warmth between Lizzie and Nils during tea, they gave no indication. As they drank tea and ate pork buns, the Carlsons and Lizzie planned the evening evangelistic street meeting. After that, they discussed with Nils his plans for a river trading business.

Because Lizzie and the Carlsons were provisionally affiliated with the China Inland Mission, Lizzie suggested Nils might do the same.

"You'll need the backing of some official group if you decide to stay in China" Lizzie said, expecting him to demur.

But he didn't hesitate. "*Ja*, sure, how do I arrange that? Do I have to belong to a specific church?"

"No," Ruth answered. "China Inland Mission members are from many churches. I think you'll need to meet with Brother Taylor. Have you heard of Missionary

Hudson Taylor? He's the head of the Mission, so is the one responsible for us and many others."

*   *   *

Two days later, Nils found himself wearing a borrowed blue cotton Mandarin long-gown and a black silk skullcap with its false black queue. It was his first outing since his head injury. Hurtling along in a rickshaw behind the others, he quickly became uneasy and nauseous.

The jolting and swerving of the rickshaw in addition to the noises and smells of the crowded streets increased his anxiety. He forced his eyes shut and focused on keeping calm, as Lizzie had reminded him to do. He felt desperate and began to pray. Suddenly, he felt a warm feeling of trust – peaceful trust like he felt when he was younger and sitting close to Pa.

After a long time, he sensed the rickshaw turn onto a quieter, smoother street. When it began to slow, he opened his eyes. They were pulling up in front of some brown tile-roofed buildings, clustered behind a tall, stone and mud wall. They stopped before the large gate. The rickshaw coolie lowered the pulling shaft to the ground. Nils, unprepared for the change in tilt, nearly fell out – to everyone's amusement and then concern.

"I guess you can tell it's my first rickshaw ride," he said, his lips in a tight smile as he stepped down awkwardly. "I'm feeling shaky."

"Here, take my arm," Lizzie said.

He felt strengthened by the warmth of her body touching his. While Bertil paid the coolies, Nils walked with Lizzie and Ruth to the thick wooden gate. Lizzie called out a few words in Chinese. In a minute, the small walking door in the gate was opened by a smiling, bowing doorman.

As they stepped through the opening, Nils saw the buildings around the courtyard were larger and more Western than the Salvation Army ones. He heard the singing of hymns coming from the large building straight ahead of them. His heart pounded faster. He wondered what Lizzie and the Carlsons would think when they heard him tell Dr. Taylor about his promise to Pa years ago.

*   *   *

Abbie's Journal
Aug 18, 2000
. . . growing up in China and Taiwan like I did, I knew Dr. Taylor's grandson as "Uncle" James, and loved listening to the stories he told when he was in our home. So it's been fascinating to read about the start of the friendship between our families a century ago. The sons of Uncle James were also my friends. Bert and I were in high school together in Taichung. Jim and I became friends as adults living in Taiwan. . .
. . . I remember Uncle James and Aunt Alice once spent several weeks with Dan and me in our Kaohsiung home. They were retired by then and visiting from the States. I don't recall why they stayed with us instead of with Jim and his family. Maybe because we had a larger home and a guestroom. Quite a dynasty of Asia missionaries, those Taylors, and associated with several missions. Makes me sad I haven't seen any of them for years. I think that's my only regret growing up an expatriate, third culture kid – special friends come and go, and are rarely seen again. . .

Chapter 6

Abbie's Journal
Sep 1, 2000
. . . today's our wedding anniversary – our 35th – and not all blissful years, that's for sure. But then is any marriage, even for committed Christians? Dan and I told the kids our trip to Rome next week is all the celebration we want. I expect they're relieved. Instead, we've started planning an early 50th celebration – a Yangzi River cruise for the entire family. In a few years, flooding from the Three Gorges Dam will change the riverside landscape so much and submerge so many antiquities. I want the kids to see the China of their ancestors before everything changes. Who knows, maybe Beijing will be selected for the 2008 Olympics and we can do both in the same trip. . .

Shanghai, 1893
Same Year of Serpent

The singing died away as Lizzie and Nils followed the Carlsons into a large reception dining hall. The familiar warmth of the greetings that met them surprised Nils. He hadn't known Lizzie and the Carlsons had all these missionary friends.

"Lizzie, where's your accordion?" someone asked in a British accent.

"I didn't bring it today. We brought our guest Nils Newquist instead."

A tall man spoke out in Swedish, then in English. "Welcome, Brother Newquist, we've been praying for you. We hope you will share your testimony of healing."

There were more words of approval and applause

for Nils. He smiled and nodded at the happy faces circling him.

"You didn't expect this, did you?" Lizzie whispered after they sat down.

"No, but I like it. It feels like church back home. Except for the Chinese clothes."

They smiled at each other, enjoying their private humor of the group's appearance.

As they sat down, the harmonious singing began again, led by several guitars and a pump organ. Lizzie pulled a Swedish hymn book from her handbag and shared it with Nils. Their hands touched under the book's cover, and neither one pulled away.

Oh min min, this feeling growing between us isn't unworthy, Lizzie thought as she sang. *It's blessed. The Lord God has brought us together and will guide us in working everything out for His purposes. I can quit worrying.*

So great was her relief, she fought back tears and couldn't sing for a time. So she followed along with the words, hearing for the first time Nils's mellow baritone singing one of her family's Swedish favorites:

> Love Divine, so great and wondrous
> Deep and mighty, pure, sublime:
> Coming from the heart of Jesus,
> Just the same through tests of time.
> He the pearly gates will open,
> So that I may enter in:
> For He purchased my redemption,
> And forgave me all my sin.

He sings like Charlie and Johann – and Papa. Is that a sign, a sign from you, oh Lord God? Lizzie prayed for Nils beside her, and for courage and guidance for both of them.

After more than an hour of songs, testimonies and prayers, Nils rose slowly to his feet, careful not to risk blacking out. A hush settled over the group, even among the restless children. All seemed eager to hear from the newcomer – from someone who might have died, but for their prayers and God's intervention.

"I don't know most of you, yet you already seem like my friends," Nils began in Swedish.

He paused and looked down at Lizzie. She stood up quickly beside him and began translating into English.

"I'm sure each of you has a story of faith or you wouldn't be here. This afternoon, some of you have shared your stories. I've been inspired and blessed.

"I am ashamed to tell you that for too long, my faith story has been a secret. Not that I haven't loved Almighty God. All my family and friends know I do. But I have been silent and reluctant about doing something special for Almighty God, something I once promised to my father. That's what I have kept secret. I planned to keep my promise someday, then kept putting it off, busy with other matters. Before long, my silence caused an awkwardness between heaven and me."

Expressions of understanding showed on many faces throughout the group, giving Nils courage to continue.

"Today I stand before you like Jonah. Like him, I've learned the cost of running away from God. Like him, God has spared my life. Like Jonah, I find myself in a heathen land. And like Jonah, I must change the direction of my life.

"I think for you to understand, I need to take you back in my life to when my father died. That was about ten years ago and a very difficult time for my family. My brothers and sisters and I were fortunate to have had a father like ours. As we were growing up, he and Mother loved God and taught us to also.

"With nine children to raise, Mother worked hard on the farm while Pa did river trading, We younger children helped Mother and the older ones helped Pa. God prospered our family, so we often had enough to share.

"Several years before Pa died, he took a couple of my brothers and me and our sister to special meetings in Stockholm. Rev. Fredrik Franson was the evangelist. Perhaps some of you have also attended his meetings and know him?"

The response to the name of Franson in the room astonished Nils. Excited remarks burst forth around the room, which were soon hushed by a reminder from the leader that Nils had more to say.

"When we went to hear Rev. Franson, I was sixteen. The others were a few years older. Even though we were young, we were awed by his powerful sermons and by the wonderful music. Never before had we attended such large, enthusiastic meetings. For a long time afterwards, we talked about them. We followed with interest every word about Franson's evangelistic campaigns as he traveled to different countries around the world. And we prayed for him in our family's evening devotions.

"Several times Pa talked alone with me about joining Rev. Franson in his work for God, like some other young Swedes were doing. Maybe he talked to my brothers about joining, too. They never said. Pa told me he wished he were young, because that's what he would do. He said he thought God Almighty was calling me. I felt so too in my heart. Yet I always told Pa I wasn't sure. I think I was waiting to hear a real voice call me, a voice like Samuel heard.

"Then Pa got pneumonia." Nils paused. He put his hand on Lizzie's arm to steady himself. His voice quavered when he went on.

"Pa had been ill with pneumonia several times before, so we weren't too worried. But this time, he just got worse and worse. The doctor said his lungs were worn out.

"I felt just terrible. I thought maybe my father was dying because I hadn't said "yes" to serving Almighty God with Rev. Franson. One afternoon when Pa was alone for a few minutes, I knelt beside his bed and whispered to him that I would join Rev. Franson's team. I promised Pa I would serve Almighty God – serve Him for both of us even though I was only nineteen. I don't know if Pa heard me or not. I have no doubt Almighty God did.

"Months ago, when my ship docked in Shanghai, everything I saw horrified me. This city looked like a place of such despair and death. As I stood with other crewmen on deck, I thought, what if I die here and never get to keep my promise? Then I really began to pray.

"In Sweden, sometimes I attended Salvation Army meetings. In my own church, the Free Church of Sweden, we often sang the hymns from the Army songbook. So when I saw the sign for the Good News Hall of the Salvation Army not far from where we were docked, I felt compelled to go there and renew the promise I made in secret to my dying father.

"How could I have known that by going there I would almost die? Or that God would use Lizzie and the Carlsons to save my life and bring me here today?"

Nils cleared his throat. Others did too and several wiped their eyes.

"Well, my promise is no longer secret. I guess by telling you this afternoon, I have started to keep it. Please don't stop praying for me. My head seems nearly well. I'm not sure about my soul."

He bowed his head, and the others in the room followed his example. In the silence that seemed holy, Nils made a second pledge to God. He vowed to give up chocolate, one of his great pleasures. It would be a private fast forever, so to speak, a secret reminder to himself of his submission to God and a symbol of his willingness to serve God.

During the rest of the afternoon and evening, Nils was amazed to learn that most of the Swedish-speaking missionaries in the group had come in response to appeals for China by Rev. Franson.

Absorbed, Nils listened to the story. How Franson had received a heavy burden on his heart for China's desperate millions by listening to Hudson Taylor, the English missionary doctor and preacher. Nils learned more about Dr. Taylor and his call from God to find one thousand missionaries for China. Nils was deeply moved to hear about Franson's response of founding a Scandinavian mission, as well as many other mission societies.

The best part of the story was that Nils heard it during dinner from Dr. Taylor himself.

Dinner, a tasty Swedish meal in Nils's honor, was excellently prepared and served by gracious Chinese servants to several dozen missionaries and their children. During tea and fruit, Dr. Taylor prayed aloud for Nils, then urged him to join Franson's mission.

"I will recommend you myself," he said. "I have heard your testimony of faith and miraculous recovery. I am convinced God has sent you to China just as He sent Jonah to Ninevah, like you shared. Brother Franson will rejoice when he hears about you."

To the earnest-faced group gathered around him, Nils said, "*Ja,* I will join. If for some reason it is not Almighty God's will for me to work here in China, I will trust Him to open other doors. It is time to keep my promise."

Lizzie stayed close to Nils throughout the evening –

interpreting for him when he conversed with English speaking missionaries, and entering freely into the discussion when they spoke Swedish.

She hoped this would become the pattern of their lives together. She hoped neither of them would ever consider the other less than equal, but as their helper and companion provided by God. She expected their lives would pass through many valleys of death and danger. On this night, she felt that together they could face any despair because they would be side by side.

Riding back to their rooms turned out to be an unforgettable experience for everyone, especially for Lizzie and Nils. It was the first evening of the Lantern Festival, and all of Shanghai seemed to be celebrating the new understanding between the two of them.

As the rickshaw coolies whisked them between the hundreds of dazzling lanterns, Nils called out to Lizzie that he'd never before seen anything like it. She called back that so far in her experience, this was the Chinese festival she enjoyed most, partly because it wasn't as noisy and frantic as the New Year's celebrations had just been.

On this night, thousands of children and adults dressed in colorful new clothes walked the streets. Each one carried a brightly decorated paper or wooden lantern alight with flickering candles. Streets normally dark and dangerous, were beautifully illuminated and festive.

When they reached the Good News Hall, they sat quietly in their rickshaws for several moments. Even the coolies looked around in wonder.

Then Lizzie said with longing, "*Oh min min!* How I long for them all to know the Eternal Light of the world."

*   *   *

Abbie's Journal
Sep 16, 2000
. . . *probably because of censorship fears, Gramma Lizzie and Grampa Nils wrote very little about the terrible political upheavals they experienced in China – things I now know, like how the Chinese struggled to survive the disastrous Opium War and the resulting Boxer Rebellion. How the revolution under Sun Yat-sen finally overthrew the oppressive rule of emperors. How Japanese aggression caused untold suffering. And all the while, how warring among greedy warlords devastated large areas of the country. No wonder Gramma and Grampa felt called to live in China to share God's message of eternal light and hope, even if it meant risking their lives – and their children's. . .*

Chapter 7

Abbie's Journal
Dec 20, 2000
. . . it's been a while since I've done anything with my
China boxes. So this morning I read a couple of Gramma
Lizzie's letters – ones her mother had saved and Dad got
after he retired. The paper is so old and brittle, I hesitated
to unfold the pages. I was touched to tears by what
Gramma wrote about her coming wedding. She longed for
her family to be able to attend! But of course, they couldn't.
Nor could Nils's family come from Sweden. She tells how
their wedding would be in three languages – Swedish,
English, and Chinese. . .

Yangtze River, 1894
Year of Horse

"A wise rule, I suppose," Nils grumbled to Lizzie, referring
to the rule that single missionaries were not permitted to
marry for two years after arriving on the China field.

"Waiting so long makes me feel like we're wasting
precious time. What if something happens and we never get
to, uh, be together?"

"Not too many more months," Lizzie soothed,
"until we sleep under the same quilt."

She smiled at his expression, and gently touched the
new mustache he was growing because he wanted to appear
more dignified and scholar-like.

"Nils, that's a Chinese saying. I didn't make it up,
so don't look at me like that. But of course, like you, I'm
looking forward to our marriage bed and having children."

He leaned over the low table between them, stroked

her cheeks and touched her lips with his. She knew he admired her openness.

With embarrassed glances, the boatmen muttered to each other about the strange improprieties of foreigners, even good ones like these two. Did they know respectable people did not converse or touch before marriage in public, at least not with a number one wife? Then to save face for Nils and Lizzie, the men pretended not to be watching.

"It is all right," Lizzie assured the men in Chinese. "We will soon be married. Look around. How many people can see us here in the boat? This is like our home. You understand, do you not?"

The men assented and eased their embarrassment with loud laughter. Nils joined in. This time, Lizzie politely covered her mouth with her hand and giggled softly, proving she did indeed know proper Chinese decorum.

With skill, the boatmen used the rudder and long bamboo poles to guide the sanpan on its return journey to Shanghai through the swift downriver current. As the boat rocked and twisted, Nils was lulled to sleep. From across the table, Lizzie looked at his tall body slumped in the chair. She smiled at the top of his blonde curly head, and a feeling of joy and tenderness spread through her. She let herself daydream about their lives together – something she never tired of doing.

Her happiness was interrupted with an uneasy thought. *Has Oliver received my letter yet? I wonder how he feels about Nils and me marrying and staying in China. Please, oh Lord God, help him to have chosen someone else. Then what I do won't matter so much.*

Lizzie looked from Nils to the River. For a moment, its appearance startled her. *Will I always expect the blues and silvers of the Des Moines River? Will I never get used to this murky brown one and its secrets?*

A bloated body came into view. She flinched, and

pressed her crossed hands over her heart. She watched the body pass in silence, certain it was a young girl. She was learning not to make a commotion over such sights. They were frequent. And no Chinese would touch the bodies for fear of harm from evil spirits or of interfering with fate. Well, she too believed in evil spirits. To dispel a disquieting sense of darkness, she went into the cabin and picked up her accordion. As the sanpan swept past a river village, the people heard her playing and singing. They looked up from their tasks to listen.

One woman washing clothes along the bank called out, "Welcome, foreigners. Next time stop at our village. Good words we hear about you."

Awakened, Nils stood and waved until the woman and her village were out of sight.

When Lizzie came and stood beside him, he said, "Let's stop at that village next trip."

She nodded and they reached for each other's hands. Every few minutes, Nils smoothed his mustache with his fingers. Lizzie smiled at the new gesture so like her dear Papa's.

For a long while, they held hands and gazed together at the sights along the passing shoreline. Sanpans and junks of all sizes were moving or moored. Signs of poverty were everywhere. Ancient temples and pagodas towered above vegetables plots and rice paddies. Small rivers and canals made their way to the River, flowing past ponds and mulberry trees. And the people, oh the people – adults and children milled about everywhere, except on an occasional craggy cliff inhabited by only a few stunted, wind-bent trees.

A loud drumming broke their pensive spell. *DUM, DUM, DUM, DUM, DUM. . .* a strange, quick drumming, not the familiar beat of trackers' drums.

"What drums are those?" they asked the boatmen at

the same time.

Chu Boatman peered behind their small sanpan as he guided it closer to shore. "It is a warning drum," he said. "Ah, now I see the boats. Yes, as I thought. Several dragon boats are practicing."

"Practicing for what?" Nils asked.

"Practicing for the race of the Dragon Boat Festival. Next week is the festival. There will be many races all over China. The races will be extra special this year to celebrate the sixtieth birthday of the honorable Empress Dowager. You must go and see the race in Shanghai. It will be the best one."

As they stared at the speeding boats coming closer, Chu continued, "Ah miserable me, several years ago I tried to join a Shanghai rowing team. I passed the strength test. Then they found out I am a eunuch and chased me away. Only whole men can row to ensure good fortune. *Ai yah!* That was one of my blackest times."

Chu said something else, but his words were drowned out by the noise of three dragon boats racing past. Each dragon head was different, yet each was huge and fierce and a brilliant red. The scaly red and gold tails whipping past them seemed almost alive. Dozens of rowers stood in the long, narrow boats, chanting and rowing their long oars in unison under billowing yellow Imperial flags.

"*Oh min min!* Just look at them," Lizzie said. "I haven't seen a dragon boat race yet. That's something we can watch for the first time together. I've heard the races can be dangerous, and in nearly every race someone drowns, often an onlooker. But the people expect that. My language teacher told me the deaths become honorable sacrifices to appease river and lake gods, and help bring bountiful harvests."

"Sounds like the legends of our Viking boat races," Nils said. "And did you see? The dragon boats even look like ancient Viking longships. Their similarity astounds me."

"*Ja,* I've seen paintings and carvings of longships. You're right. They are alike, even the dragon prows."

After a moment she added, "Last year I tasted dragon boat festival *tsongtse* for the first time. They're so delicious. I kept eating and eating them."

"You mean mooncakes?" Nils asked.

"No, those are for the Lunar New Year."

"So, what are *tsongtse* then?"

"Hmm, they're something like dumplings, made from rice instead of flour, with all kinds of tasty bits in the center. And wrapped in banana leaves, then steamed. I've had some with sweetened red bean, some with pork, and even peanuts. During the Dragon Boat Festival, the people throw *tsongtses* into the rivers and lakes as offerings for an ancient poet hero who drowned – also for the gods, especially the river dragon god. We should study the festival with our language teachers, shouldn't we? You'll like *tsongtse's.*"

"Chu Boatman, do you eat *tsongtse?*" Nils asked.

"A thousand yeses. I think they are my favorite food. Years ago I learned to prepare *tsongtse* a special way from a cook of the Imperial Family. I prepare them poorly, but would you like me to make some for you?"

"Yes! Yes, please do that," Nils said. "And thank you, thank you. You are indeed our good friend. When the time comes, shall we watch the dragon boat races together?" He smoothed his mustache.

"I would be honored," Chu said, grinning and bowing.

The other boatmen looked at him with admiration on their faces.

*   *   *

Abbie's Journal
Dec 28, 2000
. . . *how exotic – I've been reading about Gramma Lizzie and Grampa Nils starting married life aboard a sanpan junk on the Yangtze – a century ago, imagine! In a letter, Gramma describes how they were carried to the Shanghai church in decorated sedan chairs. They wore red silk Chinese wedding garments, handsewn in the old style with wide sleeves and colorfully embroidered borders. . .*
. . . they were married in the presence of many friends, and repeated their vows in Swedish. Grampa became a U.S. citizen when they married, so the American ambassador performed the marriage ritual. Missionary Dr. James Hudson Taylor preached the wedding sermon in Chinese. Hymns were sung in all three languages. Afterwards, a proper ten-course Chinese wedding feast catered from a nearby restaurant was served in the church courtyard. . .
. . . much later, as they stepped into the sedan chairs to be carried to their houseboat, Chinese friends startled them by popping off hundreds of firecrackers fastened on a rope at the end of a long bamboo pole. Both Gramma and Grampa thought for a minute they were being attacked by rebels. They posed for photographs in front of the church. I don't remember ever seeing any, so I'm guessing the photos were lost or destroyed. Maybe a cousin has one. I'll ask around. When they married, Gramma was 25 and Grampa 31. . .

PART THREE

Dreams . . . Escapes
Storyline 1896 to 1900
Journal Excerpts from 2001

To have friends come from afar
is happiness, is it not?
~ Sage Confucius (5th century b.c.)

You are my friends
if you do whatever I command you.
~ Gospel of John 15:14

Chapter 8

Abbie's Journal
Feb 6, 2001
. . . I suppose all missionaries are visionary activists to some degree or they wouldn't take on such difficult lives. Gramma Lizzie and Grampa Nils started out as river merchants. But soon were sharing about "True God" to the thousands of river people who eagerly crowded alongside their sanpan. That led to renting Good News Halls in villages along the Yangtze. Next came clinics, and then homes and schools for orphaned and abandoned children – especially girls. If they could retravel the River as Dan and I did recently, they'd see their difficult endeavors have had lasting results. . .

Yangtze River, 1896
Year of Monkey

Every minute or so, the head boatman shouted warnings towards shore where the trackers were straining with the heavy tug rope. Naked except for straw sandals, the trackers chanted and groaned to the beat of a drum as they struggled to pull the riverboat through a stretch of treacherous rapids. *DUM dum, DUM dum, DUM dum.*

Those traveling on the *Good News Boat*, with the yellow silk banner of the Imperial Empress Dowager flying high above them, had hoped to reach their destination before dark. But daylight was nearly gone, and Fengshan was still several hours away.

Everyone aboard was tense and exhausted. Monsoon rains had come early and added many days to their wearisome journey. Worried about flooding and mud slides, few people braved the pouring rain to watch them pass these days. As the *Good News* inched slowly up the swelling, muddy River, the path for the trackers became dangerously slippery with deepening mud.

"*Ai yah! Ai yah!*" suddenly burst from the trackers as several of them slid to their knees in the mud, causing the riverboat to jerk violently and be swept backwards by the wild current.

"What is the matter with you clumsy pullers," the head boatman yelled. "Do you want us all to drown? Pay attention to what you are doing."

"Do not be so harsh, Chu Boatman," Nils admonished in fluent Chinese, rapidly rubbing his fingers back and forth across his mustache. He stood braced on the open deck between the two cabins. Lizzie stood with him, tightly grasping his waist, her eyes as anxious as his.

"Did you hear me curse even once, Nieh Husband?" the boatman protested with a slight bow. "It is just that we cannot let the trackers quit now. Consider if we were forced to camp here overnight, we would face the peril of bandits and even worse, maybe Boxers."

"But we have the protection of the gunboat," Lizzie said, looking behind them.

"Ah, where is it?" the boatman said. "I have not seen or heard it for some time now. Besides, what good is a gunboat if your boat shatters on these shoals and sinks in the rapids!"

"Tell the trackers to halt," Nils said. "Then blow the horn and see if the gunboat responds." He rubbed his mustache some more.

Three times the boatman blew the horn and waited. Three times there was no response.

"I believe this is an emergency," Nils said quietly to Lizzie in Swedish and she nodded. "I'll see if gunfire gets a response."

He stepped down into their cabin and retrieved his gun from its hiding place.

At the sudden, unexpected blast so near them, the boatmen and trackers yelled out in terror and fell flat, covering their heads.

"*Wah!* Help us, gods and ancestors. *Wah!* We are frightened to death," a young man's voice sobbed.

Nils called out loudly, "*Bu yao pa!* Do not be afraid! That was my fire-sword you heard. Now listen. Is there an answer?"

All were silent.

Then from far down the River they heard a faint return shot. Upon hearing it, Chu Boatman came quickly to Nils and Lizzie.

"Now the bandits have heard the guns, it will be safe to stay here overnight. Bandits and even Boxers around here do not have guns," he said. "At dawn we can send one of the trackers back to see why the gunboat has fallen behind. Perhaps it has had engine troubles. Shall we tie up the boat and cook the evening rice? "

*   *   *

For Lizzie and Nils, living on the River never became ordinary, but some routines emerged.

When they had first started trading, Nils rented a small sanpan barge for day trips. In those early days, Lizzie accompanied him as interpreter and assistant. After his knowledge of the Chinese language and way of life increased, the trips lengthened to several days. Then Lizzie stayed behind in Shanghai and managed the shore aspects of the business. Nils and the boatman slept and ate in the only cabin, crowded next to the merchandise.

Soon after they married, the American Salvation Army headquarters determined China was not yet safe enough for a permanent mission. The Carlsons and Lizzie were recalled to the States. Because she was remaining in China with Nils, Lizzie declined her new assignment and requested a leave of absence.

The four said teary farewells on the Bund near the spot where Nils's freighter had once docked. Around them gathered Christian friends singing the traditional, yet sad, farewell, "God be with you til we meet again." Most of them did not expect to meet again on earth.

With the Carlsons' departure, Lizzie and Nils took over the Salvation Army Good News Hall buildings and courtyard. The Chinese who had served the Army, now served them, including Wang Sister and her laughing, plump little daughter.

Nils and Lizzie continued with daily evangelism efforts in the Good News Hall. The only noticeable change was the removal of "Salvation Army" from the sign in front, which they painted over as they refreshed the paint on the cross and the Good News Hall words and characters.

After a busy first year of marriage, Nils and Lizzie decided they were doing well enough to purchase their own riverboat. They found a houseboat with a small sanpan skiff in tow for sale by a warlord's widow with gambling and opium debts to pay. The purchasing negotiations took months longer than they'd expected. Finally, the seemingly endless gauntlets of red tape and bribes were accomplished.

In their eyes, the houseboat was perfect, built with two separate cabin areas – a main one for owners and a second for boatmen. A protected deck area between the cabins provided a place to cook and sit. Plus there were large clay, tile-lined water vats, along with ample storage space for their trading merchandise.

Each cabin was furnished with a large *kang* bed that could comfortably sleep six persons, and eight if necessary. The cabins also contained built-in tables, benches, cupboards and drawers. The portholes, octagonal in shape, were covered inside with special glass shutters in addition to the traditional outside wooden ones.

Lizzie was thrilled the first time she and Nils walked around the riverboat as its legal owners. Together they admired the main cabin with its mahogany paneling. Although compact in space, it was luxurious in decor compared to other places she had called home. And this really was her home. She and Nils owned it.

That same day, they joyfully dedicated their houseboat to God's service, just as they had themselves and their business. A number of missionary co-workers, including elderly Brother Taylor, came to the dedication. Inside on a shelf that had formerly held idols, they placed Bibles and hymn books. Outside in bold red paint was the boat's new name in both Chinese and English, *Good News Boat,* under a cross.

The large riverboat made longer trips upriver possible. Traveling the River was often difficult and dangerous, especially where there were seething rapids or bandits. But Nils and Lizzie knew when God beckoned at an open door, or in this case at a river, they'd better obey.

"Remember what happened to Jonah," Lizzie teased sometimes when they were pondering what action to take.

"No, remember me," Nils liked to retort, fingering the scar welts on his head.

*   *   *

The trip to the river village of Fengshan was by far their longest trip upriver yet. And they had only undertaken it after many days of persuasion by Wang Sister.

"It is time for my family to see how fortunate I am to be working for you," she had begun one day. "I have not seen my parents for several years."

"Do you need help writing a message home?" Lizzie asked. She'd arranged for a scribe for Wang Sister once before – and a messenger, as China did not yet have inland postal service. That was back when Wang Sister wanted her parents to know about the birth of her daughter, the execution of her husband, and her new home and work.

"No thank you, not this time. I want my parents to see their granddaughter, and to see how you have helped me unbind my feet."

"So, you want time off for a visit home?"

"Oh no," Wang Sister replied and waited politely.

"Well then, what do you want?" Lizzie asked.

"I want you and *sian-sheng* husband to take a trading and preaching trip to my village, and allow humble me and Shiao-mei to go with you."

That wasn't the answer Lizzie had expected.

"How far is your village of Fengshan?" she asked after a moment.

"Oh, I know it is far, far away. But you and *sian-sheng* have the large riverboat now."

"How far?" Lizzie repeated smiling.

"Maybe two months, maybe more, depending on the weather and the River."

"Yes, that is far," Lizzie said. "We have not yet taken a trip that distant."

"I will help you more," Wang Sister offered. "I will work longer every day and not take any time off."

"That is very gracious of you. However, that will not be necessary. You already work too hard and too long. I do not know what we would do without you."

As she talked with Wang Sister, Lizzie thought, *I'd better encourage Nils to go soon. Once he knows I'm pregnant, he may try to talk me out of going. This is one trip I don't want to miss.*

So it went, discussion back and forth for days, until

at last Nils agreed. Then came weeks of careful preparations. Wang Sister did work longer days. They all did. Even little Shiao-mei helped, or at least they made her think so. Although Lizzie was eager to tell everyone and especially Nils, she somehow kept her pregnancy secret until she was certain.

Nils responded with joy to the news when she told him one evening in bed not long before their departure. He wasn't at all hesitant about her going on the trip, as dangerous as it might be. She snuggled in his arms and listened with relief to his steadfast words.

"My dear, dear Lizzie, you and our child are in Almighty God's hands, whether here in Shanghai or on the River, whether in life or in death. What's important is that we're together and serving the Almighty."

Even as she agreed, she shed silent tears into her pillow. She didn't want Nils to know that although she trusted God, she still had fears. It wasn't the River that frightened her, but the threat of Boxers.

That night, their embraces were their most tender and passionate yet. In the morning when they awakened, their feet were still entwined.

In all cultures, children are a sign of blessing on marriage, perhaps nowhere more so than in China. So it was with joy they shared their good news with friends before the long trip to Fengshan. Touched by many congratulations and much advice, they promised to be back in time for the birth, God willing, of course.

For the voyage, Nils and Chu Boatman hired trackers a month early to make sure they were well-fed and fit for the arduous weeks ahead. In addition, Nils paid each man a generous advance so their families left behind would be provided for during the men's long absence.

Chu Boatman and his helper usually planned and prepared the river trip meals. With so many trackers for the extended trip to Fengshan, Nils and Chu hired two additional cooks and helpers. They chose men with reputations for honesty, men who could double as boatmen. These men quartered with Chu in the second cabin. The trackers stayed in inns or camped on shore, except when danger forced them to crowd on deck to sleep.

Wang Sister and little Shiao-mei stayed in the main cabin with Lizzie and Nils. At night, they pulled a curtain across the middle of the *kang* for privacy. They had discovered in China physical privacy was nearly non-existent. Still, they did what they could, and tried not to be bothered by crowds of people always giggling and staring, following and touching.

Even on their honeymoon, children and adults had constantly peeked at them. Knowing the Western concept of privacy was unknown to most Chinese, they had tried to adjust – grateful for the moments of privacy provided by quilted *pugais*, mosquito nets, and an infrequent curtain.

*   *   *

That first trip to Fengshan took nearly two months. Overall, it was a satisfying trip without too many unpleasant incidents or bouts of diarrhea. Since it was early fall, the weather was comfortable. Rain and mud slides didn't slow their progress until the last week.

During the daylight hours while they were tugged and poled upriver, Lizzie and Nils studied Chinese. They also read for hours from the Bible and other books, often aloud. While Nils read aloud, Lizzie sewed patchwork quilts and knitted caps and scarves for beggars. When she read, he carved wooden plaques with crosses to give to new believers.

Because summer crops were good and there was no flooding, no famine tormented the area this year. Trading was busy at the villages where they tied up each afternoon for the night. The river people were delighted to get necessities such as cloth, soap, and tools for unbelievably low barter prices. In return, they treated Nils and Lizzie and their helpers with great courtesy.

Soon after sundown each evening, Nils and Chu Boatman lit the riverboat's many lanterns and lamps. That always caused a stir – especially when Lizzie came on deck and played her accordion and sang. For years, city crowds had focused on God through her musical talent when she was with the Salvation Army. Now her musical powers persuaded thousands of river people to gather and consider the wonders of True God.

In Lizzie, the Chinese saw what seemed like a goddess come to life. She was so tall and healthy. To them, her skin was supernaturally smooth and white. She had startling blue eyes and soft, wavy brown hair. She smiled often, showing straight white teeth with no gaps.

"Look at her, just look at her," the river women marveled. Their lined faces and bent bodies were such a contrast to hers, reflecting their harsh lives.

After singing for a while in Swedish and English, she switched to Chinese. Soon Nils and Chu joined her. Then they taught the crowds to sing songs – songs about True God and his son Yeh Su, songs easy to remember and hum later.

After that, with hundreds of attentive people surrounding the boat, Nils liked to ask, "Are you tired? Do you want to go home to bed?"

"No, no" the crowds always shouted. "We want you to speak to us. Yes, yes, speak to us, speak to us."

"I will tell you some stories, may I?"

"Yes, yes, tell us some stories."

"Then you will have to make less noise."

At that, Nils crawled quickly up a ladder and onto

the top of the main cabin. The crowds always gasped at that, and quieted as Nils held up his large black Chinese Holy Book. Then he told them stories from the Bible, especially disciple stories, and finally his own story how Almighty God spared his life, like Jonah so long ago. When his story was finished, he said, "My friends, everything you have heard tonight is true. It is not legend. It is not superstition. I promise, if you choose to follow True God by believing in Yeh Su his son, your life will change in amazing ways. Next time we come, Chu Boatman over there will tell you how True God has changed his life.

"Right now, he and the others have free tracts for you. Yes, there is one for each of you. Please do not be greedy and take more than one. Do not be afraid to take one. The tracts have no evil powers. Even if you cannot read, take a tract and get someone to read it to you. Remember this announcement. Next time I come, I will bring precious Good News booklets for you to buy cheap, very cheap."

And always, his last words were the same. "Now may True God bring peace to the way of your heart."

Nils was a foot or two taller than most Chinese along the River. With his large blue eyes and light skin, even with his fair hair hidden under a black cap and queue and his body draped in a dark Mandarin long-gown, he seemed like a foreign god. Indeed, his booming voice sounded like that of a god to the river people. Most of them had never before seen Westerners, and were astounded by this white man and his wife.

In their wonderment, the people slept little during the night Nils and Lizzie stayed in their houseboat alongside a village or town. Early the next morning, the people again crowded beside the boat to watch the foreigners eat the day's first rice meal before they departed.

"Hui lai, kuai hui lai! Come back, come back soon!" the river people called to the *Good News Boat* until the trackers pulled it around a bend in the River and out of sight.

*   *   *

Fengshan

The day the *Good News Boat* finally reached Fengshan, the gunboat had caught up. Standing proudly in its prow was the tracker sent back to check on it. As soon as his fellow trackers caught sight of him, they cheered and hooted.

"What happened to slow the gunboat?" Chu Boatman called out to the tracker.

"Some worthless trackers," the tracker shouted. "They got tired of slipping in the mud so two of them died. It took time to give them to the river gods and then appease their spirits. Then Some trackers stole the spirits wine and drank too much."

"Wah!" Chu said loudly. No one else said anything. Lizzie looked at Nils and blinked rapidly to keep back her tears. He touched her arm with his hand.

The sun was high in the sky and the rain nearly forgotten when the two boats were pulled up to Wang Sister's home village. Many of the villagers were already waiting on the ancient stone embankment above the wharf. They had heard the drum and chants of the trackers long before they saw the riverboats.

When they recognized one of their own standing on deck with the foreigners, they cried out in surprise. "Look, is not she the daughter of the Lin family, the one who went to Shanghai? Is not she the one whose marriage was unfortunate and her husband's death shameful? Someone run and tell her parents to come quickly. Look at the fine boat she rides. See how healthy she is and wearing such fine clothes."

No one in the village had seen the Lin's daughter for years, not since she was given in exchange for a generous dowry to a Shanghai merchant named Wang to be his concubine. They were amazed to see again a female villager who had moved so far away. Fate rarely permitted that, especially for one whose life had turned unfavorable.

When Wang Sister saw their gestures and heard what they were saying, she said to Lizzie, "*Ai ya!* What if they are angry when I tell them I no longer worship the gods and ancestors of our village? And what will my relatives say when they see my feet? And when they see that little Shiao-mei and I wear no amulets? My heart was glad. Now it is becoming fearful."

"Do not worry," Lizzie said, patting Wang Sister's arm. "True God will guide your words. Trust True God. Even if your people are angry, we are here with you. Look, today they are happy to see you again. Show them you are happy to be here."

*   *   *

Abbie's Journal
Feb 12, 2001
. . . on our China trip year before last, we purchased a miniature mahogany sanpan. I've displayed it in our dining room. To me it's much more than a beautiful, carved artifact. It's a symbol of my heritage, especially of Gramma Lizzie and Grampa Nils's lives along the River – and of the Christlike love between them and for others. Sometimes I wish I could be a river traveler for God like they were. . .
. . . at last I found Grampa's birthdate – May 6, 1864. Yesterday I thought to look in his old Swedish Bible. There it was inside the front, along with several generations of

dates. What a magnificent family Bible! It's huge, with carved artwork on the thick leather cover. Since unpacking it recently, I have it on our coffee table. It must have been printed in the early 1800s, but I can't tell for sure. Too bad our family no longer knows Swedish. I wonder if Grampa had this Bible with him in China. All week I've been reading in his journals about his early years there —and what incredible experiences he and Gramma had. . .

Chapter 9

Abbie's Journal
Feb 26, 2001
. . . how interesting to compare what Gramma Lizzie and Grampa Nils wrote about their shared lives. Sometimes she writes about the details of living – such as bathing in a basin of water, then using that water to rinse out a chamber pot just emptied into the River. And he writes about their work – like deciding not to stop at a village because their merchandise and tracts were nearly gone. Then regretting the decision because of the disappointed cries from the people waiting on shore. Other times they switched – he writes about their daily lives, and she their work. . .

Fengshan, 1896
Same Year of Monkey

Wang Sister stood on deck between Nils and Lizzie with Little Shiao-mei snuggled in her arms. Solemnly, they all watched while the trackers pulled the houseboat up to the ancient wharf. There boatmen tied it into place beneath a steep rise of worn stone steps. By now, they had docked in many river towns and villages. But Fengshan felt different.

Lizzie turned to Nils. "Do you feel what I'm feeling? Something unusual?"

Nils nodded, opened his mouth to say something, then remained silent. The villagers who had noisily gathered on the massive stone embankment also quieted for a few moments as they stared in astonishment at the strange looking foreigners.

*   *   *

During the weeks of the long trip upriver to her remote river home, Wang Sister had answered Nils and Lizzie's many questions about her village. She told them Fengshan was settled long ago, maybe three or four thousand years ago. She described how the village's elevated location on a tributary to the Yangtze kept it safe from most floods, and how her people had clean water from the tributary – water much cleaner than the Great Long River's. With dramatic gestures, she explained how the mountain range behind the village homes and fields served like a great wall that often protected her people from bandits and warlords.

Many of the families lived in ancestral homes made of stone and mud bricks hundreds of years old. But some lived in the mountain caves behind the fields. Over the centuries, these cave homes had been fashioned into comfortable, fortress-like dwellings. On the few occasions the village had suffered attack, the villagers fled to the refuge of the caves and survived.

"When danger comes," Wang Sister lowered her voice so the boatmen wouldn't hear, "my people use a secret tunnel to get to the caves. The entrance is hidden and magical. I can't show it to you, or I might be sacrificed."

*   *   *

As Lizzie and Nils gazed at Fengshan for the first time, what impressed them was its spectacular scenic beauty. Wang Sister had never even mentioned it. Before them was a village picturesque enough to be on a scroll, a scene almost beyond belief. The canyon gorge towered above several gigantic, gnarled trees. Ancient tile roofs and stone walls were framed by rugged mountains. Through the center surged the River, chasing some low cloud puffs.

"Why, your place here is more beautiful than my home in America," Lizzie said in hushed tones to Wang Sister. "How you must miss this view in Shanghai. Why have you never told us about the beauty of your home?"

"If we speak about our home in the wrong way, we fear the river gods might destroy it. I was not sure about True God."

Just then Chu Boatman announced, "I have secured the ramp. You can go ashore."

"Is your honorable headman here?" Nils called out to the villagers.

"Yes, yes. He is waiting for you. See? At the top of the steps by the sacred tree."

Bowing low, Nils called up to the headman, "We come in peace and with the protection of the Empress Dowager."

"You are welcome. I am named Wu," the headman said and bowed low.

"Thank you, honorable Wu Headman. We are named Nieh," Nils answered. "Accompanying us are Chu Boatman over there and Wang Tai-tai here with her little daughter, along with all the others."

They all bowed towards the headman.

"Everyone is welcome," Wu Headman said, bowing again. "You are traders, are you not, and tellers of True God?"

"Yes, you are correct," Nils said. "Do you want to see our merchandise?"

"Not today, tomorrow. Today we want to entertain you because we have some questions to ask you, and because you have brought one of our people home in honor."

Wu Headman motioned to them and invited them in the Chinese deprecating manner of politeness. "Come up now. Come to my humble ancestral home where we will serve you some of our village's poor food."

Because of the many steps, Nils instructed Chu to pay extra to the carriers who would fill the boat's water vats. Then he and Lizzie crossed the ramp and started up the steep steps. Since Wang Sister was behind them, they missed the glance that passed between her and Chu.

Ascending slowly, they greeted the villagers on each side with bows and polite words. As they did so, Lizzie saw that her feet and Wang Sister's were attracting attention. Many of the women were pointing and talking behind their hands to each other.

The welcome meal in Wu Headman's courtyard turned into a community occasion, and the best entertainment the villagers had enjoyed in years. They crowded everywhere to watch, even on neighboring rooftops and trees.

However, they didn't just watch. Every minute or so, someone close enough daringly touched Lizzie or Nils, causing gasps and snickers. Finally, the headman shouted out for everyone to leave the foreign guests alone. To which Nils and Lizzie raised their thumbs in the Chinese manner of approval. At that, everyone laughed uproariously, including the headman. It was an unexpected moment of bonding.

The meal itself was a feast. The village households cooked their treasured recipes and brought them to the Wu home. Before long, the tables were crowded with delicious smelling delicacies – stir-fried dried pork with lotus roots, braised fish in black bean sauce, "one-hundred year-old" eggs nestled in tender Chinese cabbages, fishball and seaweed soup, and succulent hillside mushrooms.

Nils sat in the place of honor at an ornately carved and lacquered square table. Seated with him were Wu Headman and his eldest son, as well as Wang Sister's father. At an adjacent table sat Lizzie, Wang Sister and her beaming mother. With them were Wu's number-one wife and her eldest son's wife. Several other wives and females managed the serving of the meal. Little Shiao-mei had already been taken cheerfully away to her grandparents' home to eat and play.

After a couple of hours of eating, toasting and polite conversing, Wu stood to speak. This seemed to be a moment everyone knew was coming, for the villagers immediately quit talking among themselves and focused on their headman.

Wu carefully picked up the village's ancient carved stone ceremonial teapot. He raised it to the level of his face before bowing low to the honored foreigners. No one moved. After several moments of silence, he slowly replaced the precious jewel-embedded teapot back on its mahogany stand.

He cleared his throat several times, then said, "Today is an auspicious day, for you the foreign friends have finally come. I have been waiting for you."

Nils stood to respond. "Thank you for calling us friends. We want to be your friends. You have already treated us with hospitality far beyond what we deserve. Tell us, how did you know we were coming? We did not send a messenger ahead. Nor have we ever before come this far up the Great Long River."

"I have had dreams," Wu said.

"Ah, how portentous. Please tell us about your dreams," Nils urged and sat down.

"Do you know about the ancient and revered Jin-jiao Monument?" Wu asked.

Nils shook his head and replied he had not heard of it.

But Lizzie nodded her head and said, "Yes, I know a little about it. My esteemed language teacher in Shanghai described it one day when we were discussing Sian. Ever since I have been curious to know more."

Wu continued, "The Jin-jiao Monument is near my mother's ancestral home in the Sian countryside. We were told this antiquity was buried centuries ago to protect it and its followers from an angry emperor. In time it was forgotten, except by some secret followers known as Stone Ten Keepers. During some digging in my honorable great-grandfather's time, the stone was discovered again. Since then, it has stood in the shelter of a sacred tree. There are whispers of Stone Ten Keepers secretly coming there to worship. Who they are, no one will say.

"Several times in my youth while I was visiting my grandparents, I gazed long at this engraved stone tablet taller than I. The last time was many years ago. I hoped my honorable elderly grandfather could help me decipher its inscriptions. So I pushed him there in his old, wooden wheelbarrel. But he could not read as many of its characters as I could. The Buddhist monks from the nearby temple monastery knew only a little more than we did.

"The monks told us they had been informed by monastery brothers no longer living that the monument honored an exalted luminous religion from the fifth or sixth century. They asked me if I ever learned more, to please come back and tell them. For they sensed great sacredness and power associated with the ancient tablet's message. Even though I was still a youth, I remember sensing that too.

"So imagine my shock when last year I began to have dreams about that monument from my youth. I cannot count how many dreams, for they have all been nearly the same."

He paused and looked around. No one was moving or whispering. He swallowed several times and turned his face upwards.

"Go ahead, Wu Headman," Lizzie encouraged.

"Please tell us your dreams. We are all waiting to hear."

"Even to speak of my dreams frightens me," he said. "For in my dreams, the river gods chased me, wanting to catch and kill me, especially the river dragon god. *Ai yah*! Remembering this aloud gives me death chills.

"I tried to escape, and for some reason was compelled to run all the way to the monument – a long, harrowing journey. As I lay prostrate from exhaustion and thirst at the foot of the monument, I heard a strong, kind voice say, 'I am True God. Worship me if you want to escape the gods of darkness. Worship me and I will bring light and peace into your life.'

"'What god are you and how do I worship you?' I sobbed in my weakness.

"Suddenly, in my dreams I was standing, strong again, knowing I would soon find out about True God. Even though I no longer heard the voice, somehow I knew that foreign friends like you would come up the River to my village and tell us all about True God. Then I awakened, both frightened and hopeful.

"You see, that is why I have been waiting for you. Are you the right foreign friends? Can you tell me about True God so I can worship him? Are you Stone Ten Keepers? *Ai*, how I and my village long to be delivered from the fearsome power of the river gods."

Nils and Lizzie told Wu and the villagers they were sorry, but they did not know anything about Stone Ten Keepers. However, they did know about True God. They told the gathered crowd many stories, and answered questions until long after dark. Then they were escorted back to the wharf. Men from the village carrying flaming bamboo torches guided them through the dark, ancient alleys and safely down the steep stone steps to their riverboat.

Wang Sister and Shiao-mei stayed that night with

their Lin relatives. So for the first time in many weeks, Nils and Lizzie had their cabin to themselves. But they scarcely noticed as they talked about all that had happened in Wu's courtyard.

"What an amazing sense of Almighty God's presence!" Nils exclaimed repeatedly as they prepared for bed with lamplight shadows flickering around them.

"Yes!" Lizzie agreed. "Wu Headman and many others have hearts ready to receive God's message of Truth."

"Can you believe Wu invited us to live here? And that's after just one evening of hearing about God. You know, someday I'd like to see the monument that started his search for God. What do you make of the Stone Ten Keepers?"

"I think," Lizzie said, "the ancient monument may be one connected to the Syrian Nestorian Christian missionaries from who came here centuries ago. Maybe in time Wu will take us to see it. I'm fascinated by its effect on him. He's wise, isn't he, to know that understanding new truth takes time, especially for village people. But I wonder, Nils. This place is so far from Shanghai. Surely it can't be safe for us to live here, particularly now when there are so many Boxer threats. Do you suppose any Boxers were there tonight?"

"I didn't sense any Boxer antagonism, did you? And whether it's safe or not, we just have to trust God and obey. Like I told Wu, if we do come it won't be until after our baby is several months old. I don't want you to worry."

Nils and Lizzie snuggled closer together under the quilt, their arms tightening around each other. After a few minutes, they took turns praying. Lizzie first, then Nils. He lovingly embraced Lizzie's swollen body, and included in his prayers their softly kicking baby.

Early the next day, they began trading, wondering if

the hundreds of villagers gathered on the wharf long before dawn had gone to bed at all during the night.

It was a day that seemed unending, but a good day. Nils and Lizzie felt rewarded to see river dwellers acquire necessities. They always enjoyed hearing people exclaim over the quality merchandise and cheap prices.

At last it was time to put everything away and eat their evening rice meal prepared by Wang Sister. On this night, instead of fish with their vegetables and bean curd, they enjoyed a tasty chicken prepared for them by Wu Headman's household, along with a bamboo rack of steamed pork-filled bao-tzes and a spicy noodle dish .

As the sun set, Nils and Chu lit the boat's lamps. Lizzie played her accordion and sang to prepare the hearts of the people for Nils's stories and preaching. Since this was their second evening in the village, Chu Boatman also gave his testimony of becoming a True God believer.

"Look at me!" he began, clapping his hands loudly to get everyone's attention. "I do not know where I was born or who my parents were."

His listeners groaned aloud in sympathy and paid closer attention.

"When I was very young, somehow I reached the child market. Who knows who sold me first – my parents or other relatives. I think I remember being sold three times. Each time was for more silver than the time before because I was a strong little boy. The last time, I was healthy enough to be bought as a eunuch for the Forbidden City."

"*Ai yah!*" the crowd responded, "But better to be a eunuch in the service of the Imperial Family than starve or drown."

"Yes, so I was told back then. For several years my life was not too bad. I had plenty to eat. I learned to read and brush characters. All the skills I would use in the palace, I mastered with ease. So I was treated kindly.

"Then I began to hear whispered tales – about what happened to my young eunuch friends who disappeared in the night. Or what happened to eunuchs who displeased the Imperial Family. And how some eunuchs became beggars without eyes or arms or legs.

"Because I was a thinker, I reasoned that if those terrible things happened to others, they might happen to me. Part of my body had already been severed to serve the Imperial Family. Why should I be used for some warrior's sword practice? Or as a sacrifice to ensure the success of a military venture? Or even as a prince's whipping boy?

"It seemed clear to me that living to old age and wealth at the whim of the Imperials was extremely unlikely. So I decided to run away.

"But how could I run away and not be caught? Tell me, what would you have done?"

"*Ai!* There is no escape from fate," someone shouted.

"To turn from the Emperor is to turn from the celestial gods and invite misfortune," another called out.

"Death – death is the only escape," a woman's voice cried. "But which is worse, death or torment? And who dares to find out?"

"Yes, yes, I thought about all that," Chu said. "Still, I wanted to escape. I had reached the point of wanting some control over my own life. So when I heard the warning about bandits in the area – the fearsome Wolf Bandits – I decided to run away and offer myself to them. Surely, they would not return me to the Imperial Court because of my eunuch brand and scars.

"I once thought it was the gods and spirits of my ancestors who helped me escape one moonless night. I now believe it was True God."

"*Ai!*" the crowd exclaimed. "But are you telling us

lies just to entertain us? We can hear lies from any traveling storyteller. Tell on, tell us your true story."

So Chu told on. "To avoid being caught while I searched for the bandits, I pretended to be a girl with leprosy. *Heh*! No one dared bother me. Everyone was afraid to get near and hurried me from the city. Walking out the city gate, I left behind the only life I remembered. Though I was free, the unknown ahead was frightening. I hoped I would not soon be like the beggars heaped on a cart I had passed – grotesque and dead.

"It took me several days to find the Wolf Bandits in the hills. By then I was hungry and fearful about what I had done. When I discovered the concealed camp of the bandits, they almost killed me. First because they thought I was leprous, next because they thought I must be a spy for the army. But my eunuch scars soon convinced them I was who I said. However, if I had not stolen some gold to give them, even so they might have cut me up with their swords.

"Who knows how long I was with the Wolf Bandits. My guess is many years. For some reason, maybe because they were sorry for me or maybe because of my skills, they were good to me. I saw them beat and kill other youth, so I knew how cruel they could be. With me, they were never that way."

Then Chu paused dramatically before asking, "Are you wondering why I am not still with them?"

His listeners shouted back, "What a foolish question. Of course, we want to know the end of your story. Stop teasing us! Tell on!"

"I will tell you. That band of Wolf Bandits was finally stopped by the Imperial Army. Many times the Army let them slip away, but not that last time. Perhaps our bandit chief failed to give the officer in charge enough gold. Or maybe the officer needed to impress his commander. Who can know.

"Whatever the reason, there was a short battle. Even though the bandits were skillful swordsmen with fast horses, they were quickly overcome by the soldiers who had guns. The bandits not shot to death were soon captured and beheaded, and their heads spiked on poles as a warning to others.

"But I escaped. Was I helped by True God? Yes, I believe so, though I did not know it then.

"As I fled, I remembered a tree in which the bandits had hidden some plunder. I hid from the soldiers until night and then retrieved it – quite sure none of my Wolf Bandit companions were alive to find me and chop off my hands for taking their treasure.

"When the sky began to lighten, I set out for the Great Long River. From the bandit hideouts in the hills, I had often admired the riverboats moving along the curving waters that gleamed like ancient brown jade. Perhaps I could become a boatman, I thought. As you can see, that is what I became. For I had plenty of silver to pay the owner of a sanpan barge to hire and train me.

"That barge was the one these foreigners here named Nieh rented when they first became traders on the River. That is how they became my friends and I theirs. Best of all, they are the friends who taught me about True God.

"Because of True God, today I am a contented man. I have peace in my heart instead of fear and anger. Gambling and drinking no longer tempt me. I have extra silver without stealing. I even have friends who are like family.

"*Ai!* Now you have heard most of my story. It is very late and we are all tired. Tomorrow evening we will tell you more about True God. Come back then. Before you leave tonight, we have some Gospel tracts for you. They bear only good news, not evil. Please, everyone get one before you go home."

After the villagers were gone, Lizzie and Nils sat on deck with Chu to plan the next day. Usually as soon as their planning was finished, Chu said "sleep well" and went to his cabin. This night, he stayed on. For a while, they sat without speaking, looking at the moonlit River.

At last Lizzie asked, "Chu Boatman, is there something more you want to discuss?"

Chu moved nervously, "Yes, my good friends. True God has brought a real family into my life. Wang Sister and I desire to become husband and wife. Will you approve? We want to get married here in her Lin ancestral home before we return to Shanghai. For who knows when we will come here again."

Two afternoons later, Chu Boatman and Wang Sister were married in the courtyard of her Lin family home. The entire village was invited, and everyone crowded as close as possible, just as they had for Nils and Lizzie's welcome dinner. Those too far away or too short to see, made do with the gleeful accounts shouted out by the lucky ones in the trees.

At such short notice, a full wedding feast was impossible. But Nils and Lizzie added sweets and oranges to the hot jasmine tea and peanuts provided by the Lin family. Speeches, songs, and laughter filled the afternoon. And for the first time, the villagers heard an explanation of the Christian view of marriage.

In the end, the wedding turned out to be a more festive celebration than anyone could have predicted. The guests, who enjoyed themselves immensely, just hoped the gods and ancestors were not offended by the lack of traditional offerings and incense. Or if so, that True God was powerful enough to dispel any affront.

Some villagers made snide remarks about Lin Daughter marrying a eunuch. But they were quickly hushed by Wu Headman who saw the marriage as fortuitous.

He said in the hearing of many, "Be careful how you talk! If a husband and wife make plenty of money working for generous foreigners who worship True God, what does having sons matter? If they choose, Chu and Lin Daughter can raise one of her nephews to care for them in old age. What a lucky boy that would be, growing up with these people! And remember, Lin Daughter from now on will be called Chu Sister."

"You have spoken what I was thinking," a woman said, whose face revealed her painful life. "If I could marry such a good man as Chu, I would not care if he was a eunuch or that he worshiped a foreign god."

"Yes, yes of course," other villagers nodded, eager to see what came next in this unusual drama occurring right before their eyes – a drama so unusual they would surely talk about it for years to come.

When the soldiers on the gunboat escort were first informed about the delay in departure to accommodate the wedding, they had become impatient and scolding. But gifts of merchandise from the *Good News Boat* soothed their tempers. They promptly agreed that staying until the tenth day was just fine. Had they ever said otherwise?

However, they hoped no trouble from bandits or rebels occurred in the area while the boats were docked. When trouble came, it was better to be moving on the River, did not the Niehs agree? Had not the foreign friends noticed more bodies than usual in the River the past few days? That was a sure sign of conflict upriver.

At Nils's insistence, the gunboat soldiers promised to increase their vigilance. From then on, at least four of them would always be on guard, two facing upriver and two down. They hinted that working such long hours meant a few extra worthless gifts would be appreciated when they reached Shanghai.

*   *   *

Abbie's Journal
Mar 15, 2001
. . . Gramma Lizzie and Grampa Nils often read aloud to each other from the Bible and other books – sometimes in English, sometimes in Swedish or Chinese. How cozy, especially when I imagine their long days of travel on the Yangtze. I wonder if they also read their journals to each other like the Tolstoys did – probably not something I'd want to do with Dan. Besides, he doesn't journal. "Dagbok" they called their journals in Swedish. One thing's for sure, their daybooks are giving me glimpses of an extraordinary couple. They were so brave and compassionate in the face of great danger and suffering, yet wrote of their lives as victorious and joyous because of God's grace. . .

Chapter 10

Abbie's Journal
Mar 29, 2001
. . . as they say – some things never change. It seems the Chinese government still doesn't like the American government. But I'm pretty sure most Chinese like us Americans – just as most Americans like the Chinese. These days, the U.S. and China are in a words war over the spy plane incident. China's downed fighter pilot is undoubtedly dead. So our heroic crew – who landed their rammed plane on Hainan Island "without authorization" after being rammed by the pilot – are being "detained." China surely won't dare harm them – not like the dreadful things done to so many "foreign devils" and their Chinese friends in Gramma Lizzie and Grampa Nils's time. . .

. . . probably because of censorship and retaliation fears, Gramma and Grampa wrote essentially nothing about the terrible political upheavals they experienced in China – things I now know, like how the Chinese struggled to survive the disastrous Opium War and the resulting Boxer Rebellion. How the revolution under Sun Yat-sen finally overthrew the oppressive rule of the Imperial emperors. How Japanese invasions caused untold suffering or death for millions. And all the while, how greedy, battling warlords devastated large areas of the country. No wonder Gramma and Grampa felt called to live in China to share God's message of eternal light and hope, even if it meant risking their lives – and their children's. . .

Fengshan, 1896
Same Year of Monkey

The year her older sister Mei-lee gave herself to the hungry
gods of the Great Long River, Hui-ching was seven years
old.

She was fourteen when the foreigners named Nieh
came in the *Good News Boat* to Fengshan. To her
excitement, her Lin cousin who had been gone for many
seasons arrived with the Niehs.

Soon Hui-ching had another reason to be excited.
As she held her returned cousin's hand in greeting and
hugged little Shiao-mei, she felt sudden eagerness. Here
might be the opportunity she was awaiting. Maybe she
could accompany her cousin on the *Good News Boat* when
the foreigners returned to Shanghai.

Later that day, when Hui-ching looked at her
mother, she could tell her mother was having the same
thoughts. Perhaps she could become her cousin's helper.
Ai! Perhaps here was her chance to attend school. For in
Shanghai, there were schools for girls.

To Hui-ching's both joy and fear, her mother did
arrange for her to leave with her cousin and the foreigners
named Nieh. When she said farewell to her family and
friends, she wistfully tried not to think about how long it
might be until she saw them again. Instead, she tried to
think of her good fortune – of being the first girl from
Fengshan to go away to school.

As the *Good News Boat* headed back downriver
towards Shanghai, Hui-ching stood on deck beside her
cousin, newly named Chu Sister, and the Niehs. As long as
possible, she gazed with the eyes of her soul at her home
and the beauty surrounding it – a beauty too special and
sacred to be spoken.

Tears choked her throat as she thought of Ma and

Ba and the others she was leaving behind. In farewell, she had repeated to Ma her vow from years ago. Diligently she would study, so one day she could paint the landscape of the gorge and restore honor to Mei-lee's memory. As she watched her home village disappear in the distance, how she hoped she would not fail.

The trip to Shanghai was one frightening experience after another for Hui-ching. Though she had grown up by the River, rarely had she been on it – and never for days and weeks at a time. She wept often from fear and homesickness. Each time she was consoled by her cousin or Nieh Wife, as she respectfully called Lizzie. Each time she felt more secure.

At first, she had been terribly frightened to be so near the foreign devils. But Chu Boatman and Chu Sister chided her whenever she referred to the Niehs that way.

"Not these foreigners," they said reprovingly. "These two are like benevolent gods. Except they are not gods, remember that. They are the kindest people we have ever known. You do not need to fear them. Because they worship True God, they are different from the fearsome foreigners in Shanghai. Those foreigners we will point out to you later so you can avoid them."

In spite of their reassurances, Hui-ching scarcely slept her first few nights aboard the riverboat. She lay tense and wakeful under her *pugai* on the *kang,* just a short distance away from Lizzie and Nils on the other side of the curtain. She remembered dreadful foreign devil stories, and imagined things like that happening to her.

"Why, they even smell strange," she whispered to her cousin the third night, trying to explain her fears.

"You will soon get used to them," comforted her cousin, whose sleeping arrangements on the riverboat had not changed since she became Chu's wife. "Did you know we smell strange to them too? They told me so."

At that, Hui-ching nearly laughed aloud. She covered her mouth tightly with her padded quilt, laughing inside as she thought about the smells of people. That night she slept soundly for the first time aboard the *Good News Boat*.

Two weeks downriver from Fengshan, Hui-ching had her worst fright of the journey. They all did.

Passing cautiously through a stretch of perilous rapids, they came suddenly upon a wrecked boat partially submerged in the water. The boatmen struggled with their poles while the trackers held tight to their rope to keep the *Good News Boat* from ramming into the vessel. They succeeded, but not before Hui-ching began sobbing hysterically.

"*Ai yah!* Protect me, spirits of my ancestors! Do not let me drown in the River like Older Sister!" she cried out repeatedly.

Lizzie and Chu Sister tried to calm her. Soon little Shiao-mei was also crying in fear because of Hui-ching. Moments later, they were all horrified to see bodies from the sunken boat caught in the jagged rocks of the lower rapids. Quickly they looked around for survivors, but saw none. Not that they really expected to, knowing few who traveled the River could swim.

To Lizzie's surprise, Hui-ching quieted at once after seeing the bodies.

Lizzie raised her eyebrows in question, and so Chu Sister explained, "Hui-ching thinks the river gods have been appeased by those deaths back there. So she feels safe for a while. Of course, that is what she was taught to believe, like I was. Now I understand the River better. I try not to think about my old superstitious beliefs. Someday, Hui-ching will also understand. I am teaching her True God's ways like you have taught me."

By the time they reached Shanghai, Hui-ching had

become accustomed to being on the riverboat and away from her family. No longer was she easily frightened. She even liked living with the Niehs.

One day she said to Chu Sister, her cousin, "How can I not like them and their kind ways? They treat me as if I am as worthy as a male." It was a new and pleasing feeling for Hui-ching.

Near the end of their journey, she even permitted Lizzie to massage her feet with a soothing aloe vera ointment several times a day, and to help her move her toes in special ways – just like her cousin did. In a few days, Hui-ching's newly unbound feet hurt less and were stronger.

When her mother had unbound her feet, they had not used any ointments, just warm water and looser strips of cloth. She remembered how upset she had been to discover unbinding her feet hurt as much binding them. Now thanks to Lizzie's treatments, she no longer felt the crunching pain in her feet when she walked. The day Lizzie said her feet would someday be nearly normal, Hui-ching smiled all day long.

"Will my feet be as good as my cousin's?" she asked.

"Even better," Lizzie said, "because your bones and flesh are young and heal better."

Later Hui-ching said to little Shiao-mei, "You are so fortunate. You have unbroken feet, just like Nieh Wife. Your mother will never let anyone use a stone to break your toes and bend them under your feet. Never will you have to smother your cries of pain at night so your father will not beat you. You will always be able to run and climb, and no one will dare say you are undesirable because your feet are big and ugly like a farm worker's."

"Yes, I am lucky lucky lucky!" Shaio-mei laughed, jumping up and down on her strong little feet in their handsewn padded cloth shoes.

*   *   *

Shanghai

At last, the day came when the *Good News Boat* reached its spot at the Shanghai wharf. After the houseboat was safely docked, everyone joined Nils and Lizzie for prayer.

Chu Boatman prayed. In a loud voice, he thanked True God for protection and blessings. Hui-ching thought he sounded like he was talking to a good friend, not to some fearsome, angry god. With eyes half shut, she peeked at him. Then she peeked at the crowd of people gathering along side them on the wharf. She was dismayed to see a group of foreign devils among the people. With them were soldiers armed with guns and swords.

Is there trouble? she thought with apprehension. *Are these the fearsome foreign devils my cousin warned me about? I hope True God's ears are open to Chu Boatman's words.*

When she worried about the foreigners to her cousin, she was told they had come to meet the Niehs, like always.

"How do they know when to come?" she asked.

"When we get near Shanghai, Chu Boatman sends a shore messenger to their compound," Chu Sister said.

"*Ai*, I understand," Hui-ching said. She knew about shore messengers. One of her brothers earned silver doing that whenever he could.

Unloading didn't take long. Most of the merchandise and food supplies were gone, and Lizzie and Nils and their helpers traveled light. The bedding and meal utensils remained on the houseboat, protected day and night by Chu Boatman and armed guards.

Lizzie and Nils walked home behind a mule-drawn cart carrying their belongings. They were escorted by their friends and the guards who had met them – the very ones who had alarmed Hui-ching. As they walked, they heard the tragic news. Just three days before, a missionary couple and the Chinese Christians traveling with them had been brutally attacked by Boxer rebels outside the West Gate. Four Chinese died during the attack. Whether the missionaries and the other injured Chinese would live was still uncertain.

"Perhaps," one of the men said, "it would be best if God took them quickly to heaven and spared them unspeakable suffering and memories. We're troubled because these attacks by Boxers and other secret anti-foreigner groups are increasing. May God grant our Chinese friends and us wisdom and courage for these times."

"*Oh min min!*" Lizzie said. "I wondered why so many of you met us, and why no women came. I thought at once something must have happened."

She sighed, tightening her grip on the hands of young Hui-ching and Shaio-mei walking beside her. Neither of them had wanted to ride on the cart, afraid the mule might run away with them. Now they saw fear in Lizzie's eyes, and thought she too was afraid of the mule.

"So," Nils asked, "are Westerners and other foreigners leaving the country?"

"Perhaps we should wait to talk about this when we're safe inside your walls," another of the men replied. "The women are waiting for us. They've prepared a welcome home tea for you."

They hurried the rest of the way not speaking, instead listening to the crowds they passed in the street. A few Chinese shouted out threateningly, "Kill the foreign devil imperialists. *Sha, sha!*" But mostly, the crowds were stony faced and silent. They too feared the uprisings that always left many of them dead and destitute.

This is scary, Lizzie thought. *We may have to leave China. We may even be the next ones attacked. Oh Lord God, help us. We need your grace.*

Once safe inside the courtyard, Lizzie and Nils and the others relaxed. With smiles, they exchanged the hugs considered unseemly in public. The women patted Lizzie's stomach, and asked how she and the baby were after the ordeals of the long river trip. Everyone wanted to know when the birth would be and where. As they chatted, they took turns washing their faces and necks, hands and arms with carbolic soap in an enamel basin with warm water from the bathing area vat. The men dried with one towel, the women another.

Refreshed, soon all were seated in the front room. Cheerful servants served them British tea and hot cocoa, along with homemade bread and jam and Swedish butter cookies. To Lizzie and Nils who hadn't tasted such treats for months, everything was extra delicious.

During tea time, conversation centered mostly on safety concerns. But even though she was worried as the rest of them, Lizzie kept eyeing the small pile of mail stacked on the desk in the corner of the room.

She was relieved when one of the women said, "Go ahead, read your letters. You must be eager to hear from your loved ones after all these months. Besides, we want to hear the news from overseas too. It will do us good to think about something besides danger."

There were nods of assent throughout the room.

"All right then," Lizzie said. "Just remember, you're the ones who persuaded me to be rude."

As their friends laughed, to Nils she said, "Which country shall we open a letter from first, America or Sweden?"

While Lizzie and Nils took turns reading aloud the news from their letters, Hui-ching had her first lesson in a foreigner's kitchen.

Again and again she said to her cousin, "*Wah!* What is this?" as she pointed to the ice box, an oven, a cupboard full of canned foods, and the stove-top toaster. "*Wah!* Who would believe all this?" as she examined the dish washing area, a silverware drawer, the shelves of dishes and pans, and stacks of folded clean cloths.

Barely modest by Western standards, in Hui-ching's eyes the Nieh home seemed as wonderful as the dwellings of magistrates and warlords which she had heard about but never seen. She wondered aloud to her cousin if the Nieh home was as grand as the palaces of the emperor.

Chu Sister laughed at her. "My poor young cousin, you think like I once did. We are ignorant because we are from so far inland. The Westerners and many people living here in Shanghai seem rich to us, like my wretched first husband and his family seemed. I have learned the Niehs actually have little compared to many others like them, even though they have much compared to us and our people."

She laughed some more. "As grand as the emperor's palaces? How little you know. Just ask Chu Boatman to tell you about the palaces he has seen. You will not believe the splendor his words describe."

That night, Hui-ching slept for the first time with padded quilts on a bed made of wood and woven rope. She was given her own room. But too fearful to sleep alone, she dragged the bed into her cousin's room. And for the rest of her time in Shanghai, Hui-ching slept there, often with little Shiao-mei snuggled next to her. This arrangement suited everyone, as it permitted Chu Sister to spend time occasionally on the *Good News Boat* with her new husband Chu Boatman.

To Chu Sister's great chagrin, that's where she was the evening tiny Hilda Cecilia was born, several weeks earlier than expected. She had to be content with her young cousin Hui-ching's story about the strangeness, yet sameness of a foreign woman's birthing.

*   *   *

Abbie's Journal
July 16, 2001
. . . "55 Days in Peking," that old movie was on TV today. Parts of it are ludicrous. Still I've enjoyed watching it several times because parts of it are so realistic and reminiscent of Gramma Lizzie and Grampa Nils's time. Violence, cruelty, filth and desperation abound, but so do loyalty, sacrifice, and hope. What courage Gramma had – to give birth to their first baby in such a setting, and only Grampa and a young servant to help her. . .
. . . Gramma wrote later she was so thankful for the babies she had assisted her Mama deliver. That plus her Salvation Army medical training helped her know what to expect and do. She called little Hilda a gift of love and joy from heaven in the midst of China's dreadful turmoils. The 55-day siege of Peking hadn't happened yet, but already Boxers were terrorizing and killing Westerners and Chinese Christians. As the movie clearly shows, the Empress Dowager hoped to drive out all "barbarians." Slyly she aided the Boxers by night, even as she spoke against them by day – truly a woman with a snake-split tongue. By the time Western powers forced her to halt the Boxers, hundreds of Westerners had been murdered as well as thousands of Chinese. What tragic chaos! Oh my my, poor little baby Hilda. . .

Chapter 11

Abbie's Journal
July 26, 2001
. . . sorting through my China boxes has me on a China reading binge. We're in Paris this week, in a gorgeous hotel with marble everywhere, and my bedtime reading is Peter Hessler's River Town. *So ironic, the contrast! What a compelling account of his two years as an English teacher in Fuling – a Yangtze river town that hadn't seen a "foreign devil" for fifty years. Talk about haunting! His narrative and descriptions take me right back to my childhood and probably to Dad's. An online reviewer who questioned his impressions obviously hasn't lived in China inland. . .*

. . . one incident in the book especially grabbed me – when Hessler described meeting an elderly man who showed him an old Bible given him long ago by a missionary from Sweden. The man said "yes" when Hessler asked him if he was a Christian. Wow – I wonder, did that old man's Bible come from Grampa Nils. . .

Fengshan, 1897
Year of Rooster

After Christmas, Nils and Lizzie sent a messenger to Wu Headman with the news of baby Hilda's birth and their plans for returning soon to Fengshan. They hoped to arrive around Chinese New Year, their message informed him. With them would be Chu Boatman, Chu Sister and little Shiao-mei, along with several others. Hui-ching, who was diligently studying in a school for girls, would stay in Shanghai and board at the school.

Unknown to them until later, the messenger never delivered their message. He was a trusted friend, they thought. Thinking bandits or Boxers had waylaid and murdered him for the money they had given him, they mourned for Li Brother when they found out he was missing.

The *Good News Boat* reached Fengshan late one afternoon in March after a cold, fairly routine two-month trip upriver. Since their message had not reached him, Wu Headman was surprised at the arrival of the Niehs. Nor this time had his dreams foretold their coming.

When he hurried down the ancient stone steps of the wharf to greet them, he didn't seem like the same man who just a few months before had urged them to come back as soon as possible. Besides being surprised to see them, he was openly anxious and barely courteous.

The next day, the gunboats that had escorted the *Good News Boat* upriver turned around and headed back to Shanghai. Cheering onboard were the trackers willing to spend a portion of their earnings from Nils for a ride home. The other trackers called farewell from the wharf where they waited, hoping to be hired by a passing barge or junk.

From her cabin porthole, Lizzie watched the gunboats leave with a sinking feeling. She looked down at three-month baby Hilda nursing hungrily at her breast and said softly, "You are Lord God's, my darling, like Saint Hilda whose name we gave you. But I'm frightened and can't seem to put aside my fear. May Lord God help me be brave for your sake and the others who need me strong."

Her tears coursed down her cheeks and onto Hilda's tiny brown curls. Later, when her tears had stopped, Lizzie discovered her fear was gone as well. God had answered her thoughts even before she spoke them in prayer.

Oh Lord God, why do I ever forget, she prayed with a deep sigh. *Your grace is always greater than my needs.*

Thank you, oh Lord God. Forgive my lack of trust.

In the middle of that night, Lizzie awakened to care for Hilda. She was concerned to hear wolves howling in the hills beyond Fengshan. She recalled what Nils had told her earlier about his disturbing day in the village with Wu Headman.

"Everyone's fearful," Nils had said. "The atmosphere doesn't feel at all the same as when we were here last fall. I'm sure Wu and the other villagers I talked with intended to be welcoming, but they were distracted and agitated."

"What's the problem?" Lizzie asked. "I questioned Chu Sister when she came back to make our meal. I could see she was upset, but she wouldn't talk about it. She said you'd tell me everything better than she could. She did say she was worried about leaving Shiao-mei on shore. I reminded her that staying at her family's home was her choice, and maybe they should return here to the boat."

Nils nodded. "They should. It's dangerous for them in Fengshan."

"Boxers?"

"Partly that. Bandits are in the high hills sending menacing messages. They might be Boxers or maybe other rebels – the worst kind because they're fighting for a cause. Wu Headman is terribly distraught. But there's another, more immediate danger – wolves. Wu says winter was bad. The wolves are hungry, very hungry. Already two packs have run through the village and snatched away children, including two baby boys. He says once the wolves taste human flesh, that's all they want. Even more upsetting, many villagers think these things are happening because they have somehow angered the river god. Maybe by inviting us to come here to live."

"*Oh min, min!*" Lizzie gasped. She tried to keep eating, but nearly choked until she sipped some tea.

"What should we do, Nils?" She pressed a trembling hand over her heart.

"Pray. Pray lots. I think you'll have to stay on board for a while. Chu and the other boatmen will be here with you. They have their swords. As well, Wu's guardsmen are patrolling. I'm joining them soon with my gun. Wu says no one else has one."

"No Nils, no! Don't take your gun! What if you kill someone? How Christian is that?"

"Lizzie, I've told you before. I'll use my gun until Almighty God stops me, and pray for quick fingers and accurate aim – for wolves, of course. I don't want to kill anyone and hope I never have to."

"Nils, you frighten me. Whatever will I do if something happens to you?"

"And I feel the same about you and dear little Hilda. So with God's help, I'm going to protect you. Pa often served God with a gun handy, so will I."

Nils patrolled for several hours that night. Just before heading back to the houseboat and bed, he shot his gun twice at the sky. He knew it would give the bandits pause, but probably not the wolves. Beside him, Wu Headman swore and said he was not sure if Nils's fire-sword made him less afraid or more afraid.

"Unless it is pointing at you," Nils reassured him, "pretend it is firecrackers – just a frightening noise."

"*Wah*! What a good idea!" Wu said. "We should throw firecrackers at the wolves to scare them away."

"Or anger them into attacking," Nils countered.

But no wolves came close enough that evening for the men to use either weapons or firecrackers.

Next morning while the sky was still heavy and grey with the passing night, Wu Headman called out loudly beside the *Good News Boat*. "Wake up, Nieh Friend. Get dressed! You must come with me to the Temple. Bring your fire-sword. Awaken your boatmen to be on guard. Come, come with haste!"

"What's happening?" Lizzie asked, dressing hurriedly in the dark beside Nils.

"I was afraid of something like this," he replied, then pointed to the hiding spot. "Lizzie, use my small gun if you need to."

She shook her head. "Only if it's wolves, and you know they won't come down here."

"I mean for attackers."

"I couldn't, Nils. You know I would rather die myself than shoot someone, even a bandit."

"Lizzie, think! Think of baby Hilda!"

"I am, Nils. Maybe we shouldn't have come with you. Maybe I wasn't listening carefully enough to God."

Wu Headman called again, "Hurry, Nieh Friend! Hurry! We must stop them!"

Lizzie watched him rush to join Wu and several dozen guardsmen waiting impatiently on the ancient stone wharf. In a moment, Nils was close behind Wu. They dashed up the steps with the others following, and tramped swiftly towards the Temple.

Lizzie backed away from the porthole and still dressed, lay down on the warm *kang* beside little Hilda. Was Nils angry with her? She hoped not, but he had left without saying goodbye or any endearments. She couldn't remember him doing that before. For a few moments, ache replaced fear in her heart.

Suddenly, she realized Chu Boatman was talking to someone in low tones. She sat up on the *kang*. Should she take out the gun like Nils had said? But she was too late.

Someone tapped on the door, then slowly opened it. She had forgotten to slide the stout wooden bolt after Nils left. To her relief, there stood Chu's wife.

"Chu Sister, how you startled me! Why are you here

so early?" Lizzie's heartbeat thumped loudly in her ears and her hands trembled.

"Wu Headman told me to come. He said you need company and I need safety. There is trouble at the Temple. I have brought my daughter. I was afraid to leave her with my family."

Lizzie felt calmer as she hugged little Shiao-mei. "My precious, you are always welcome. This is your home too. Tell me, Chu Sister, what is happening? Nieh Husband did not tell me. I do not think he knew when he left in such a hurry."

Chu Sister was silent until she had bolted the door and helped Shiao-mei onto the warm *kang* beside baby Hilda. In spite of everything, Lizzie couldn't help smiling as she heard Shiao-mei begin to chant softly, "My cute little white sister. My cute, cute little white sister."

Above the soft chanting, Chu Sister told Lizzie what was happening at the Temple.

"I am so shamed by the people of my village. I told my family and neighbors, Nieh Husband and you are not bad fortune. No, you are good fortune. Look how Chu Husband and I prosper because of you."

Lizzie nodded in sympathy, as together they prepared the morning rice meal.

Chu Sister continued. "Some accept my words, but many say it is up to Temple Priest to decide whether or not the foreign devils have caused the misfortune of killer wolves and bandits to the village. That is what is happening right now. Temple monks are burning incense and presenting food offerings to the gods. At sunrise, Temple Priest will receive a message from the gods when he throws the oracle sticks."

"What will the villagers do to us if Temple Priest says we are to blame?" Lizzie asked, surprised how calm she felt.

"I am not sure about Shaio-mei and myself. Since you and Nieh Husband are foreigners, maybe you will just have to leave. But there are those who want to kill you to appease the river gods. Some think the gods can be appeased in another way, maybe with a special sacrifice to the god they call Fire Belly – maybe with little Shiao-mei."

"*Ai ya!* That is terrible to hear! Your precious Shiao-mei is so young to be involved, and of course, she is innocent."

Chu Sister nodded, and kept chopping the breakfast pickles and slicing the brown soy eggs. "But look at me, her mother. I live with you. I married Chu Boatman. And we worship True God."

Lizzie stood motionless a moment, then asked, "What if Temple Priest says we are not to blame?"

"That would be good. Still, some people will blame you in secret. That will not be good, especially if Temple Priest favors their words."

Chu Sister took a bowl of rice gruel with toppings and a porcelain spoon to Shiao-mei. She sat beside her daughter on the *kang* and helped her eat. After a few minutes, she asked, "What are you thinking, Nieh Wife?"

Lizzie had served herself a bowl of rice gruel. She was sitting at the narrow foldout table and gazing through the porthole above it.

"I feel peace," she said. "I am sorrowed there is trouble, but I feel peace. This feeling is from True God, otherwise I would be afraid. Today I am not distressed. Last night I was. I know if True God wants us to remain in Fengshan, He will take care of us and the trouble."

"You truly believe that, do you?" Chu Sister asked.

Lizzie nodded and smiled.

"Then I do too. *Wah!* What a good feeling to trust True God!"

Up at the Temple, Nils was wondering if anyone

around him was on his side. He hoped Wu Headman was. However, the older man's face was inscrutable – as were the other faces in the Temple courtyard.

How rapidly things change, he thought. *Not long ago these people were honoring me, laughing with me, listening to my stories. Now they are blaming me and seeking vengeance. Please Almighty God, give us wisdom. Protect us for your glory, according to your will.*

Nils shifted his heavy gun, causing those closest to him to back away. He could tell he alarmed them. They had probably forgotten how large and white he was compared to them. He guessed his gun frightened them too. No doubt they had heard guns were magic and more powerful than a thousand swords.

Nils smiled and bowed often to the growing crowd. When no one returned his bows, he quit smiling. He wondered if he appeared to be baring his teeth like some sort of demon. Instead of staring at him and talking about him, the people ignored him and looked silently to the hills in the distance. Nils looked in that direction too, nervously smoothing his bushy mustache.

Suddenly, one of the men shouted. "*Hai! Hai!* Look over there! Wolves are running down High Hill Three towards our village. Look! Men on horses are chasing them. Now we know who the bandits are. The Wolf Bandits. *Hai! Hai!* Gods and ancestors, help us! A double wolf attack! What shall we do?"

In an instant, all eyes looked at Wu Headman and then at Nils. Seeming to forget Nils was a fearsome foreign devil, they honored him with rapt attention. Nils shifted his gun some more before responding to the request in their eyes.

"Do the bandits think they are attacking the village by surprise? And that we are in bed asleep? *Heh!* Instead, we will surprise them. We will frighten away the Wolf

Bandits by killing the wolves. True God will help us! True God will guide my fire-sword. Those who have weapons, follow Wu and me without noise. Those who are not armed, return quickly and quietly to the village. Tell everyone to lock themselves indoors, and to pray to True God for victory and protection."

*   *   *

The sun was just beginning its rise when Temple Priest strode importantly from his sacred room. Expecting the veneration of the villagers while he pronounced the oracle of the gods, he was shocked to find an audience of only a few monks.

"Most Honorable Priest," one of the monks said, bowing low, "the people have followed Wu Headman and the white Chinese giant. They go to protect the village from attacking wolves and bandits. Look yonder. You will see them approaching High Hill Three."

A second monk added, "Venerable Holy One, the white Chinese has a fire weapon. Did you hear? He has a fire-sword and the protection of True God. *Ai!* This time our village will not be plundered."

"How do you know the message of the oracle?" Temple Priest asked, his eyebrows raised.

"*Ai!* I do not know the oracle. Instead, I saw the fire-sword myself and heard the words about True God from the mouth of the foreign devil who sounds Chinese."

"Amazing!" Temple Priest said. "Is it possible True God is indeed the Most High God of Heaven? I will watch and see."

Nor was he the only one who watched. Although they had been warned to stay indoors, many villagers climbed up trees and onto roof tops to watch the attack. Down at the River, Lizzie rushed on deck when she heard the first gun blast. Her view was blocked by the village, so she listened for return blasts. There were none. Relieved, she knew then these bandits were not armed with guns and probably would not fight. Soon she heard more shots from Nils's gun, then shouts from the villagers watching.

"*Wah*! Another one is dead, and another, and another. *Wah*! That one is a mighty wolf killer. That giant is not a devil; he is a savior. Another one is dead, and another, and another. We are saved. The village is saved. See, the wolves and bandits are fleeing. The white Chinese giant has saved us. *Sha, sha!* Kill, kill all the wolves!" they shouted with increasing excitement.

Hours later Nils returned to the *Good News Boat*. He returned a hero, no longer a foreign devil to be driven away or worse. When Lizzie heard the crowd nearing, she climbed on top of their cabin with her accordion and began to play and sing. On the deck below, Chu Sister stood with baby Hilda in her arms. Beside her carrying Shiao-mei stood Chu Boatman, relief spread across his smiling face. Loudly he sang along with Lizzie and the others on the boat.

Before long, hundreds of villagers were also singing the words of Lizzie's simple song over and over in joy and victory:

> True God loves us, this we know,
> For Book Holy tells us so.
> To True God, we should belong.
> Weak we are, True God is strong.
> Yes, True God loves us,
> For Book Holy tell us so.

When Nils reached the houseboat, he climbed up beside Lizzie and tried to speak to the people. But they kept shouting and chanting. He soon gave up. Laughing, he and

Lizzie climbed down to stand on deck beside the others. Before long, he took little Hilda and raised her high in his arms.

"True God loves my precious daughter!" Nils shouted to the people. "True God loves boys and girls the same. Today True God has protected us all, male and female the same!"

"What a marvelous idea," Lizzie said in Swedish. Following Nils's example, she took little Shiao-mei from Chu Boatman and held her high in the air beside baby Hilda.

*   *   *

Abbie's Journal
Oct 7, 2001
. . . BT and I just had our daily walk through the woods to the lake. Fall – what a colorful, radiant time. It's easy to forget the terrible wars and suffering in places like China, the Mideast and Africa when I'm outdoors with BT – when we're surrounded by peaceful sights and sounds and smells. All so unlike what I read earlier today in Grampa Nils's memoirs – about the time he protected Fengshan's terrified villagers from both bandits and wolves. He wrote about killing 30 or more Siberian wolves with his gun – imagine! Doing so frightened away the bandits. Although he didn't mention killing any bandits, I can't help but wonder, especially since there is a blacked out line, probably by Dad. . .

. . . in gratitude, the villagers made fur coats from the wolf pelts for him and Gramma Lizzie, and for Wu Headman and his number-one wife. To honor Grampa and Gramma for "a thousand fragrant years," Wu Headman gave them the village's ancient carved stone teapot – the one they had

used for important ceremonies for centuries. Grampa always called it his Bandit Teapot. My cousin Joy has this treasure from old China, inherited from her father, Dad's brother Oliver. She's had it appraised. It's over 500 years old and may be jade, the ancient brown jade. . .

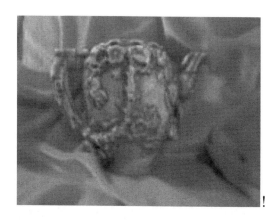

Chapter 12

Abbie's Journal
Oct 10, 2001

. . . New York and Washington and Pennsylvania have been attacked – how shocking and still unbelievable! Certainly haunting and stressful for war survivors like me. Watching TV, I'm overwhelmed by memories and weep for the new survivors. In spite of the attacks, I know America is the safest, freest, most wonderful place on earth. Yesterday Phil emailed me a piece called "Myths of the Taliban." One of the myths is thinking the people of Afghanistan support the Taliban. The truth is, they are weary of oppressive warlords, bandits and terrorism. Sounds like China a century ago. Sometimes Gramma Lizzie and Grampa Nils halted bandit and rebel attacks other times they fled for their lives. . .

Fengshan, 1900
Year of Rat

"*Wah! Ni kan!* Look!" Chu Boatman announced excitedly from between the cabins where he was checking the water level in the vats. "A messenger on horseback rides along the riverside!"

Nils, about to leave the houseboat for a meeting at Good News Hall, headed instead towards the messenger. Half way up the steps, he called down to Chu, "Please tell Nieh Wife where I am going. Tell her I will come back before I go on to the meeting."

Messengers this far upriver were rare, especially ones flying the protection of the magistrate's banner. Soon villagers were running through the alleys of Fengshan to hear why this one had come.

At the communal water cistern, the messenger dismounted, as messengers had for centuries. A waiting villager took his horse's reins. Others watered and fed the horse. Wu Headman welcomed the messenger as he handed him a wet cloth to refresh his face and hands, and then a bowl of steaming tea.

Squatting, the messenger sipped the tea and looked around. His eyes were red from exhaustion, and he squinted and blinked. When he spotted Nils standing in the midst of the villagers, he rose slowly to his feet.

He bowed and said, "You! You are the foreign Good News man of Fengshan, are you not?"

Nils returned the bow and replied he was.

"*Ai!* Then the message I carry is for you. Come here. For you, I have risked my life."

"A thousand thanks!" Nils said and walked over to the messenger. "You will be well repaid. What is the message you bring me?"

"I do not know. I am a poor man and read too few characters. Besides, this message is not written in characters, but in the scratches of a foreign devil."

The villagers laughed nervously.

Nils took the envelope. Its red seal was broken but he said nothing. He did not want the messenger to lose face.

"What is the message?" the people murmured, louder and louder.

"It is a long message. Please wait," Nils answered.

To himself, Nils read in Swedish:

My Dear Brother Nils and Sister Lizzie:

How I pray you will receive this message in time to save your lives.

Do not tell the people of Fengshan anything it says until you read to the end. Then tell them that Christians here in Shanghai rejoice to hear that in Fengshan you now have a school and clinic next to your Good News Hall.

Next, warn that Boxers threaten all Christians these days, both foreigners and Chinese. The Christians in Shanghai are praying for all True God followers to be faithful during suffering and death. Please join our prayers.

Dear co-laborers in God's vineyard, you must leave the night you receive these words. Do not tell anyone in the village lest someone betray you. Trust no one!

Flee down the River as quickly as you can. Disguise yourselves. Stop only when necessary. I pray you will meet a gunboat or convoy for escort, but do not trust anyone with Imperial connections.

May God Almighty be with you until we meet again on earth or in heaven.

Your brother in Christ,
J. G. Nelson
Field Director
May 7, 1900

After telling the people crowded around him what he could from the message, Nils reminded everyone to meet in the Good News Hall as the sun sank behind the river gorge. "Tonight we must prepare for persecution," he announced.

"Yes, yes," the people agreed. "We want to be brave for True God if Boxers come."

A few minutes later, Nils was back aboard the *Good News Boat*. As he read aloud Brother Nelson's grim message, Lizzie nursed their infant twins, just three weeks old, while little Hilda snuggled close to her papa.

"*Ja!* We were afraid this was coming, weren't we," Lizzie said softly, surprising Nils with her calm as she nuzzled the tiny heads of Alfred and Adolph. "But it's come much sooner than we expected, hasn't it!"

They were quiet for a few moments, then she added, "Even if Brother Nelson says not to tell the villagers we're leaving, we have to tell Chu Boatman and Chu Sister, don't we?"

Nils nodded. "They'll have to choose whether to stay here or go with us. Oh Lizzie, my heart is heavy for what may be ahead." He rested his chin gently on Hilda's head and rocked back and forth.

*   *   *

Late that night, the *Good News Boat* slipped away from the ancient stone wharf where it had anchored for more than a year.

For this journey by stealth down the Great Long River, the Imperial banner was not raised. Long lengths of white cloth, the sign of mourning, were fastened over the boat's sides to hide its name. During their flight, Lizzie and Nils and the children would remain in their cabin and not venture on deck to greet those they passed as was their custom. Nor would they dare hang their laundry to dry on deck on bamboo poles.

With grave face, Chu stood at the steering rudder and peered into the darkness. His two helpers worked the sails silently, wondering why they were leaving secretly in the night and why Chu told them nothing.

On the bank above the wharf, Chu Sister stood alone beneath the old sacred tree. Weeping silently, she lamented to True God the departure of her husband with their foreign friends and the three little ones she loved as if they were her own. Waving her white neckcloth in farewell to the soundless shadows on the disappearing boat, she could not control her shivering.

When Chu Sister had first heard the frightening message from Shanghai, she had knelt before Nieh Husband and Wife. Along with Chu, she begged them to hide with their children in the caves behind the village. "My village will take care of you and defend you," she urged.

Sadly, Lizzie and Nils shook their heads. "We must do as our director requests," Nils said. "Besides, how can we even think of endangering the lives of people in Fengshan by staying?"

Choosing to stay behind had been a difficult choice to make within an hour's time. However, once Chu Sister realized Wu Headman needed her help to keep the school and Good News Hall open, her decision was firm. She raised her clasped hands towards heaven and prayed to True God for courage. The others joined her, all praying aloud together for strength and guidance.

But when Nieh Wife gave her potted aloe and comfrey plants to make ointments for the clinic, Chu Sister had protested, "*Bu neng! Wo bu neng!* No, I cannot keep the clinic open too. I do not know how to bring healing to people in the same way as you and Nieh Husband."

"Of course you can since you have to," Lizzie assured her. "You have learned from us. You know more than you think you do. And you know how to pray. That is the best healer of all."

Watching the boat disappear, Chu Sister worried the

most about the clinic. But she knew that at least she could help girls and young women unbind their feet. And she could keep persuading families not to bind the feet of their young daughters. Focusing on what she could do helped her to stop worrying about what she could not do.

After she could see nothing down the River but darkness, still she waited, not yet ready to return to her home where Shiao-mei was sound asleep on the family *kang*. For a long time, she watched and listened. She wanted to be sure no one else knew until morning that the *Good News Boat* had sailed away.

*   *   *

Lizzie and Nils had not risked sailing the River at night before. Traveling upriver would have been impossible for trackers. Traveling downriver at least was possible, though perilous. Since every eye was needed to watch for dangers, Nils spent the night on deck with the boatmen.

In their cabin, Lizzie, too, was sleepless.

I'm learning what the Bible means when it says to pray without ceasing, she thought. *Oh Lord God, I wonder which death is worse, the River or the Boxers. Oh Lord God, if it be your will, please spare our lives. There's so much to do yet in China. And our children are just babies.*

For five nights and days, the *Good News Boat* did not stop. Many times someone on another boat or from shore called to them, "Why do you not stop? What do you mourn?"

To protect the identities of the Niehs in case Boxers were around, Chu Boatman was the one who replied. "We hurry to Shanghai. We mourn the loss of family."

"How? By what misfortune?"

To that, Chu never replied. He just bowed. When pressed, his helpers shouted they did not know. They were nothing more than hired hands and did not know their master's business.

"Who is your master?" someone usually shouted back.

Then the boatmen became silent. They focused on their tasks with the poles and sails, their eyes averted from the inquisitors.

On the fifth day fleeing downriver, Little Hilda became feverish and dehydrated from an attack of dysentery. Lizzie treated her hourly with diluted comfrey tea. Nils anointed her with oil and prayed. By the next day, Hilda was better, but their twin babies were sick.

"*Oh min min*, where did they get it from?" Lizzie moaned, weary and worried. "I've tried so hard to be careful."

"It's not your fault," Nils said. He helped her clean away the foul matter seeping from the little bottoms of their infant sons, then gently smoothed aloe ointment on the red, blistered skin.

"These things happen, we both know," he said. "We must commit little Alfred and Adolph to Almighty God for whatever is His will."

A day later, Baby Adolph died peacefully in his sleep. One minute he was breathing softly, and the next he wasn't. Almost as quickly, baby Alfred recovered.

As the *Good News Boat* hastened downriver, Chu and the other boatmen watched. Lizzie heard them asking each other what Nils and she would do. Would they cry out against True God for letting their son die? And their son's body, would they give it to the River? Or what would they do with it? What did foreigners do with their dead?

Nils heard Chu tell his helpers that foreigners buried their dead in special cemeteries just for white people. The two other boatmen said foreigners sent the ashes or bones of their dead back to the country they came from.

"And what about a baby conceived and born in China, where does he come from?" Chu asked the men.

For that, his helpers had no answer. And neither did Nils.

Finally, numbed and exhausted by their children's illness and Adolph's death, Nils and Lizzie told Chu to pull ashore for a few hours. There they would decide what to do with their son's tiny body.

As the boatmen maneuvered the boat to the riverbank, in the cabin Lizzie cuddled Adolph and Alfred in her arms. She told little Hilda her baby brother had gone to heaven to wait for them in a pretty place with Jesus.

Hilda didn't understand. She just smiled and patted both babies' faces. "Jesus, Jesus, pretty, pretty," she chanted to them.

All at once, loud shouts and sounds of horses and men pounding along the shore broke upon them. Before Chu and the other boatmen could do anything, dozens of yelling Boxer rebels waving swords were beside the boat and jumping on board.

Nils leaped down from the *kang* to where his guns were hidden beneath the floor.

Should I take them out? No, he decided. *The guns might be forced from me and used against us.* Instead, he picked up Hilda and hugged her close.

"Papa has you safe, my sweet Hilda girl," he said into her soft little ear. "Papa has you safe."

The next moment, rebels burst into the cabin with swords drawn and cursing foreign devils. "Come with us!" they shouted. "Come with us to our commander. Come with us or die. *Sha, sha!* Kill, kill!"

"Listen, please!" Nils said sternly, towering over the men crowding into the room. "Bring your commander here. Our infant son has just died from sickness. We are in mourning."

"*Hai!*" The rebels stepped back. "What disease?"

"We are not sure," Lizzie said. She stood up and started walking towards the men, still cradling a baby in each arm. "Yes," she added fiercely. "Bring your commander here. He may not want us on shore."

Backing away from the foreigners who looked like strange giants but sounded Chinese, the rebels muttered to each other, arguing over who should go and who stay. Fearing the dead baby's spirit as well as his disease, no one wanted to stay in the cabin.

"Why stay down here with us?" Nils suggested. "If you stand guard on deck, how can we escape before your commander comes?"

"Are you not the foreign devil with the fire weapon that never misses?" one of the rebels asked.

"Can you not see I carry no weapon?" Nils replied. "Nor will I carry any when your commander comes."

Listening and praying, Lizzie and Nils waited near the closed door of their cabin. Minutes later, they heard the commotion of the commander arriving.

"If we are to be killed," Nils said, "I hope the little ones will be killed first."

Lizzie nodded, too drained to speak or weep.

"Come up on deck!" a voice shouted. "Come up at once or die, you despicable foreign devils, spoilers of China!"

"We come with our children. We carry no weapons," Nils called as he helped Lizzie up the stairs and onto deck.

On shore to meet them was the Boxer commander, astride a restless, black horse. Dozens of men surrounded him, wearing the black headband of the Boxers and armed with swords. The rebels clinched fists were raised to signal righteous harmony. A more frightening sight, Nils and Lizzie could scarcely imagine. Then their eyes met those of the commander, and they nearly cried out. For they recognized their lost friend and messenger, the one they had called Li Brother.

Immediately, the commander stopped them with harsh words. "Do not speak unless told to!"

They bowed, and he said more kindly, "My men say your infant son has died."

Lizzie nodded and bowed again, raising the tiny body of Adolph in one arm.

"And you have a son who yet lives?" the commander asked, looking down at Lizzie's other arm.

"Yes, True God spared the life of one twin," Nils said.

"Today your god is good," the commander replied.

"True God is always good," Nils said bravely.

At that, the commander shouted at his men, "What were these people doing wrong? Why did you stop them? What did you catch them doing against China?"

"Do you not see, honorable commander?" one of the rebel soldiers replied. "They are foreign devils invading our country. For that we must kill them. *Sha, sha!*" he cried out and others joined his cry.

Whimpering, little Hilda buried her head in Nils's shoulder. Baby Alfred slept peacefully in Lizzie's arm beside his dead twin.

Lizzie looked straight at the commander who had not acknowledged them as friends. She said to him and his men, "You did not catch us doing wrong because we have done no wrong. Like you, we want only good for this country. It is now our home and the birthland of our children."

"Attention!" the Boxer commander shouted and extended his right fist. His men straightened and raised their fists in return salute.

"Look around! Where are the foreign devils? I hear

none. I see none. I see only *bai-zhong-ren* white Chinese. Release them and their boat."

Then he commanded several of his men on horses. "You and you and you, ride ahead and announce my words along the River. The boat with mourning cloth travels in safety."

Late that afternoon, Nils and Lizzie stood again on deck. The *Good News Boat* had reached a deep, slow-moving spot in the River where the shore was empty of people. In her arms, Lizzie carried little Hilda and baby Alfred. Nils carried a clay water jar, its sides now etched with a cross and the words, Beloved Baby Adolph Newquist, Safe in the Arms of Jesus, 1900.

Nils walked to the side of the boat and leaned over the edge, then carefully lowered the jar into the River. He watched it sink out of sight before he stepped back. With their heads lifted towards heaven, he and Lizzie and Chu recited the Twenty-third Psalm in Chinese.

"Shall we not sing?" Chu asked after a pause.

"Not today," Lizzie said. "Today I can only weep. Tomorrow, Chu Brother, tomorrow we will sing again."

On their way back to their cabin, Nils turned to Chu. "The Boxer commander, did you not recognize him?"

"*Ai!* I did," Chu said. "When I saw who he was, I prayed at once. I begged True God to touch Li Commander's heart with mercy for you according to His will. I knew you and Nieh Wife had pain enough in your hearts. You did not need more pain and death. Praise be to True God! He answered my prayer for you, and He included unworthy me and my helpers. Thanks be to True God."

"Amen! Thanks be to Almighty God," Nils said.

*   *   *

Shanghai

Soon after their Boxer rebel scare, Nils and Lizzie caught up with a convoy of boats traveling downriver. Six gunboats from the European settlements were in escort. A week later, they reached Shanghai safely, their sadness deepened by the scores of bodies they saw in the River.

In Shanghai, they heard the terrible news of thousands attacked and massacred by Boxers, and hundreds held in siege in Peking. With protection by the Imperials so uncertain, they decided to join the great exodus from China.

Their first step back to Western culture was to change from their Chinese garments into their former clothes.

And so on a sweltering August morning, no longer dressed as Chinese, they departed with little Hilda and baby Alfred aboard a crowded steamer headed for New York. Fearful of Boxer spies, they told their Chinese friends farewell in secret, including their faithful friend Chu Boatman, who they left with their name chops to serve as caretaker of their business, property and boat.

Home, Lizzie thought, watching their adopted home shrink smaller and smaller in the distance. *Where's home? We say we're going home to America. But no one knows we're coming and Nils has never been there. And we haven't had any letters for so long.*

"Do you think Almighty God will bring us back?" Nils asked, startling Lizzie from her reverie.

"But of course. Millions along the River still need to hear about God. *Oh min min!* But what will our lives be until we return?" Lizzie lay her head on Nils's shoulder and sobbed.

*   *   *

Abbie's Journal
Nov 22, 2001

. . . *in her journals, Gramma Lizzie tells how the Salvation Army* War Cries *were a wonderful source of courage for her. And I remember Dad telling how his mother treasured her* War Cries, *how she saved the magazines in neat stacks by her desk, and how he liked to looking at them. In one of her journal entries I read today, Gramma notes that Catherine Booth in one of her sermons urged mothers to be thankful even when their children die, and not to mourn too long. For children who die go straight to heaven, a far better place than earth. . .*

. . . *based on several biographies I've read, Mrs. Booth lived what she preached. Hmm – what a thought, especially today, Thanksgiving Day following 9-11. Dan and I have not personally experienced the grief of "losing" a child. And today we feasted in comfort and safety with our family and four scholar professors from China who are studying at the College. All day we ate and talked and played games, and gave thanks to God for America's freedoms and blessings. We also prayed for those who suffer in many place around the world. . .*

PART FOUR

Secrets . . . Calamities
Storyline 1901 to 1922
Journal Excerpts 2001 and 2002

Ten foot tall Stone Ten Keepers Monument,
China's Nestorian Monument.

The secret waits for the insight
of eyes unclouded by longing.
~ Sage Lao Tzu (6th century b.c.)

There is a God in Heaven who reveals secrets.
~ Daniel 2:28

Chapter 13

Abbie's Journal
Nov 27, 2001
... in church today, Pastor Terry asked who would go back in time to 1900 if they could. No one raised a hand, including me. But I said yes, yes, yes in my heart. I'd jump at the chance to go back then, just for a while. I'd love to spend time with Gramma Lizzie and Grampa Nils in person and join them on some River travels. And get some questions answered – like, whatever happened to valuables they buried all those times they fled ...

Des Moines, 1903
Year of Hare

A year passed.
Then another.
     To Lizzie and Nils waiting for word it was safe enough to return to China, their past lives on the Yangtze seemed more distant every day. In their daily prayers, they remembered Chu Boatman, Chu Sister, Shiao-mei who was now old enough to be called Ta-mei, Hui-ching and their other friends there.
     "*Oh min min!* Do you think they're still alive?" Lizzie sometimes asked Nils late at night.
     His answer was always the same. "Whatever is happening, Almighty God is with them."
     Near the end of their second year in Des Moines, they gave thanks to God for the birth of another son, their first truly American child. They named him Oscar Charles after two of their brothers.

"Beebee O," Little Hilda and Alfred called him, patting his tiny face and laughing with delight.

Lizzie's mother was a doting, loving Grandmama. She made it easy for the Newquists to share the family farmhouse where she and Charlie still lived. As the months passed, Lizzie and Nils talked less and less about finding a place of their own.

Lizzie happily resumed some of her former life. Occasionally she dressed in her new corset and uniform to play her accordion with the Salvation Army band. While Nils worked on the family farm with her brother Johann or rode horseback to churches and schools to speak about China, she and the little ones took a farm wagon to visit her friends and their children.

As they caught up on each other's lives, they shared hugs and tears. But mostly they laughed together and agreed nothing between them had really changed.

During this happy and peaceful interlude in their lives, Lizzie and Oliver became good friends once again. And Oliver and Nils made peace with each other.

Oliver was now a widower. He hadn't married one of Lizzie's friends after all, rather a newcomer to the area. When his wife Dorothy died during childbirth in their second year of marriage, Oliver named the baby Dorothy Elizabeth. Little Dottie and Hilda were nearly the same age, and soon became inseparable. Lizzie and Oliver often smiled at each other over the heads of the two young friends, both parents somehow comforted by the companionship between their growing daughters.

"When will you marry again?" Lizzie asked Oliver one Saturday afternoon when their families were enjoying a picnic by the river.

"I doubt I will," he said. "*Ja!* This time I really will wait for you."

Everyone laughed, but more in friendly

understanding than humor.

"I have my Dottie," he added. "I'm happy enough. But I've missed you so much, Lizzie. You were my best friend for so long and I loved you. After you left, at first I thought about following you to China. But who would have cared for my parents and the farm? And what would have happened to you, Nils, eh?"

Lizzie sighed. She patted Oliver's arm and reached for Nils's hand. "God guided each of our choices," she said. "He blessed us and gave us extra strength when we needed it. That's what matters most, isn't it?"

Nils nodded. "You're a fine friend to us," he said to Oliver, "like a brother. I'm glad you and Lizzie can be good friends again."

Would I ever have felt the same passion for Oliver I feel for Nils? Lizzie wondered. *Poor Oliver, he's had it so much harder than I have. But Nils is right. It's so good to be special friends again.*

In silence, she and the others watched the clear waters of the Des Moines River dance by, spraying grand arcs over boulders along its way. On this afternoon, no one felt like repeating the story of Oliver rescuing Lizzie. But they remembered. They remembered also that Nils owed his life to Lizzie. And that no one had been able to save Oliver's Dorothy or sweet baby Adolf.

After a time, Nils began to hum *Love Divine so Great and Wondrous,* their favorite hymn. One by one the others joined in, first harmonizing softly and then singing in Swedish with fervor.

We sound like a fine choir, Lizzie thought, looking at the faces of the children who had paused in their play to listen. She felt a huge sense of joy within. *I'm so blessed, thank you, oh Lord God, thank you. It's so wonderful to be here at home – oh Lord God, it's so hard to think about going back to China.*

Then she thought about what she had chipped onto the nearby bluff boulder so many years ago.

"Come," she said to Nils, taking his hand, "I want to show you a secret, something important."

*   *   *

Every day, something reminded Lizzie of her dear Papa. She hoped he was looking down from heaven to watch his grandchildren eating and playing where once she had been his happy daughter. She hoped precious little Adolph was in his arms.

"See Papa," she said sometimes, looking up. "You would have had so much fun with them. They would have loved you and your stories."

One time when she did that, Hilda asked, "Does your Papa hear in heaven like God does?"

"*Ja!* I hope so, my dear. If he doesn't, I think God hears and tells my Papa."

"Then I want to go to heaven. With Dottie. She wants to see her Mama. Maybe God will come and get us soon, do you think?"

Lizzie pressed her hand hard over her heart. She wanted to say something, but felt such a stab of foreboding she could only smile. After a moment, she hugged Hilda and kissed her forehead.

*   *   *

When baby Oscar was not quite a year old, Nils decided it was time to visit his family in Sweden. Before they returned to China, he longed to see his aging mother and other relatives. He wanted to take his family with him, but finally agreed with Lizzie it would be safer to wait until the children were older. She urged him to take her brother

Charlie instead.

Charlie's arms had been shattered in the Philippines during the recent Spanish-American War. There was little on the farm he could do anymore. Everyone agreed a special trip to Sweden might brighten his outlook on life. Like Lizzie, Charlie had not been back to his birthplace since the family came to Iowa all those years ago.

"But of course, money for his trip isn't your real concern, is it?" Lizzie asked Nils one night in their bedroom after Hilda and the little boys were asleep.

"No, you know Almighty God has been good to us that way. I guess I'm hesitant because I wonder what the trip will do to Charlie's health."

"When I see the light in his eyes at the possibility of going, I think the trip can only be good for him," Lizzie said. "Let's tell him tomorrow, shall we?"

"*Fint,* all right then. If you and the children aren't going, I agree Charlie is next best."

They snuggled close in the soft bed, a real bed they fondly called it, remembering all those hard Chinese *kangs.* Something Lizzie didn't tell Nils that night before they went to sleep was she might be pregnant again. Nor did she plan to tell him yet. She didn't want anything to worry him or shorten his trip. When he rejoined them next year, he would have a welcome home surprise – maybe a new child named Oliver Nils or Nils Oliver.

*   *   *

Sweden

Two months later, Nils and Charlie's ship docked in Goteberg. Long before dawn, they went together to the railing to watch the ship come into harbor. For hours they said little, silenced by the beauty of their nordic homeland and by deep emotions.

"Many times I've wondered if I'd ever see this sight again," Nils said at last, his voice and mustache trembling.

"And I – I'm thankful to be here too," Charlie said. "You know something, Nils, I can't shake the feeling I've come home. It's all just as I pictured it from Father's stories and some of my own memories. Seeing it again after so many years almost makes me forget my arms. Curse that war! I've been thinking what I wouldn't give to be a sailor again. *Ja!* A sailor in this port."

"Me too, Charlie. But all those years on the Yangtze have nearly erased my life here." Nils paused. "I wonder if the *Ericsson* is in port. I'd sure like to see Captain Johnson again if he's still around."

"Is there a place you can ask?"

"*Ja.* See that big building over there? Looks like it's still the central shipping office. We can ask there."

Several hours later, they were about to enter the building when they heard a woman's voice calling, "Nils, Nils Newquist, is that you? Nils, Nils, can you hear me? Stop! Is it really you? Nils!"

Nils stopped and turned around. He recognized the voice, but couldn't believe his ears. Sure enough, there running towards him was Ruth Carlson. In a moment she reached him, and they hugged each other like a long-lost brother and sister – which in a way they were. They backed away, looked at each other and hugged again.

Nils remembered his manners and began to introduce Ruth to Charlie, but she interrupted him. "Ah, you must be one of dear Lizzie's brothers You look so much like her. Let me guess, are you Charlie or Johann. I guess Charlie because of your curly hair. Am I right?"

Charlie and Nils both nodded and they all laughed. Then Nils told Charlie who Ruth was.

"Just think, you two running into each other here, today, after all these years," Charlie said.

Nils explained to Ruth they had just arrived, and had walked over to inquire about the *Ericsson* and Captain Johnson.

She stared at them and shook her head. "You won't believe it," she said. "I'm here to ask about the *Ericsson* too. It's due in any day, and sails next for Shanghai. I'm booked on it. I was returning to China to look for you and Lizzie."

"Look for us? Why?"

"Did you know? I'm a widow now, without any children, sad to say. Bertil died here two years ago. I can still hardly believe he's gone. When he became ill, we came back to be with our families and take care of inheritance matters. At first I thought maybe I would stay here. It's been so wonderful to be back. But I cannot shake China from my heart. So I decided to find you and Lizzie, and work with you once again."

When the men just looked at Ruth, speechless, she continued, "Let's go see about the *Ericsson*. After that, I invite you to stay with me while you're here in Goteborg so we can talk and talk and talk. You haven't made other arrangements yet, have you?"

"Well, no," Nils said slowly. "Is that all right with you, Charlie?"

"Sure. I'd be honored to stay with you, Ruth. I've heard so much about you and Bertil from Lizzie that I almost feel like we're friends already. I don't think Lizzie knows about your husband, does she?"

"Maybe not. I haven't heard from her since he died. I've been wondering if my last letter ever reached her."

As they walked the two miles to Ruth's home, a hired porter followed behind with their luggage. On the way, she explained to them that her home was a suite of rooms in her brother's city place. The guest suite next to hers was theirs to use for as long as they needed. She told them other things about herself that Nils hadn't known before.

Or maybe, he thought, *she told me some of this when I was recovering from my head injury and I just don't remember.*

To his astonishment, he and Charlie learned her family was nobility and related to the royal family. Her grandfather, a count, was a close friend and adviser to King Oscar II. So her family enjoyed many privileges.

"Ruth," Nils asked, "how can you leave a grand life like this and go back to China alone? Back to the poverty and destitution there, and maybe even death?"

"I already left it years ago. I left it when I joined the Salvation Army and married Bertil in America. You should know my family is pleased I'm going again to China to serve God. They will provide whatever I need for as long as I need it. Afterwards, I can always come home."

Servants, carpets, embroidered linens, fine dishes and silver, plush chairs, books and more books, gardens and fountains – Nils and Charlie had never before enjoyed such luxurious living. To their surprise, Ruth's family was also rich spiritually. Her family took their wealth for granted, but not their worship of God.

Evening dinners were occasions for entertaining scholars and theologians, as well as nobility and government officials. Intense religious discussions often absorbed guests until late at night, although never past midnight at the insistence of Ruth's brother.

"God's workers need rest," he liked to say. "Come, let's have today's last word from the Holy Book and then bid each other pleasant dreams."

For a fortnight, Nils and Charlie stayed in Goteborg waiting for the *Ericsson*. When there still was no definite date for its arrival, they decided it was time to travel on. After discussing with Ruth the best way to get to Nils's home, they chose train. While boat would have been cheaper, traveling by train would give them an enjoyable day of inland scenery – picturesque farms, flashing waterfalls, and rivers with colorful boats. In Malmo, they would hire a horse cart to take them to Nils's home in the heart of Smaland.

Once they had their tickets and schedule, Nils sent a telegram to his mother. He tightened his fingers to keep them steady as he wrote the brief message. Then he and Charlie said grateful farewells to Ruth and her family, with plans to reunite in several months, God willing. For now Ruth was no longer going alone to China on the *Ericsson*. Instead, she had agreed to return to America with Nils and Charlie. From there, she would travel to China with the Newquists.

"Let me join your family as your children's auntie," she had said to Nils one evening while they were awaiting the *Ericsson*. "I can help Lizzie and you with the mission work. Then I can return to China with dear friends and not by myself. That would please my family."

Indeed, Ruth's brother was so pleased with the new arrangement, he offered to fund as many schools and orphanages as they could establish in river towns. Nils knelt beside the guestroom bed in thankful prayer for a long time that night. He fell asleep smiling about the surprised look of joy on Lizzie's face when she saw Ruth again and heard about the brother's great generosity.

*   *   *

Nils and Charlie spent four wonderful months with Nils's mother, his brothers and their families. His sister Cecilia, who had not married, still lived at home to care for their mother. Nils's other sister had married and moved to Norway several years before. When a reunion with her didn't work out, his gifts for her of intricate ivory carvings from China and framed family photographs from America, the same as he gave the others in his family, he left with Cecilia.

Nils was a strong man and not often emotional in public, but he wept with sorrow when it was time to tell his family goodbye. Should another ten years pass before he came again, who would there be to greet him? Surely not his frail mother, who he preferred to remember as a strong woman riding horseback about the countryside, directing and encouraging her sons and hired hands.

In his own sadness at leaving, Nils didn't notice how Charlie and Cecilia kept extra close company with each other the final days. Nor did he think it unusual when Charlie waved his handkerchief from the train window as Cecilia ran alongside until the last possible moment. Sure, Nils was sad to leave his dear sister. But he expected to see her again. He missed that this time it was Charlie's departure bringing tears to Cecilia's eyes.

By the time Nils and Charlie boarded the train in Malmo, they had added two large wooden crates to their luggage. One contained gifts for relatives in America – handsome wool sweaters, tasty cheeses, along with many other lovingly packed items from the "old country." The second crate held a precious chest. Nils had protested this gift, but his mother and Cecilia both insisted until he accepted. It was his mother's treasured wedding chest, artfully crafted and painted in blues, reds and yellows by Nils's father more than fifty years before.

"Please take it for your darling Hilda," Nils's mother said with tears in her eyes. "I love her and pray for her. I know I will never get to see her on this earth. So you tell her that her grandmama hopes she will one day marry a fine, godly man like her grandpapa."

"But Cecilia, isn't the chest rightfully yours?" Nils

had asked.

"Yes, but of course I gladly give it to my namesake. I am happy to give her some other things as well – a few for now, a few for when she is older. They are in the chest along with my gifts to Lizzie and your boys. Tell little Hilda Cecilia I pray she will one day visit her auntie in the house where her father was born."

From the town of Malmo, Nils and Charlie traveled to Jonkoping where they enjoyed a month-long reunion with their mother's Beckman relatives. Many aunts, uncles and cousins came from throughout the area to see them, and to send love gifts to Thor's widow and the family.

Nils's China stories were soon as popular with his wife's relatives as they had been with his own family. "Tell us more," he heard again and again – and not just after the evening meal, but nearly every day in the country buildings that doubled as churches and schools.

He told his listeners stories about Chu Boatman, the eunuch, who became a Christian and married Wang Sister, now called Chu Sister. He acted out how her first husband had nearly killed him, Nils, and as a consequence brought Lizzie Beckman into his life. He described the thousands and thousands of destitute and spiritually hungry river people living along the Yangtze, a river so very different from their own.

He told about the mission work in Fengshan, and how he and Lizzie had barely escaped with their lives during the height of the Boxer Rebellion. He explained the plight of hundreds of thousands of children in China, especially the little girls. Then he told about dear little baby Adolf, safe forever in the arms of Jesus.

Nils never asked for money for the mission work in China, yet many gold and silver pieces were quietly pressed into his hands by both relatives and strangers. In his *dagbok* journal, he marveled at Almighty God's provisions, and this unexpected opportunity to enlist prayer and support for China. Sweden had been blessed in recent years, and the Swedes responded with thankful generosity for people they didn't know and would never see on earth.

I'm so glad I kept my promise to Pa and Almighty God, Nils thought more than once during his afternoon walks with Charlie through the countryside. *I never envisioned such blessings. May I be granted strength to keep my promise always, no matter what God permits for his glory.*

*   *   *

Abbie's Journal
Dec 25, 2001

. . . when Gramma Lizzie and Grampa Nils returned to Fengshan in 1905, they were stunned to see the terrible effects of floods and mud slides all along the River. The Fengshan villagers had suffered, yet nothing like those in other villages with lower locations, and probably because they ate hundreds of Grampa's goats. I can hardly bear to read Grampa's accounts of devastation, disease and starvation. He writes that hundreds of thousands, maybe millions drowned in the raging waters. An angry river dragon god had demanded appeasement – everyone said in fear. Thousands and thousands of homes disappeared. Planting and harvesting were disrupted. Disease and famines followed, and millions more died, especially old people and children – sometimes eaten by desperate relatives. . .

. . . Grampa and other missionaries tried to distribute food in the villages. Mostly it was rejected. The people feared the foreigners and hid in their houses, saying they had to accept the fate of the gods. Besides, perhaps contact with the foreign devils were to blame. That was the year

Gramma and Grampa starting having Christmas festivals in the villages, and eventually for other holy days too. Festival food thousands of people accepted without fear for some reason. From then on, food distribution was part of their mission work, and later for my parents as well. . .

. . . one of my haunting memories from childhood is of pitiful, hungry beggars, many near death, reaching out and crying for food. Beggars were everywhere during my China childhood – hundreds, maybe thousands of them. I remember cringing and crying when they grasped me. How wonderful not to see anyone that desperate during our trip to China last year. . .

Chapter 14

Abbie's Journal
Jan 9, 2002

. . . such a disturbing dream I had last night. I was lost in a strange place – a town ancient and scary. The streets were dark alleys, narrow and winding. Peculiar old houses closed in around me. As I hurried along, I kept stumbling into a smelly street-side gutter. People crowded against me from all sides, taunting and laughing. None could help me find my way because I didn't know where I was going. . .

. . . mixed in my dream was a frantic feeling for a lost child. I kept calling the child's name – was it one of my brothers? One of my children? What a relief to wake up! It took me til this evening to realize the dream was of my childhood memories of Fengshan. I've been sitting here thinking the town probably hasn't changed much since my grandparents' time. But the new river town being built because of the Three Gorges Dam will be different. It will be a modern, more pleasant town, I think, and no longer a place of nightmares. . .

Fengshan, 1909
Another Year of Rooster

"Mama," Hilda called, "Oliver and Johann have been in my room long enough. Can Alfred or Oscar play with them now? Please?"

"Your mama went to the clinic," Mother Ruth said, coming to Hilda's door. "And I think the big boys are with your papa at the children's home. Oliver and little Johann, come with me. I'll read to you from the story book. You know Hilda leaves for boarding school in a few days. She needs to get her things ready to pack into her trunk. Let's give her time to be alone."

"But we were helping," Oliver said. "Besides, Mother Ruth, I don't want to hear a story now. I've heard them all. I'm going to see Cook."

He skipped and jumped down the hall to the kitchen at the back of their home called Great House. Now that he was six, he was allowed to be in the kitchen because he had promised to sit on a stool by the bread table and obey Cook. That was easy. Cook gave him fun things to do and taste, like brown sugar lumps after the sugar had been boiled clean of bugs and dirt.

Little Johann took Mother Ruth's hand and walked importantly with her to the front room. He loved being read to, especially in the front room – the pretty room where adults talked, where his sister and brothers did their English school work. Johann guessed the front room was almost like heaven. At least that's what his Chinese playmates suggested when they peeked in the door and saw the smooth cement floor with its colorful rugs and strange-looking furniture.

*   *   *

Two years after returning to China, Nils and Lizzie, along with their children and Ruth, had moved into Great House. Before building *Ta-Chia* or Great House, they lived for a year aboard the *Good News Boat* with Chu Boatman.

During that time, Chu never tired of telling them about True God's protection for everyone while they were away. A faithful caretaker of their Nieh property, Chu made many trading trips between Shanghai and Fengshan. He had avoided disaster, and made both money and converts to True God. He had also provided well for his wife Chu Sister, her daughter Ta- Mei, her cousin Hui-ching, and hundreds of homeless boys and girls.

With the return of the Niehs, more than a dozen of them lived together in crowded conditions aboard the boat. Their sense of adventure changed to an urgent longing for space and privacy. Soon Nils and Lizzie were praying, and making plans for a permanent home in Fengshan. Ruth generously did more than her share. She frequently telegraphed requests to her brother in Sweden. Because of his status, he was often able to supply what they needed through direct and privileged routes.

During the year of Great House's construction, Nils and Lizzie's household moved from the boat house to an abandoned house. For years, villagers had been unwilling to live in the old ancestral place of the Ling family, claiming it was haunted by demons. Since it was the only unoccupied place in the village, Chu Sister suggested they might live there.

When she discussed the matter with Wu Headman, he replied, "But the demons, I do not think even Christian foreigners like the Niehs can live with Chinese demons!"

"They will pray to True God who will drive the demons away," she said. "I have seen them do it before. Your prayers and mine may not be strong enough, but theirs are. Do you not remember how they always say True God is more powerful than demons?"

Wu Headman cautiously agreed. Later that day, he offered the place to the Niehs.

When Nils and Lizzie went with Wu to inspect the haunted Ling home, Chu Sister and Chu Boatman accompanied them. Hundreds of fearful, excited villagers followed along behind. It turned into such a notable occasion that Temple Priest sent some monks to watch what happened, wishing he did not have to save face by staying away.

When they reached the front courtyard, Nils asked

Wu, "Are any Ling descendants living in the village?"

Wu thought for a moment. "No, only a few females. They are married, so belong to other families."

"Are any of the Ling females here right now among the village onlookers?" Nils pursued.

Wu Headman called out several names. The villagers shoved each other this way and that as they looked around, then moved aside and gestured towards a middle-aged woman suddenly standing alone. She bent her head over her cane in embarrassment.

Lizzie walked to the woman's side, then gently said, "Peace, Ling Daughter. Will you come with me to your former courtyard? You see, we need your help. Nothing will harm you, we promise."

With reluctance, the woman assented. She followed Lizzie as quickly as she could on her crippled bound feet, balancing with her cane.

Entering the courtyard she had fearfully avoided for many years, the woman felt a tinge of hope. What if these foreigners could cure her ancestral home? Even though it was no longer hers, its curse had tormented her life by bringing shame to her husband's family through her. As the eldest surviving Ling daughter without any brothers, each year she presented offerings to the river gods, and entreated Temple Priest to trick the demon ghosts into leaving.

All in vain.

Year after year, Temple Priest repeated the same words, "Maybe next year. We will try again next year. Next year double your offerings."

Once inside the courtyard, the woman forgot her momentary hope. She began to breathe in gasps and strike her heart with her fist. *"Ai yah!"* she moaned. "Being here again after so many years brings the dark fear of death to me. How can you be so calm? Do you not sense the evil? Let us leave quickly before the demon ghosts strangle us like they did my father. *Ai yah! Ai yah!*"

Nils walked over and stood with Lizzie beside the woman. In one hand he carried his open Bible, in the other a small capped container of oil.

"Have you heard about True God?" he asked the woman.

"*Ai!* yes, yes. I have come many times to the Gospel Hall and listened to the stories. I wonder, if your True God is indeed the True God of Heaven and Earth, then why does not Temple Priest lead us to worship your god instead of the river gods?"

"Ah," Nils replied, "because Temple Priest's heart has not yet been changed by True God. But what about you? Would you like your heart changed by True God?"

"Yes, yes! If that will help cure the demons' curse on my family's home here."

"Then I invite you to listen carefully to True God's Holy Words."

Nils raised high his Chinese Bible and read loudly so everyone could hear. "Jesus, the Son of True God, rebuked the demons and they came out." He paused and added, "These Words are from Saint Matthew's Good News Book."

He turned some pages and read more. "From the Good News Book of Saint Luke. Then the seventy who followed Jesus, the Son of True God, returned with joy saying, 'Lord, even the demons are subject to us in your name.'"

Nils asked the woman, "Do you understand what I have read? Or do you want me to read the Holy Words again?"

"I think I understand," she said. "Because you are a follower of True God, if you ask, True God will drive away the demons from here because He is more powerful than they are."

"That is right! That is right!" Chu Sister and Chu Boatman exclaimed together. "Praise be to True God for bringing understanding of the truth to the heart of Ling Daughter."

Nils placed his open Bible on the ground. The six of them held hands and formed a circle around the Bible.

Following Nils's example, they lifted their eyes to heaven and repeated over and over, "In the name of *Yeh Su*, Son of True God!"

At the same time, Lizzie voiced aloud a prayer of exorcism. She ended with the words, "Oh Holy True God, cast out the demons from this place to a dying tree high in the hills, and bind them there forever and ever. For your glory, protect everyone and every place in this village as the demons pass. In the name of *Yeh Su* Thy Son, Amen!"

What would happen?

Hundreds of eyes stared at the old deteriorating house with its tiled front rooms and thatched back rooms. Suddenly, a few people gasped, and then more and more did as they heard shrieks and curses coming from the house. Something like black smoke began to pour from the windows and doors opened earlier by Wu and Chu at Nils's request. The ugly smoke and sounds rose and gathered above the house and hovered there – a dark, raging mass, seemingly reluctant to leave.

Lizzie shouted loudly to it, "In the name of Jesus, be gone and be bound forever! Amen! Amen!"

The dreadful mass circled the courtyard once, then streaked up and away to the hills. In horror, the villagers fell to the ground. Many cried out, "Save us, True God and *Yeh Su* of the foreigners! Save us, Jesus! Save us!"

And they were saved. The Ling ancestral home was saved, along with Ling Daughter and the reputation of her husband's family. From that day on, she was no longer shunned. She became a woman honored and asked to tell again and again the story of this day and her family's old home. After restoring the Ling place to usefulness, Nils and Lizzie and their household passed a happy year there while their own house was being built. When they moved out, Wu Headman sold it for a fine price to a retired scholar from the Imperial household. By long-standing custom, Wu could have kept most of the money for himself. Instead, he kept only one portion. He gave a second equal portion to the Niehs, a third portion to Ling Daughter, and set aside the fourth for the village's annual payment to their warlord.

"I am a True God believer," Wu said. "So I want to do what is fair and pleasing for everyone."

*   *   *

Because of its size and its importance in Fengshan, *Ta-Jia* Great House was what most villagers called Nils and Lizzie's new home. But there were some villagers who called it "house of the foreign devils," although not in the hearing of Wu Headman. These same villagers confided their fears to Temple Priest. He told them to wait and watch, and to give extra offerings at the Temple to appease the river gods.

Most of the villagers thought *Ta-Chia* was astonishing, even greater than the houses of the magistrate and warlord farther up the River. For hours at a time, the people liked to stand outside the open gate or climb nearby trees to stare at the spectacle and to laugh at the activities of the foreigners. They tried to imagine what it was like to live in one house built on top of another. They had heard of such houses, though few had seen one before. Every day they expected the house to collapse, and wanted to be there watching when it happened.

One unexpected result from building *Ta-Chia* was

the added prosperity it brought to Fengshan. As the villagers stared at the completed compound, they never tired of talking about the thousands of bricks and roof tiles they had learned to make and now continued to make and sell. They told many stories about gathering stones and lumber from the hills, and about their long days of well-paid labor following the strange building instructions of the foreigner Nieh.

Another result was Nils's discovery that he had instinctive building skills. He enjoyed using these new skills to work with the men of the village. For years to come, he used these skills in Fengshan and other villages along the River. The buildings that resulted housed many abandoned children, school classes, clinics, and Good News halls.

No wonder Jesus was a carpenter, Nils often thought as he worked. *He probably enjoyed doing this as much as I do, maybe more.*

*   *   *

When the Newquists moved into Great House, Hilda was delighted to have her own room for the first time in her life. Her cozy room was one reason she was not excited about going away to boarding school soon. She would miss her room. She could not even imagine what it would be like to live in a dormitory room with several other English-speaking girls. If she made at least one really good friend, like Dottie back in Des Moines, then maybe it wouldn't be too bad.

Hilda knew she would miss her family, too – maybe not her younger brothers so much, but of course, Mama and Papa very much. Her stomach and throat felt tight when she thought about not seeing them for ten whole months. And Mother Ruth who was always so kind and loving, with fun ideas, Hilda would miss her. She would miss her Chinese friends, too, though missing friends was different from missing family.

Her trunk stood at the foot of her bed. Actually, it was Papa's old trunk from Sweden. Papa had told her wonderful stories about his travels – stories to keep her brave and smiling when she was away from home and by herself.

One of her favorite stories was about the hope chest with the pretty red and yellow and blue designs that Aunt Cecelia had sent her from Sweden. Hilda wished she could take it to school, but it was safe in America waiting for her to grow up. Sometimes at night she dreamed she was with Dottie and her chest. Just as they opened it, she would awaken. That was the disappointing thing about happy dreams, thought Hilda, she always woke up too soon.

Tomorrow Mama would help her pack. Today it was Hilda's job to make sure she had everything she wanted to take arranged in piles. She also needed to make sure everything had her name sewn on it, something Mama and Mother Ruth had been helping her do for weeks.

Now that China had trains, land travel was much easier and faster than it used to be when they had to journey by mule or oxcart, especially to cities like Sian. Papa was escoring Hilda to Cheungking where she would board a train. Chu Boatman was taking them in the *Good News Boat.* She was meeting other children and some teachers in Cheungking. They would all ride the train together to Sian where the school for English speaking children had been built in a large compound just outside the city wall.

Mama had reminded Hilda several times to inquire about Wu Headman's ancient monument when she got to Sian. If it was near the school, they would go to see it when Mama came to take her home at the end of the school year.

During her journey to school, coolies would be

hired to carry Hilda's trunk. She would carry her new travel bag with her important travel documents and money, food and drinking water, her English Bible, some clean clothes, and a small tin with two baby aloe plants.

For months, Mama had been showing Hilda how to use aloe treatments for burns and other afflictions. She also was learning how to care for her little aloe plants so they would flourish and become large like Mama's. As she paid close attention to Mama's instructions, Hilda hoped someday she would know as much about healing as dear Mama. If she studied hard, maybe she could even become a doctor. China needed many, many more doctors. Both Mama and Papa said that these days, girls could dream about becoming doctors, just the same as boys.

*   *   *

Abbie's Journal
Jan 31, 2002
. . . among my vivid memories from childhood is Dad's collection of aloes. Wherever we lived, he soon had dozens of plants in all sizes for medicinal purposes. When the plants became too many and got in the way, Mom would protest and Dad would give some away. As a kid, I thought of Dad's aloe vera remedies as his. Since reading Gramma Lizzie's journals, I've discovered Dad's aloe cures were first hers. I wonder how many homes in China still have aloe plants because of the two of them. I used to have a few myself. But these days, you can buy aloe-everything here in the States – probably in China too . . .

Chapter 15

Abbie's Journal
Feb 9, 2002
. . . *last night the Winter Olympics opened in Salt Lake City. Dan and I watched the ceremonies, fascinated. We kept looking for Jeanne and James and the girls, but the cameras never caught them – ha! Commentators noted the modern Olympics were started in 1896 to encourage world peace and friendship. That year had a family connection I couldn't recall. Then this afternoon it came to me – 1896 is the year Gramma Lizzie and Grampa Nils traveled up the Yangtze to Fengshan for the first time. If they knew the Olympics, they didn't mention it in anything I've read. They would have been keenly interested. Peace and friendship were their life goals. What happened to two of their dear children must have felt like the worst kind of betrayal. . .*

Cheungking, 1911
Year of Swine

With difficulty, young Alfred and Oscar clambered up the steep metal steps of the smoking, hissing train. Wishing the train was more like an oxcart and not so frightening, they clutched their travel bags, and ducked their heads to keep the cinders from their eyes. They were excited to be going with Hilda to school in Sian, but at the same time teary-eyed about saying goodbye to Papa. To comfort them, he boarded the train and helped them settle.

This trip, Hilda didn't need comforting. She was happily greeting classmates. By now, she was used to saying goodbye to her parents. She knew their loving presence was always with her, almost like God's Holy

Spirit. She enjoyed being at school with others her age, and learning from the kind teachers and dorm parents.

The Sianfu School for English Speaking Children had reserved an entire train car. So for this departure, there were nearly as many Westerners as Chinese crowded onto the platform in Cheungking. On many faces, happiness was mixed with sadness. For at the same time friends were greeted, tearful goodbyes were said. Parents and children would not see each other again for many months. And as always in China, death's shadows lingered near.

*   *   *

Fengshan

Two weeks later when Nils returned to his family at Great House, he described how the boys had waved goodbye. "Just as brave as Hilda," he said.

"*Ja,* but of course," Lizzie said. "Being with Hilda helps them not feel so alone." She smiled and blinked rapidly as tears overflowed her eyes.

"Don't cry, Mama," young Oliver said. "Johann and I are still home. You can spend more time teaching us. Now you can get us ready for school too."

"And then who will care when I'm sad and missing you?" Lizzie asked.

"Maybe you can get some Chinese children," Oliver said. "There are too many of them at the children's home. I heard Chu Sister tell Chu Boatman so."

"And what did Chu answer his wife?" Mother Ruth asked, lay her hand on Oliver's shoulder.

"He said to choose two more boys to live with them, that six sons would be good for their old age. Then he laughed and said Johann and I were almost like sons, so that made eight. He said he felt as blessed as honorable old Jacob in the Bible."

Nils smiled. "What a fine Christian brother Chu is. No wonder so many in Fengshan and along the River are believers."

For Lizzie, these were distressful days. Smiling and laughing did not come easily. No matter how much she prayed and sang, she couldn't shake free of worries. She was far more worried than Nils about China's increasing political upheavals. She hadn't wanted to send the children away to school this year. Nils had insisted. When she suggested taking them back to Iowa for school instead, he looked at her with shock on his face, then said surely she wasn't serious .

His words made Lizzie feel almost ill. Sometimes she didn't even want to be in the same room with him. She wondered why he wasn't more understanding and reasonable. Not for the first time during a rift between herself and Nils, she thought about Oliver. But she didn't allow herself to think about him for very long. She had chosen, and she hadn't chosen Oliver.

Forgive me, oh Lord God, she breathed, *I don't want to be ungrateful or have unfaithful thoughts.*

Instead she made herself think about how strong and steadfast Nils was. How he always said, "God Almighty will be with us whatever happens. And with our children." Usually his words reassured her, but not these chaotic days.

Lizzie knew God allowed suffering, and she didn't want her children to suffer. Every day she worked to soothe the suffering in others. Every day she prayed that the suffering she saw in Chinese children and women wouldn't happen to her children. After all, she and Nils chose to live in China. But what choice did their children have?

Ruth tried to uphold Lizzie even as she shared the same worries. And Ruth had reasons Lizzie didn't know about. Her brother in Sweden kept urging her to come home. Didn't she know, he asked in his letters, how unstable China was from the mushrooming rebellion against the Imperial Court, and the warlords and bandits out of control?

Of course she knew, and Lizzie and Nils and all the Westerners knew. They had endured their uncertain lives here for years. These days, every ship leaving a China port was filled to capacity. Those who didn't leave, hoped and prayed the situation would somehow be resolved without too much horror and bloodshed. Yet deep in their hearts, as they watched millions of peasants reach for a life better than the brutalities of feudalism, they knew the coming conflict might be China's worst ever. They knew they weren't the only ones watching. So was Japan, ready and waiting to take advantage of China's internal turmoil.

Several nights after Nils returned from taking the children to the train, Lizzie awakened with a start. She had heard her children screaming for Mama and Papa. She rushed to Oliver and Johann's room, but they were sound asleep.

Back in bed beside Nils, she lay awake praying, anxious and filled with dread. When she finally fell asleep, she heard the children screaming again. And they were running. She could sense they were running from danger. Once again she awoke, her pulse pounding in her ears. This time she shook Nils awake.

They didn't go back to sleep, but lay in bed until dawn, praying for their children and for China. By the time they got up, Lizzie had decided.

As they dressed, she said to Nils, "I'm going to Sian. I'm leaving this morning, and taking Oliver and Johann with me. I expect Ruth will go too. I know you can't go now with us. Chu Sister and the others in the schools and clinics need you too much."

Lizzie could see her decision stunned Nils.

He walked to the window and stood with his back to her. No words of comfort came from him. She knew he wasn't used to her making a momentous decision like this without first discussing it with him, and then praying together for God's blessing. But something within her forced her onward in spite of Nils's silent, yet obvious objection. He said little during the next few hours as he helped her and the boys and Ruth hurriedly prepare to leave in the *Good News Boat* with Chu Boatman.

Word spread quickly among the Fengshan villagers that Lizzie and Ruth were leaving. No one knew exactly why or for how long, just that their departure was urgent and somehow involved the children they all adored.

Hundreds of villagers hurried to the ancient stone wharf to bid farewell to their friends who no longer seemed like strange foreigners. They wondered about the women leaving without Nieh Husband. At the same time, they were relieved that their defender, whose fire-sword kept wolves and bandits and warlords away, was not leaving.

Just before Chu and his helpers raised the sails to start downriver, Nils quieted everyone for prayer. In a determined voice, he asked True God to bless and protect the travelers as well as those who stayed behind. He prayed for grace for all of them during China's troubled days.

Then he embraced Ruth, his sons, and finally Lizzie. The villagers had rarely, if ever, seen such a tender demonstration. Watching, they felt the seriousness of the moment. This time, no one dared gesture or laugh at the strange foreigners who were their friends.

*   *   *

Cheungking
    Five days later when they reached Cheungking to take the train, Lizzie and Ruth heard the news about the

terrible attack in Sian. Although full details were not yet known because travel was hazardous, the missionary friends they stayed with had heard about the massacre of children and teachers in the school by rioting rebels. Unfortunately, the school compound was outside the protection of the city wall – that ancient wall, two houses high and one house wide, built of stone, bricks and mud pounded together. Although soldiers from within Sian had rushed to quell the attack, most at the school were already slain or injured by rebel swords when the soldiers arrived.

Neither Lizzie nor Ruth slept that night. Their missionary friends had not known the names of the dead and injured. But Lizzie knew. In her heart she knew – and she cried out to God in anguish throughout the night.

Ruth tried to comfort her. "Dear, dear Lizzie, we don't know for sure who was killed. Wait until we know before you sorrow. Tonight lean on God. Reach out for God's grace and strength."

No one could dissuade Lizzie from immediately journeying on to Sian. So her friends did the next best thing, and found volunteers from the Chinese Christian community to travel with her and her group. By midmorning, a dozen men and women had gathered to accompany Lizzie and Ruth and the boys to Sian. These were Chinese who had experienced faith and its spiritual freeing. They were ready to defend with their lives any foreigners who had helped bring the Good News of True God to China.

The train trip took several days – long, agonizing days. Because of rumors of more rioting and attacks, armed soldiers patrolled the train, causing numerous delays. Lizzie and her young sons and Ruth were the brunt of many anti-imperialist remarks and hateful looks. But thanks to their Chinese companions and the soldiers, there were no violent outbreaks.

*   *   *

Sian

The missionaries in Sian had received word by telegram that Lizzie and Ruth were arriving. When the train pulled into the station, a delegation of missionary men with soldier escorts waited on the platform. As she stepped down from the train, Lizzie looked into the waiting faces and knew the news was what she had feared. In that instant, she heard again the screams of her children in her dreams. She put her face in her hands and sobbed.

One of the men came quickly to her side. "Sister Elizabeth," he said, "your son Alfred is safe and waiting for you at the mission station."

"What?" Lizzie gasped. *"Oh min min!* Is one of them alive? Praise Lord God!"

"Yes. Your son Alfred is spared, though God took dear Hilda and Oscar to heaven along with others. Come now, Sister, a crowd is gathering. We'll tell you everything at the mission." He took Lizzie's arm and led the way to waiting rickshaws.

An hour later, she and Alfred were reunited and seated in the midst of comforting friends, who were telling them about the attack. It was a gruesome account. But Lizzie insisted on knowing every detail of the massacre.

She listened intently. Alfred was hunched securely between her and Ruth, his face pale and his young body shaking from time to time with dry heaves. Young Oliver snuggled against Lizzie's other side, and little Johann sat on her lap. She was not the only parent in the room whose beloved children had been cruelly killed. As other grieving parents and Alfred recalled for her what had happened, in her heart she begged God to reach down and touch them all with a promise of grace so they could bear the wrenching pain of their horrendous loss.

The magnitude of the attack by the rebels had been a surprise, as was the place. A school for missionary children had never before been attacked. There had been warnings and many incidents of violence. But in China, that was nothing new.

The attack happened several weeks after school started and late at night when everyone was asleep. By then, parents from other places in China had returned home, and the soldiers from inside the city had grown lax in their guarding. The school compound had been built outside the city walls to provide a healthy environment. It became instead an unprotected target for a secret society of anti-imperialists whose goal was to reclaim the Middle Kingdom for Chinese people.

On the surface, life in Sian had seemed peaceful enough – a deceptive lull before the deadly storm. For the moment, the fighting between General Sun Yat-sen's soldiers and the Imperial Army had seemed distant and non-threatening. With the brutal quelling of the Boxer Rebellion a decade ago, who could have guessed there was yet secret remnant ready to strike again. This time, at defenseless children of so-called Western imperialists.

The first sign of the attack had been the cries of the gatekeeper's wife from the gatehouse.

"Awaken, awaken!" she had screamed. "Bandits are upon us. With swords they kill us! Save us! Save us!"

Her cries, even as she was stabbed to death, aroused the other servants. Some ran and hid. A few rushed into the dormitories to warn the teachers and children, then paid with their lives.

"Run! Hide! Run! Hide!" adults shouted to the dazed, frightened children wearing only pajamas. In safety drills, the children had been taught to scatter and hide if bandits or rebels attacked the school. And to stay hidden until soldiers came and the school bell rang the "all safe."

That dreadful night, the bell never rang. Teachers and older children grabbed the hands of younger ones and ran. Soon there were screams of fear and pain as torch-carrying rebels caught the slower ones, broke their arm bones, and thrust their swords into them.

In the darkness and confusion, Hilda somehow managed to find Alfred and Oscar. "To the Christian cemetery!" she hissed frantically.

They held hands and ran faster than ever before in their lives to the small gate in the back wall – a new wall of mud bricks and plaster and as high as a house. The gate was open. Others had already fled the compound through it.

The cemetery wasn't far. Hilda said maybe fear of night-roaming ghost spirits would keep their attackers away from the cemetery.

It didn't.

"*Sha! Sha! Sha!* Kill! Kill! Kill!" sounded louder and louder behind them.

"When we reached the big tree," Alfred said, his voice quavering, "Hilda told me and Oscar to hide in it. She ran on. I tried to push Oscar up to a branch, but he couldn't hold on. So I climbed up and reached down for him. We climbed higher in the tree. Then Hilda screamed. Oscar said we had to help her. Right after he jumped out of the tree, a man grabbed him and sworded him. I didn't know what to do. Oh Mama, I couldn't move. I didn't know what to do. I didn't know what to do. And I waited too long to help them."

Lizzie and Ruth tightened their arms around sobbing Alfred to comfort him. And they assured him over and over that he did the right thing.

Finally, finally, soldiers had come running to the school and cemetery. The swords of the rebels were no match for the soldiers' guns. Soon the rebels were dead or captured. Alfred didn't remember coming down from the tree or what he did next. When missionary men found him later, he had carried Oscar over by Hilda and was crouched between their bodies, holding their bloodied hands and praying for help.

The people of Sian had responded with outrage to the attack. Chinese Christians and non-Christians worked together to avenge the awful deed. Within hours, family coffins were given and new ones made. Men volunteered themselves or their servants to dig the graves. Women and their servants worked in the Good News preaching tent, now a funeral tent. They provided enormous quantities of tea and steamed meat *baotse* buns for everyone.

By late afternoon, thirty-three coffins were ready for burial. Missionaries and other Westerners had lovingly prepared the bodies as best they could, weeping at the dreadful death wounds.

But as they worked, they observed something amazing about all the bodies, and told about it for years to come. Each face had a peaceful expression, even those with cruel slashes and broken, protruding bones. God's angels had been with the children and their teachers as they died – just as with Stephen, the first Christian martyr.

When Lizzie heard about her dear children's faces, she was comforted. She covered her heart with her hands crossed and cried out softly, "Oh Lord God, thank you! Thank you, oh Lord God!"

At that moment, a gentle perfume-like fragrance wafted throughout the room. Everyone looked around in wonder, then at Lizzie with her sons nestled close to her.

"But of course, it's God's sign," she said, tears streaming down her face. "It's God's sign of His grace. We need it, don't we? God knows how much we each need it during this terrible time."

Then she heard how the mass funeral had taken place while it was still light. While some suggested waiting another day, most felt it should be that very day, for both health and safety reasons. So not quite twenty-four hours after their brutal murders, God's young warriors were buried in the Christian cemetery near their school – in the very place where some of them had died, and beside those who had died for the Kingdom at other times and in other ways.

The next day, even as the graves were mounded with more earth and permanently marked, the surviving rebels were executed. Their heads were displayed as a warning outside Sian's main gate, jammed atop spiked poles alongside the heads of their comrades. Onlookers told how one of the rebels had recanted his deeds before his beheading. Because of all that had happened, hundreds of Chinese were now asking how to worship True God.

As conversation around Lizzie turned to what to do next, one of the teachers limped across the room and stood before her and Alfred. He was the one whose wife and two children had been killed, the one who escaped with seven children and hid with them overnight in a fish pond.

"Hilda told me a few weeks ago she wanted to become a missionary doctor here in China," he said to Lizzie. "Did you know that?"

Lizzie nodded, so he continued. "At first I felt that made her death extra tragic. Now I realize that she and my family and the others have led more people to God by dying than most of us do in a lifetime. Dear sister, I mourn with you. We all mourn for Hilda and Oscar and the others."

He kneeled down in front of Alfred and put his hands over Alfred's trembling hands. "You are very brave," he said. "You have had a terrible experience, more terrible than anyone can imagine. So have I."

Alfred nodded, tears streaming down his face.

"But Alfred, you and I and the others here today are

alive for a reason. And those who died, died for a reason. Remember that, Alfred, and listen for God's voice in your life and obey."

The teacher embraced Alfred and Lizzie, young Oliver and Johann, then limped back across the room to his place beside his only surviving child.

*   *   *

After resting for a day and night, Lizzie and Ruth went to the cemetery to visit the graves. Others went with them, enough to fill seven donkey carts. Many of them carried bamboo branches and fall peony blooms from their gardens. They sang hymns as the carts bounced along. Chinese lined the streets to watch the procession, marveling at the happiness of Christians even in mourning. Soon hundreds were following on foot.

They rode out the city gate and past the grotesque sight of bloody rebel heads.

All at once, Lizzie shouted out in Chinese, "Halt! Please halt the cart!"

Then she pointed at a head and said in English to those beside her, "I want to look more closely at that man's head. Yes, yes, that one! I know him! I'm sure he's the one Nils and I called Li Brother. He was once a Christian. Later he saved our lives during the Boxer Uprising when he was a rebel commander."

"This time he took lives," one of the missionary men said, "many innocent lives."

"See that blue cloth with the characters tied around the pole under his head?" another missionary said. "That means he recanted before he was beheaded. I heard one of them said something about being sorry for his wrong doings, then something about True God and Stone Ten. Doesn't make sense, does it? He also said something about wanting his spirit to rest in heaven and not wander around tormenting people. When I heard that, I wondered what his background was. How did you and Brother Nils know him?"

"I'll explain later," Lizzie mumbled. "Let's move on." She covered her head with her shawl, and the boys snuggled closer to her.

Several minutes later, Alfred put his head under her shawl. "Mama, I just remembered something. Now Hilda won't get to see Wu Headman's monument. She said it was very important. She wanted to find it with you."

"*Ja*, that's right son." Neither of them said anything for a few minutes until Lizzie added, "Maybe you can find it with me instead. In heaven, Hilda will know and she'll be glad."

Alfred looked at her with a small smile.

That's his first smile since the attack, Lizzie thought. She smiled back, even though she could scarcely see through her tears.

*   *   *

Not long after, word came from Shanghai urging all Western women and children to evacuate from China immediately. Rebellion and fighting were breaking out all over. Perhaps this time General Sun Yat-sen's army would defeat the Imperial Army, the missionaries said to each other. That seemed like a good thing. General Sun was a Christian and known for baptizing whole regiments at once with water from a hose. But who could know for sure if the revolution would win? Meanwhile, Western embassies issued high states of alert, and large numbers of women and children and a few men left China daily, filling every departing ship.

Ruth agreed to escort two young sisters from the

Sian school back to their relatives in Sweden. The girls'
parents and baby brother were among those killed in the
attack. After praying and fasting for a day, Lizzie decided
to travel to Sweden with Ruth without returning to
Fengshan before leaving China.

She sent a long letter to Nils with two missionary
men who agreed to visit him on their way to mission
stations further inland. It was the most difficult letter Lizzie
had ever written, and she was grateful Nils would have
comforting friends with him when he read the gruesome
details of Hilda and Oscar's deaths.

She explained her decision to the boys. "We'll visit
my birthplace and your Papa's too. You'll like Sweden.
Being with relatives will be good. *Ja,* you'll get to know
your Swedish cousins, and you can even go to school with
them. After that, maybe we'll go to Des Moines and visit
our other relatives before we return home to Fengshan."

And I want to spend some time with Oliver, she
thought. *I want to talk with him. Maybe I'll even leave the
boys with him like he's offered. Nils won't disagree now.
And it will be a comfort to see Hilda's dear friend Dottie.*

"What about Papa?" Alfred asked, breaking into her
thoughts. Young Oliver and Johann looked at her too, their
faces solemn like Alfred's.

"He visited Sweden a few years ago with Uncle
Charlie, remember? Just before Uncle Charlie moved to
Sweden to teach English in schools and marry Aunt
Cecilia, remember? Anyway, Papa can't leave the work
right now. Lots of missionary men have decided to stay
here like Papa while their families leave like we are."

"When will we see Papa again?" Johann asked, his
eyes filling with tears.

"Only Lord God knows," Lizzie said. A sob rose in
her throat and she hugged her boys. "We might not see him
for a year, maybe two, maybe longer. But you can talk to

him in letters and he'll write back."

If God grants him to stay alive, Lizzie thought.

*   *   *

Shanghai

A month later and for a second time in her life, Lizzie watched China become fainter and fainter on the horizon. She thought about arriving in China for the first time twenty years before. Then she had stood beside Ruth on another ship deck. This time they were leaving China, side by side again. This time, neither one had a man to lean on. Instead, young children with anxious faces leaned against them, silently watching the only country they could remember fading into the distance.

Oh min min! What lies ahead? Oh Lord God, please, please, no more deaths if it be your will. Be with Nils and the others in Fengshan. Be with us aboard this ship. Thank you for your mercy in sparing some of our lives one more time.

*   *   *

Abbie's Journal
Feb 14, 2002

. . . when we Newquist relatives get together, someone always mentions our China martyrs. The memory is still an anguish, though none of us alive today knew Hilda and Oscar. We shudder, even as we cherish what they died for. Not long after their deaths, Gramma Lizzie wrote in her dagbook that she feared she could never again play her accordion and sing. But she did. For God's healing grace came to her, a grace she always said only those who experienced it could understand. With it came a special sign – not only once, but several times. . .

Chapter 16

Abbie's Journal
Mar 6, 2002

`. . . this morning in one of my China boxes I discovered an envelope of old, fragile letters – all in Swedish. If Dad left translations of these letters he saved from his father, I haven't found them yet. With a dictionary, I'm figuring out bits of what they say. I really should have them translated. Growing up, I always took Dad's extensive letter writing for granted. Now I realize he was rather unusual. So was Grampa. They exchanged letters regularly over the years – starting soon after Dad was nearly killed with Hilda and Oscar and the others – back when the family separated because China was terribly unsafe. So Dad felt close to his father, even though they were separated for years after his parents returned to Fengshan with Johann and Abigail, and left Dad and Oliver in Iowa with "Uncle" Oliver, as they called him because he was Gramma's good friend. . .`

Cheungking, 1922
Year of Canine

Lizzie boarded the express train for Shanghai, trailed by her two youngest children and Chu Sister. They chatted happily as they arranged their belongings in the first class sleeper compartment. When they were seated, they washed their hands and necks with the warm, scented wet towels brought to them on a silver tray by a bowing porter.

"Don't wash your eyes or mouth," Lizzie cautioned. "Might be germy."

"*Ja*, Mama," Abigail said. "We remember." She

raised her eyebrows at Johann and he winked back.

For a few minutes, no one spoke as they sipped hot tea from the tall Chinese tea cups with lids, their teeth gently closed against the floating Jasmine petals and tea leaves. Later, Abigail and Johann picked out the cooled delicate petals and ate them, smacking their lips and laughing at their mother's expression.

In recent years, travel privacy was a luxury Lizzie arranged whenever possible, especially if the children were along. The first time she suggested it, she had expected Nils to protest the extravagance. However, he too liked the idea of privacy and comfort.

"Almighty God knows we have given up much in our lives," he said. "It is God who provides for us. We will enjoy this blessing with thanks."

So they did. No longer did they dread train trips. Gone were their days of riding in grimy cars, crowded uncomfortably on wooden seats, eating cold snacks from their travel bags. Train trips were now holidays to anticipate – especially the delicious hot meals served in an elegant Westernized dining car with starched table linens, lovely dishes and silverware.

But how can I enjoy this trip, Lizzie thought. She leaned back against the cushion to rest. *My last two children are leaving home. Oh min min! How can I bear it? At least I'm spending these travel days with Johann and Abigail. Poor Nils, having to stay with the work.*

Closing her eyes, she thought about their youngest son Johann, nearly a man and soon on his way to America. Because of the Great War, he had not gone to America when he was ready for high school as they had originally planned. Instead, he had started high school in Sian. The torpedoing of the Lusitania and similar recent incidents were still topics of concerned conversation between them and their friends discussing overseas travel.

But now at last, Johann was on his way to live with Uncle Oliver in Iowa and finish high school, just like his brothers had. She hoped he would also follow them to college, even though he wasn't attentive to studying.

Once Johann was on his way, she had some business to attend to in Shanghai. She needed to collect payment from the merchants renting their bund property, and to make numerous purchases. When her business was finished, she and Chu Sister would be free to visit Hui-ching for several days. They hadn't seen her for years, and were looking forward to spending time in her new art scroll shop, the place she had described with such delight in a letter to Lizzie last year.

Then on their way back home to Fengshan, they would take Abigail to Sian, and leave her there at the boarding school for her first time.

Lizzie often thought what a blessing it was that Abigail had no frightening memories of the school. She had not personally known her sister and brother who were killed there, only the family stories. She had never expressed any fear, just eagerness to be with others her age who spoke English and Swedish. As they had with their other children, Lizzie and Nils assured her she could come home if she became too homesick. Since Mother Ruth who was like family would be her dorm mother, no one expected Abigail to suffer from homesickness.

Lizzie was startled from her thoughts by the departing blasts of the train whistle. She jerked and gasped. Her eyes popped open. Johann and Abigail giggled at her. She smiled back. As the train pulled away from the station, the three of them leaned out the window, waving goodbye one last time to their friends on the platform.

It's been ten years since the attack, Lizzie thought as the train rolled along faster and faster. *Why do I still feel fresh sorrow every time I'm on a train? But thank you, oh*

Lord God, for granting me grace to live with joy anyway. Thank you for my dear children here, for my dear sons Alfred and Oliver in America, and dear devoted Nils.

She grasped Chu Sister's hand – precious Chu Sister who was once her servant and now her dearest friend and co-worker – and said to her in Chinese, "Chu Sister, we should pray for travel mercies, should we not? I have not heard of any bandit or soldier threats along the way, have you? But who can know for sure. Since my heart is sad because my youngest children are going away to school, will you be the one to pray, please?"

Chu Sister nodded and said, "This heart inside me is heavy too. It also feels happiness for the opportunities of your children."

She reached over and patted Johann and Abigail. "*Ai yah!* I will miss you. Like my own children you two are. I hope you will not forget your old auntie and her daughter."

"Chu Sister," Johann assured her in polite Chinese, "How can we ever forget you and your daughter Ta-mei? You are always so good and kind. You are like family to us. We will think of you often. Mama will read our letters to you. And you can send messages to us in Mama's letters, is that not so?"

Beside him, Abigail nodded, her face solemn.

Chu Sister beamed at her foreign children. "You are the offspring of my cherished Nieh friends. What would have become of me and my daughter without your family? We might not have survived. And what about the many others your family has saved? Your family has brought True God's mercy to Chinese like me. A thousand fragrant thanks forever!"

She folded her hands and began to pray aloud. Lizzie, Johann, and Abigail bowed their heads close to hers.

*   *   *

Shanghai

Waving farewell to friends from Shanghai's Bund always saddened Lizzie. But waving goodbye to her youngest son nearly crushed her. Who knew how many years would pass before she saw him again?

After Johann sailed away in the care of missionaries also returning to America, Lizzie collapsed into bed. For days she stayed there. Chu Sister cared for her faithfully, and Abigail came to sit beside her bed several times a day.

The first day Lizzie got up, she was weak and pale. Before long, however, she was once again her strong, cheerful self.

Abigail was relieved when her mama rallied even though she was enjoying the extra attention of missionary aunties and uncles. Each evening, she excitedly told Mama about everything she had done that day, and then wrote it all to Papa in a journal-like letter that Mama would take to him.

Abigail loved telling her parents about attending the Shanghai school for English speaking children. Even though she was only attending for a brief time, she quickly made two new American friends who were her same age. In a secret ceremony hidden by some flowering bushes, they promised to write to each other for the rest of their lives.

On several occasions, Abigail was taken to worship services. For the first time in her life that she would remember, she sat in a large, beautiful church building that looked like pictures of churches she admired in books. Never before had she felt such awe to be in the presence of God, her heavenly Father. Now she knew why Papa always said Almighty God.

The Chinese seamstress who worked on the mission

compound made Abigail some new dresses. These were dresses made just for her from brand new cloth. They weren't from a missionary barrel or cut from one of Mama's dresses. Every time she dressed in one, she felt a special happiness and smiled at herself in the mirror.

I didn't realize how much she was missing in Fengshan, Lizzie thought as she lay recovering in her guestroom bed, watching Abigail. *Ja, it will be good for her to go to school in Sian. I must remember her joy here when I miss her. Oh Lord God, keep me from selfishness about wanting to be with my children.*

When Lizzie was herself again and ready to visit Hui-ching with Chu Sister, Abigail begged to stay instead at the mission compound.

"Mama, I don't remember the Lin lady at all," she said. "Why can't I stay here with my friends until you are ready to go to Sian?"

"Hui-ching is a special family friend and she's Chu Sister's cousin. She knows you even if you don't feel like you know her."

Abigail was quiet as she fiddled with the pockets on her new dress. After a bit, she said, "I know, Mama. How about this? How about if I visit the Lin lady with you the first day and then come back here? Please, Mama? I would so much rather be here and attending school than listening to you and Chu Sister talk and talk in Chinese with someone I don't even know."

So Lizzie agreed. "But of course, my dear. That's a good idea. *Oh min min!* You're so clever to think of it."

Several days later, hired rickshaws whisked the three of them to Hui-ching's place, in a district on the other side of the Huang Pu River.

*   *   *

Ten days later, the three of them were together again, this time seated on the express train headed for Sian. Lizzie noticed Abigail looking around their compartment with a strange expression on her face.

"What are you looking for, my dear?" she asked.

"I miss Johann," Abigail said. "I didn't think before how strange it would be to travel without him. Do you think he's missing us on the ship?"

"I'm sure he is. But soon he'll be with Alfred and Oliver." Lizzie struggled to smile and not weep.

"That's good, I guess. You know, Mama, I don't really remember Alfred and Oliver that well. I just remember what you tell me about them. When I look at their photographs, they don't even seem like my brothers."

She hummed and tapped her feet on the floor, enjoying the smartness of her new leather shoes, unaware of her mother's sad face. After a bit, she opened her travel bag to choose a book to read. Her favorite store in Shanghai had been the one with all the books. She had four new books and it wasn't even Christmas.

One book she had chosen because it had Papa's name on the cover, *The Wonderful Adventures of Nils.* Papa sure would smile when he saw that, and be pleased it was in Swedish. Maybe he would put it next to his favorite book in Swedish, the one about a pioneer missionary to China, Robert Morrison. Papa sometimes read to her from that book, and now he could read to her from this new Nils book.

For a few minutes, she looked at the Nils book about a boy in Sweden and a flying goose, then put it away and started reading another book that was in English. Before long, she was far away with a girl her age named Anne, who also traveled by train to a new school and to a home called Green Gables.

While Abigail read, Lizzie and Chu Sister relaxed

and talked.

"Did you like Hui-ching's scroll shop as much as you said, or were you just being polite when you told her so?" Chu Sister asked.

"Yes, yes, I liked her place," Lizzie said. "I was a little disappointed at first, but not after we went upstairs to her living quarters. The art rooms downstairs are not what I had imagined from her letter. However, her rooms upstairs are nicer than I expected. The people in the neighboring shops are very friendly. I can see why she is pleased. Can you not?"

"*Ai!* Yes! But I wonder how old she is now. I think maybe she is getting too old to marry."

"Sometimes it is right not to marry." Lizzie smiled. "Do you not remember that for a few years when I was young I thought I might not marry? Besides, what if Hui-ching marries and the man turns out to be like your first man? What then?"

"True, true. That would be unfortunate. Yes, I was cursed with a misfortune I pray Hui-ching will not experience. How old do you think she is? I did not want to ask her or talk about marriage."

"Well, let us add the years and see. She was fourteen, was she not, when she came with us to Shanghai? And that was, hmm, that was more than twenty years ago. So she is about thirty-five. I say that is still not too old to marry."

"You think not? *Heh!* I think it is." Chu Sister chuckled. "At her age, she might only be asked to be a second or third or fourth wife. And I have learned from you that is not the best way for marriage, according to the Holy Book of True God."

"Yes, and I am glad you tell young women so. You know what I think about Hui-ching? She may have taken an artist's vow not to marry."

"*Wah!* What vow is that? Alas, there is much I do not know since I did not go to school."

"I know only a little about the vow even though I went to school." Lizzie smiled at her good friend. "I have heard there are artists who take the vow, sometimes to gain favor with heaven. Not all artists, just some. Like priests in several religions do. Probably women take the vow more than men because it is harder for women to be artists after they marry."

They sat in silence for a few minutes.

Then Chu Sister said, "Being married to Chu is almost that kind of vow. Except with Chu I have a loyal friend and protector. He does not act like he owns me. I like him more than any other man I know. Because of his kind ways, I have not missed the togetherness under the marriage quilt. Since we have no children of our own except my Ta-mei, we have shared our home with many poor boys, as you know. And that is good, is it not?"

"Oh yes, a thousand yeses! You and Chu Husband are indeed wonderful followers of True God. Your lives are miracles, and you bring miracles to others. Nieh Husband and I give thanks daily to True God for you. We pray you will always be courageous for True God."

Chu Sister nodded and smiled.

"Do you know what one thing surprised me very much at Hui-ching's?" Lizzie asked..

"What did? What surprised you?"

"The way she signs her scrolls."

"I cannot read characters, so I did not notice anything. What did you see?" asked Chu Sister.

"She does not inscribe her own name on the scrolls she and her apprentices paint."

"I saw the characters of a name."

"Yes, but the name is not Lin Hui-ching. I asked her what name it was and why she did not use her own name.

She said she would tell me someday. That the name she signed was to honor me, and to comfort her mother's spirit by restoring beauty to the memory of her sister Mei-lee."

Chu Sister was thoughtful. "I think maybe she uses another name from fear. Perhaps because she is female and not male. Heh! What about that?"

"No, I do not think so. No, I did not sense any fear in her words to me."

"But without her name on the scrolls, it is as if she has disappeared."

"Yes, that is what I think too. And I am puzzled. Why does she not want to be known by her own name?"

"If her mother were still alive, we could ask her."

Lizzie nodded, then took a scroll box from her bag. She lifted out the scroll, and Chu Sister carefully helped her unroll it.

Abigail became interested. She closed her book and leaned over to look at the scroll.

"See, the name is in this corner," Lizzie said. "But I cannot read the characters. They are too artistic. Though I can tell the first one is not Lin."

Abigail stood up to see the scroll better. She touched the painted silk gently in several places.

"Why see, Mama, it's a scroll of home," she said with delight. "It's so pretty. How nice of the Lin lady to give it to you."

"Yes, it's a thank you gift. She gave one to Chu Sister as well. I think they will be very valuable one day," Lizzie said.

"Oh, Chu Sister, I want to see yours too, please," Abigail begged.

"Yes, yes, I want you to see it."

Chu Sister helped roll up Lizzie's scroll before opening her own scroll box. Together they unrolled the second scroll. It was similar to Lizzie's. They looked at the name characters in the corner, brushed with artistic calligraphy strokes. Again Lizzie shook her head as she puzzled over the characters.

Just then the porter knocked on the door. He opened it to announce ten minutes until their seating in the dining car for the evening meal.

"Good," Abigail said. She stood up and smoothed her hair and dress. "I'm hungry, and eating in the dining car is such fun. Maybe we'll sit by Americans tonight."

*   *   *

The next day, Lizzie and Abigail took turns reading aloud from *Anne of Green Gables*. When they apologized to Chu Sister, she laughed. She assured them she liked the sounds of the words even though she could not understand.

And she added, "When we live in heaven, I will be able to read too. I look forward to that. Perhaps then I will read and you will listen."

"I look forward to heaven too," Lizzie said. "Look, Chu Sister, the book I am reading to myself is about heaven. It is a comforting story. When we return to Fengshan, I will translate it for you."

The three of them looked for a few minutes at her book with *Intra Muros* engraved in gold on the cover and many surprising sketches of heaven inside.

Later, lying in her new silk pajamas between the smooth, white sheets of the narrow train bunk bed, Abigail said, "Mama, I think I'm like Anne."

"Whatever do you mean, my dear?" Lizzie asked sleepily.

"I almost feel like you adopted me – because I was born in Sweden and Papa didn't even know. Last week Auntie Aasta asked me some questions I couldn't answer. Then she said to Auntie Angie that my birth circumstances were mysterious."

"Well, there was nothing mysterious about your birth. It was a sad time in our family's life, but you filled our arms with great joy. Don't you remember the stories I've told you?"

"Not much. Nobody in Fengshan talks about when I was born. I think before you leave me at school, you should tell me again. People who aren't Chinese often ask me about where I was born and what country I'm from."

"But of course, my dear." Lizzie yawned. "I'll tell you tomorrow after breakfast, all right? I'm exhausted now. I'm sure Chu Sister is too. Goodnight, Abigail. Don't forget to pray."

"*Ja,* I remember. Goodnight, Mama and Chu Sister."

Chu Sister did not answer.

The next morning when they returned from breakfast in the dining car, their compartment was ready for day travel. The beds were now cushioned seats, and fresh tea steamed in the tall cups under the window. As soon as they were seated, Abigail said, "I'm ready, Mama. Tell me now, please."

Lizzie raised her eyebrows in question, so Abigail reminded her.

"I haven't thought about your birth for quite a while," Lizzie mused. "I wonder how ten years could have passed so quickly." She hugged Abigail. "Lately, I have thought about Johann's birth. I guess because he was leaving home. He was born in Fengshan, you know."

She turned to Chu Sister. "Remember how the whole village celebrated another baby boy in our family? With red banners all over? The believers said Johann was a sign of True God's blessing on the village. The others said Johann was a sign the river gods were no longer angry at the foreigners."

Chu Sister nodded, and looked up for a brief moment from the small shoes she had handsewn and was now embroidering for her daughter Ta-mei's youngest child. These were cute cloth shoes, just like the ones she used to make for Ta-mei years ago when she was still little Shaio-mei.

Abigail leaned against her mother. She loved it when Mama told family stories, especially ones about her.

"Back to when you were born, my dear," Lizzie said, putting her head for a moment against her daughter's. "When I left China with young Alfred and Oliver, after your sister Hilda and brother Oscar were martyred, I went with Mother Ruth to Sweden. Papa didn't feel he should leave the work and our friends along the River, so he stayed in Fengshan. Lots of other missionary men also stayed. One reason we went to Sweden was because Mother Ruth was taking two orphaned sisters to relatives there."

"Orphan girls?" Abigail asked. "That really is like Anne. I hope they got to be bosom friends with someone the same as Anne and Diane. Then being orphans wouldn't matter."

"I think they did. I met their relatives and liked them. Anyway, on the ship going to Sweden, we were very crowded. Hundreds of women and children were evacuating from China. I was sick and throwing up the whole trip. I thought it was because I was so sad and the smells were so bad from all the people. Poor dear Mother Ruth. She had to take care of four children plus me. After we arrived in Sweden, I found out I was sick because I was pregnant with you. *Oh min min!* What a surprise you were!"

"I didn't know being pregnant makes you sick," Abigail said. "I hate vomiting. I guess I won't have any babies."

Lizzie interpreted to Chu Sister what Abigail had

just said so strongly, and the two women looked at each other and smiled.

"After your babies are born," Lizzie said, "you're so happy you don't care you were sick. That's how I was after you were born. We stayed with Mother Ruth in her family's beautiful home in Goteberg for nearly two years. Everyone was so good to us when I couldn't decide what to do and where to live. By then my own Mama was in heaven, so I just kept staying on month after month. The Swedish relatives of mine and Papa's came to visit. Sometimes they took Alfred and Oliver back to their farms. Your brothers really liked Sweden. After we left, they used to beg to go back."

"I want to visit there some time," Abigail said. "I should see where I was born, don't you think, Mama?"

"Yes, I do. I did that for myself after you were born. I traveled with you and your brothers to my birthplace in Sweden. I hadn't been there since my family moved to America when I was little, too little to remember much. But when I visited, I could feel in my heart that place was my motherland. It was the place where I started life, and so a special place."

"Tell me about baby-me. Did I like traveling then too?"

"You were an absolute darling and so good. You were my best baby. I always said you must have been born with extra blessings from God because of our family's sufferings. Hilda would have loved you dearly. She always wanted a little sister. You looked so much like her. That's one reason I gave you Hilda for your middle name. Your baby hair was curly like hers, although lighter in color. Your eyes were the same blue, and still are."

Lizzie's eyes had a faraway look to them as she took one of Abigail Hilda's hands in hers and wrote H-i-l-d-a in the palm.

"I remember how everyone wanted to cuddle and play with you. They were surprised you smelled so sweet – like a gentle perfume fragrance, they said. Someday I'll tell you more about that. You rarely fussed, even when you were sick or teething. Although you drooled terribly, all down your clothes. That's when Mother Ruth made you some pretty bibs."

Abigail had a pleased look on her face. "I'm glad everyone liked me. I don't see why Auntie Aasta thinks what you've told me is mysterious."

"It's probably because she's single and doesn't understand about Papa not being with us and all that. Don't worry about what Auntie Aasta thinks. Sometimes she says strange things. It's just her way of being caring."

"Why didn't Papa come to Sweden to be with us when I was born?"

"He would have come if he had known about you. That's why I kept you secret for a while. We had many people taking care of us, and Papa needed to be here in China with the work and the people. When at last we went to Iowa and I told him about you, he came as quickly as he could to be with us. You were almost two years old when you and Papa first met. You loved each other instantly. For a long time, your favorite place was Papa's lap. It took your brothers longer to get used to Papa that time."

"Even Johann?"

"Especially Johann. He was the youngest and didn't remember Papa nearly as well as your other brothers did."

"Then it's good you didn't leave Johann with Uncle Oliver like you did Alfred and Oliver."

"You're right, my dear. Back then, he was too young to leave with someone else. I hope you aren't too young to leave in Sian."

"I don't think I am. I'm still in China near you. Besides, Mother Ruth is there. Oh Mama, I can't wait to see her again. She's my special grownup friend. I hope she'll read my Anne book with me like you are."

*   *   *

Sian

The next afternoon, as the train pulled slowly into the Sian station, Abigail put her head out the window to look for Mother Ruth.

"She's here!" Abigail shouted. "I see Mother Ruth! On the platform over there! Do you see her, Mama? Do you see her, Chu Sister?"

Lizzie saw her dear friend. Though she waved and smiled, she felt a pang go through her. She pressed a hand over her heart, and looked away from Abigail.

*   *   *

Abbie's Journal
Mar 9, 2002
. . . Cousin Joy emailed me last week. She thought she might have the scroll I've been asking about. I was so excited. Then she called today to say it was not painted by an artist named Lin Hui-ching. She had taken it to a Chinese antique store in Seattle. They sent her to a scholar who deciphered the artist's name, and it was Chiang Mei-lee, the Chiang for fragrance. How disappointing! Looks like it's not the scroll by our family's special artist friend! Something good, however – the scholar said the painting is definitely a Yangtze gorge scene, though he had not heard of Fengshan – phone's ringing. . .

Mar 10
. . . Joy didn't say anything about having the scroll's value appraised and I forgot to ask. She wondered if I wanted it,

said she just keeps it in its box because it's so old. Of course I said yes. It must have belonged to Gramma and Grampa, and maybe even Mom and Dad when they were in China. Maybe they mailed it back to Joy's parents before the war started. It is a river gorge scene – and likely Fengshan. That's enough to thrill me and erase my disappointment about the artist. . .

PART FIVE

Surprises . . . Triumphs
Storyline 1923 to 1931
Journal Excerpts from 2002

Dying embers may glow again.
~ Ancient Chinese proverb

Without God, hope evaporates.
~ Job 8:13

Chapter 17

Abbie's Journal
Mar 17, 2002
. . . I guess I grew up both respecting and fearing Chinese medicine. I remember once having a terrible cough that bothered everyone in our household night after night. Mom and Dad tried everything, but even Dad's aloe syrup didn't help. There were no missionary or U.S. military doctors near, so finally the folks took me to our house helper's father who was a doctor. He examined me, then gave me some neatly folded little paper packets containing a white powder. I took a packet with a drink of water whenever I had a coughing spell at night. And did that powder ever work! I recall Mom saying something to Dad like – should we worry about the opium? And Dad answering – shh, Abbie's still awake. . .

. . . that experience made me wonder why Chinese people needed missionary clinics when their own medicine worked so well. What I didn't realize until I was older – most Chinese couldn't afford their own doctors and medicine, only the well-off could – and that China had many fake doctors and cruel superstitious practices. But missionary medicine was kind and safe and free to the needy. . .

Fengshan, 1926
Another Year of Tiger

Lizzie hummed hymns as she sorted and packed – something she found she did more slowly these days. She noticed her thoughts and hands didn't move as quickly as they once did.

Tomorrow, ah tomorrow, she and Nils would start

on their way to Shanghai to meet Alfred. But first they would go to Sian to pick up Abigail. Lizzie knew Abigail could hardly wait to be with the brother she hadn't seen since she was three and he fifteen.

How wonderful, Lizzie thought with joy, *by this time next year, dear Alfred will be here in Fengshan with us. Thank you, oh Lord God! And thank you for the time we will soon have with Abigail. Thank you for these family blessings.*

Alfred's childhood friends, now grown young men like him, were eager to see him as well. Nearly every day, one or two of them with their new Western haircuts and clothes came to ask if the news of his return was correct. Of course, what they really wanted was an excuse to see his photographs again, and to express how pleased they were he was coming back to Fengshan.

One of them was sure to ask, "Has our friend Fu-de changed? What is he like now?"

And Lizzie or Nils would answer, "We really do not know. We think he will be the same friend you knew, just grown up. We ourselves have not seen him for more than ten years. But he sounds the same in his letters."

"Does he still play his harmonica?"

"Oh yes, and he's bringing back many harmonicas for any of you his friends who want to learn how to play."

"Ah, that sounds like our generous friend Fu-de." The young men cupped their hands around their mouths and pretended to be playing harmonicas. Then they all laughed.

"And you say he is not married and has no children?" was another frequent question.

"No, the young woman he wants to marry does not want to live in China," Lizzie said.

"Then why does he come? We hear that to live in your country is beyond belief, that everybody is rich and everything is beautiful and wonderful."

"He comes because the voice of True God tells him to come," was always Lizzie's answer. Alfred had expressed that in his letters. In her heart, she hoped it was true. Because without God's call – well – without it to live happily as a foreigner in China was impossible.

A few hours later as Lizzie and Nils were finishing their noon rice meal, someone pounded loudly on the front gate. Their houseboy hurried to answer. He was soon back at the dining room door.

"A messenger from Yang Magistrate awaits you in the front room," he said. "I will tell Cook to prepare tea and sweet cakes."

"Thank you," Lizzie said.

Watching Nils hurry down the hall towards the front room, she had a sinking feeling. *Something has happened,* she thought, *something that will keep Nils from leaving tomorrow.*

Her intuition was right. He came mid-afternoon to their bedroom where she was stretched out on the bed, resting and reading. He lay down beside her and smoothed his mustache for several seconds.

"The magistrate requests me to come to his private home in Shenli," Nils said in a tired voice. "He has heard about our cure for opium addicts. He wants me to cure those afflicted in his household. He asks me to start right away for his place. The messenger informed me the magistrate's favorite concubine is dying. I told his messenger that my helpers and I must first prepare ourselves with fasting and prayer for this difficult work. But we will come in a few days. And to tell the magistrate that sometimes people are cured, sometimes they are not."

Lizzie sighed. "*Oh min, min!* I knew it. I knew in my heart something like this was happening. I was looking forward so much to this trip with you. But of course, you have to go to Shinli. I will go on to Sian. And you'll join us in Shanghai?"

"You know I'll try to."

Lizzie nodded her head against the pillow, and reached for his hand.

"Since you can't go, Nils, I think I'll ask Ta-mei to travel with me."

"Instead of her mother Chu Sister?"

"*Ja.* Ta-mei's youngest children are old enough now for her to be away. I think for this trip Chu Sister will gladly care for her grandchildren so Ta-mei can travel with me. I'll ask Cook's wife to help Chu Sister. For pay of course. You know, this time I'm in Sian, I really want to locate Wu's monument. It's too bad you won't be along. But Ta-mei has keen interest in the monument too. She's heard things about it I haven't. Earlier I almost asked her to go with us. Now it seems like this is a clear sign to ask her. If she can go, I'll delay departing for a couple of days while she gets ready. I'll still have plenty of time for everything, don't you think?"

*   *   *

Two days later, Nils and a team of believers were escorted by Lizzie and a crowd of villagers to the road for Shinli. After prayer, Nils and his Bible man mounted their horse. As usual, Nils briefly raised his Bible in one hand and his gun in the other before the two men cantered away. The others followed in a cart pulled by two donkeys, along with a second cart carrying provisions. The journey would take several days. The team hoped to find available inns at night, but was prepared to camp out if necessary.

Oh Lord God, when will I see him again? Lizzie wondered. It was a question she had asked God more times than she could count. It was one of her questions God never answered, but just asking gave her assurance and peace. And now she felt an echo from Nils's words earlier that day. "Whatever happens, Lizzie, we know Almighty God will be with us."

Long after most of the villagers had returned to their homes and work, she sat on the edge of the ancient stone cistern, enjoying the cool shade of a young bamboo grove. With an awe that hadn't lessened over the years, she gazed at the familiar beauty of the river gorge around her.

Turning her head to the foothills, she watched their herd of goats – some running, some grazing – all guided by the long bamboo poles of the herders who understood each snort and bleating. Recently, Nils had remarked their herd now numbered more than three hundred. So they had decided to give each village elder a gift of thirty goats at the coming Lunar New Year to celebrate thirty years of friendship.

Thirty years, she thought. *They've passed so quickly – and yet they've taken forever too. I came to rescue little girls. Oh Lord God, you've helped me rescue many. But there are so many more. Oh min min! Help me, Lord God, help me rescue many more.*

Walking back to Great House, she chatted with women along the way, thankful for the hundreds of women and girls in Fengshan who no longer suffered from tiny, mutilated feet. Chu Sister had been a tireless crusader in the cause. And recent government edicts were helping, along with the efforts of the Anti-Footbinding League.

As she passed the school, she gave thanks for all the boys and girls who had learned to read the Holy Bible and Hymn Book. Some had even advanced to schools in larger towns.

When she stopped in the orphanage courtyard for a few minutes, she was reminded of the hundreds of abandoned girls and boys who had been rescued, and the many adopted by Christian Chinese families like Chu Boatman and Chu Sister.

But it's not enough, she thought. It's not enough. There are millions more.

She paused in front of the clinic where thousands had been treated in the name of Yeh Su. Where so many had learned better health practices, like teeth brushing. She smiled, recalling how funny it was to watch someone brush their teeth for the first time.

As she turned the corner by the Good News Hall, she chided herself and pressed her hand over her heart. She should have been thankful first for the spiritual rescues. Nothing else really mattered. How surprised she and Nils had been several years ago when Wu Headman observed that the temple was no longer the center of Fengshan. Instead, the Good News Hall was, and they hadn't even noticed.

Wu died not long after that comment. Lizzie thought now of her promise to him over the years – that one day she would visit the monument that had directed his life to True God. Yes, she had tried to discover the secret Stone Ten Keepers, but so far without success.

"When I reach the monument," she remembered saying to him, "even if you are in heaven, I think you will know. And I hope the monument will help me find the Stone Ten Keepers."

*   *   *

Shinli

The afternoon of their third day traveling, Nils and his team of believers reached Yang Magistrate's private residence. Shinli was larger than Fengshan, and those who had never been to the city before were visibly impressed. As they rode into the center of town on its main street, they couldn't stop exclaiming about the sights that accompany growth and prosperity. Riding into the magistrate's compound, they were even more impressed. Compared to this place, the Great House of the Niehs was indeed humble, they whispered to each other.

"Is this a palace?" one of the women asked. In wonder, she looked at the immense, luxuriant garden surrounding red and gilt trimmed brick and stone buildings.

She had never seen a palace, and a place this magnificent probably seemed it must be one, Nils thought, but remained silent.

Nor did her companions answer. They were too busy scrambling stiffly out of the cart. Hastily smoothing their dusty, disarrayed garments, they were preparing to greet Yang Magistrate who was coming swiftly towards them enthroned in an open sedan-chair carried by eight uniformed servant-bearers.

For once, Nils bowed nearly as low and long as those around him. He knew this man could just as easily kill as honor him. Even so, Nils had secured his gun in the cart. Although he was accustomed to trusting God in every circumstance, his surroundings here made him feel imprisoned. He did not want to risk his life unnecessarily or fumble this unusual opportunity for witness. So he kept bowing, although he did not touch his forehead to the ground as the others were doing.

Help us, Almighty God! Grant me, grant us your wisdom and power! This silent prayer he prayed over and over. From the looks on the other believers' faces, he knew they were praying similar prayers.

"Welcome to my modest, unattractive home," the magistrate said loudly. "Thank you, True God believers from Fengshan, for coming on such a long, arduous journey at my humble request."

"It is our privilege, honorable Yang Magistrate."

Nils spoke for all of them. "Thank you for inviting us. We have come to bring healing to your household in the name of True God." Nils gestured politely towards the assembled servants and guards.

Those with Nils nodded and bowed low again. This time, Nils stood straight, a tall, fearsome-looking foreigner with a bushy mustache.

"I apologize for what may seem to be rudeness," the magistrate said. "Please begin the cure at once. Several members of my household are near death from opium. If she – if they die, my heart will die too. Tell us what to do. I have ordered immediate obedience to your words."

Thank you, Almighty God, Nils breathed. *I didn't expect to reach this point so easily. You are already at work, thank you, thank you.*

After a brief rest and refreshments of hot tea and sweet delicacies, Nils and his team began to do what they had done many times, not just in Fengshan but also in many other river towns and villages.

They met with the afflicted, one by one or in small groups of three and four. They told the stories about True God and his power over evil. They read from True God's Holy Book. And they sang soothing, comforting hymns.

Every evening for six days, each afflicted person was anointed with oil and prayed for while the believers placed their hands on that one. During those days, the afflicted were encouraged to sleep regularly and eat specially prepared vegetables along with their rice and small portions of meat. They were invited to confide their sorrows and misfortunes. Hourly, they drank comfrey tea. Twice a day, the opium intake from their elegant, silver pipes was reduced.

On the seventh day came the harrowing part – the true test. In the afternoon, Nils asked Yang Magistrate to bring all the idols and ancestor worship items from his household to a central place for burning.

"What?" the astonished magistrate shouted. "How dare you make such a request! Do you think I am a fool who has no regard for the anger of my ancestors and the gods?" He began to stomp about, cursing Nils and his team of believers.

Their response was quick. They formed a circle around the magistrate and prayed aloud. Soon, he stopped ranting. After some moments of silence, in a low voice he gave the order to his head servant.

How could he not? He was getting old, but he was not yet blind. He could see the cure was working. That very morning, his favorite concubine, the mother of his only two living sons, sat up in bed, smiling and eating.

Idol burnings made Nils think of the walls of Jericho tumbling down. And this burning was a great victory in a powerful household. When the flames consuming the idols became smolders, Nils and his team led a prayer service. The magistrate's entire household was present, even the children.

After a time of singing and listening to Nils preach, those being treated for addiction were brought to the front near Nils. They were anointed for a seventh and final time. Then the believers prayed together aloud, and in the name of Yeh Su commanded any demons of addiction that remained to be cast out and bound forever far away by the power of *Zhen Shen* True God.

The resulting commotion – both terrifying and victorious – was never forgotten by anyone there that night. What happened was enough to make a believer of any doubter. And just like in the days of the New Testament, testimonies of release and joy lasted long into the night.

For two more weeks, Nils stayed with the magistrate. During that time, he secured a store front for a Good News Hall. There he and his team daily told Bible stories, counseled, and prayed with the crowds that gathered.

When he left for Fengshan, several members of the team remained in Shinli. They had cheerfully volunteered to teach Bible lessons from Saint John's Good News booklet, and conduct evening street meetings. In his departing words to Yang Magistrate, Nils promised to send more evangelists when these returned home, and to bring Lizzie the next time he himself came.

Hundreds of townspeople walked with Nils and his team through town and to the road outside the city gates. He was the last to depart. Finally, he too bowed a last time.

"Now may True God bring peace to the way of each of your hearts," he said. In farewell, he raised his Bible high, but not his gun this time.

Then he galloped away on his horse and soon caught up to the carts.

God's miraculous salvation work here is worth everything, he thought. *Ja! Even missing the trip to Sian with Lizzie. Thank you, Almighty God. Bless my dear family today, and these dear new believers in Shinli.*

*   *   *

Sian

Outside the fort-like walls of Sian, along a road that was more ruts than road, bumped a small convoy of mule carts. In the first cart, rode Lizzie, Abigail and Ta-mei, along with a British teacher from the boarding school for missionary children, a Chinese guide, and Mother Ruth. Three more carts followed, carrying an assortment of missionaries and older students, as well as an American diplomat. Armed Chinese soldiers escorted them in front and back.

As they searched the area, the sounds of their

talking, laughter and singing drifted over the countryside, drawing clusters of people from their farms to stare at the strange procession. Small children looked, then burst into frightened tears at the sight of the foreigners.

From time to time, Lizzie and others called out greetings. They handed Good News Gospel tracts to those brave enough to come close to the carts. As they jostled along, they talked excitedly about what they were searching to see. At least what they hoped they would find to see. The guide thought he could find the ancient monument, though he had made sure he would be paid whatever happened.

Several times the carts stopped. Mules as well as riders needed rest breaks. While they eased their sore joints and muscles, the adults discussed what direction to search next. These were moments of eager exploration for Abigail and the other children.

Lizzie had hoped to find the monument before noon. But noon passed, and they were still searching. The guide had an uncertain air as he and the mule drivers talked about where to look next.

"We should have seen it by now," he kept muttering.

After a while, Lizzie asked, "You mean we can see the monument from the road?"

"No," the guide said. "But we can see the sacred tree it stands beneath."

When he said that, everyone starting looking for an old, tall tree. In this area, because trees were not plentiful enough for the needs of the people, only sacred trees grew old and large. The others were cut down young for firewood and other uses.

At last Lizzie said, "Let us stop. We will have our picnic lunch now and decide what to do while we eat."

Mother Ruth pointed to a pleasant, shady spot not far from a pagoda that looked like it had been guarding the area for centuries. The carts stopped and everyone gathered around the cart with the lunch provisions. Mother Ruth was in charge, not a small task for nearly thirty people, counting soldiers, mule drivers, and everyone else. But Mother Ruth loved picnics, and was used to large groups. And she purposely brought along a couple of servants to help. Before long, everyone was enjoying a meal that was part Chinese and part Western.

After lunch, most of the adults stretched out on blankets to nap. A few joined Abigail and her young friends for some exploring. To the annoyance of the nappers, in a few minutes the explorers came rushing back.

"Mama," Abigail called. "Ta-mei and I have found something important. Come and see it. It looks like a cemetery grave stone. And it has writing on it."

Lizzie sat up quickly. In Chinese she asked the guide, "Could it be the monument is near here? Is it possible they have found it?"

He looked around and shrugged his shoulders. "Where is the sacred tree?"

"Tree or no, let us see what they have found," Lizzie said. "Up everyone! The monument may have been found. *Oh min min!* Isn't this wonderful! It's something I have longed for years to experience."

When they reached the engraved stone, everyone crowded close to stare at it. Lizzie and a couple of others knelt down to examine it.

With obvious disappointment, Lizzie shook her head. "This is not it. This stone is much too small and not nearly old enough." She pulled an old photograph of the monument from her pocket so the others could compare the two.

The American diplomat kneeling beside her asked, "What do these characters say? Can you read them?"

"No easily," she answered. "I hope the guide can.

But look, here's a cross, like the one on the monument in my photograph."

They made room for the guide to squat between them.

Haltingly, he read aloud the characters. "For Protection – Ancient – Luminous – Religion – Tablet – Removed – to Sian."

No one spoke for a few moments. They gazed in awed silence at the stone and what remained of a jagged, decaying tree stump.

"Well, whatever this stone is," the British teacher said, "it appears that after the monument was removed, someone cut down the tree. Strange indeed! I didn't think Chinese cut down their sacred trees."

"Well, it's gone. They're both gone," Lizzie said. "I wonder why none of us heard about it being moved to the city." She paused. "Would you like for Ta-mei and me to tell you why we want so much to see the monument?"

There was a chorus of "yeses."

Speaking back and forth in English and Chinese, so the soldiers and mule drivers could understand, she and Ta-mei told the story of Wu Headman's conversion. How his contact with the monument years ago in his youth and then later in his dreams had opened his heart to believe in True God. They also told the little they knew about the mysterious ones called the Stone Ten Keepers who were somehow connected to the ancient monument.

The return ride straight back to Sian with no searching detours was much shorter than the morning ride. But because they were tired and the ride was rough, it seemed as long. As they bounced over the ruts and stones in the road, Lizzie and the American diplomat talked about the monument. He said he thought he could find out where it had been taken.

"Oh, please do," Lizzie said. "When we bring

Abigail back for school in the fall, I hope you can take us to see it."

The others were listening and nodded. They had been deeply moved. Like Wu Headman long ago, they had felt something spiritual in the place where the monument once stood, where according to tradition a thousand years ago a Christian temple had thrived.

The guide said he, too, would check on the location of the monument.

To ease his loss of face, Lizzie thanked him for directing them to the sacred place of the monument. That was indeed memorable, she assured him, an experience none of them would ever forget.

Again the others nodded, and bowed to the guide.

They reached the school compound in time to hear the evening dinner gong. Everyone was silent as they rode up, for they had just passed the walls of the Christian cemetery. Over the front gate hung a white banner. On it were large black characters quoting from Proverbs: "The Memory of the Righteous Is a Blessing."

Ja! That is true. Oh Lord God, thank you. Lizzie smiled at Abigail and Mother Ruth. Just yesterday, they had placed fragrant jasmine buds on the graves of Hilda and Oscar and their young friends. In silence, too emotional to speak, Lizzie had remembered a clay jar somewhere at the bottom of the River.

Early in the morning two days later, Ta-mei headed home for Fengshan. That same afternoon, Lizzie and Abigail eagerly boarded the express train for Shanghai. If Alfred's ship docked on schedule, this time next week they would be standing on the Bund, waving welcome. How Lizzie hoped Nils would be there too.

*   *   *

Abbie's Journal
Mar 27, 2002
. . . I heard the folks say more than once how more females than males were opium addicts in China, partly because women and girls suffered so much physically. Their agonies started early with foot binding around age four – which meant being in pain the rest of their lives. I don't even like to think about Dad's stories of going to sleep at night as a boy and covering his head so he wouldn't hear the little girls crying all over Fengshan. I didn't experience that as a child since foot binding had ended by then, but I do remember lots of weeping and tears associated with unbindings. Females suffered so much! Last week I read that suicide percentages among females in China are the highest in the world. If it's that bad now, think how much worse it used to be. . .

Chapter 18

Abbie's Journal
May 17, 2002
. . . stirring the swirling ingredients of a custard this afternoon made me think of Dad. He was the one who taught me this special Swedish custard he learned from his mother. Custard was a rare treat in Fengshan when he was young, for Gramma seldom had enough eggs, milk, sugar and vanilla to make it. Since the custard takes two hours and patience to bake it correctly, it's still a treat for my family. . .

. . . and vanilla reminds me how early in his missionary career, Dad learned to make imitation vanilla – a recipe he had promised to keep secret. So he always made it mysteriously late at night after everyone else was in bed. Dad's vanilla made him a popular guest among Westerners in inland China where it couldn't be bought. In my China boxes, several days ago in Dad's small worn black pocket notebook, I discovered the secret vanilla recipe in his neat, tiny printing. I rather think he wanted Phil and me to know the secret, or he would have torn out that page. . .

Windridge, USA, 1931
Year of Ram

Chesterton College in Windridge, Indiana, was a perfect place for students whose parents lived overseas, like the Newquist family. For them, tuition was waived even during the Depression years, thanks to generous donors.

The college campus was located in a wooded area with sand dunes and wetlands, just a few miles from the southern tip of beautiful Lake Michigan. Students loved to roam the beach with its spectacular dunes and sunsets. Romances often began under the spell of the Waters of Michigami, the campus's poetic nickname for the lake. Alfred and his brothers had experienced the spell, and in their letters teasingly warned their sister Abigail.

The town itself was as ideal a community as can be found. Camelot – alumni wistfully called it after they graduated and moved away. Its quaint downtown stores and parks were surrounded by streets of charming homes and lawns with flowering trees. Compared to Fengshan, well, each Newquist expatriate loved Windridge from first sight.

To them and all students, a bonus was the inexpensive commuter train running regularly to and from Chicago. What more could a college student want?

Nothing, Nils and Lizzie's children each decided when their turn came.

After Alfred had spotted the college advertisement in a church magazine with its enticing free tuition offer for children of missionaries, he applied and attended – even though MIT had offered him a full-ride scholarship. But he had wanted a college with missions and Bible classes, and so he chose Chesterton College. His brothers followed his lead, and years later so did Abigail.

One by one, they wrote to their parents describing how wonderful Chesterton College and the town of Windridge were. When they couldn't go home for breaks – which was all the time – or to Uncle Oliver's farm in Iowa, they were warmly welcomed by families from the Methodist Church in town, fondly called the College Church.

When Abigail was in her second year of the college's nursing program, she thought often about going back to China as a nurse. She hadn't told anyone yet – not even Mama or Mother Ruth. In her heart, she felt that's what God wanted her to do. But in her mind she didn't want to if it meant being a single nurse. She wanted to experience love and marriage, and the missionary nurses she knew in China were single.

Just thinking about returning to China as a nurse excited her and helped her not to feel so homesick. She didn't want to go to the small clinic in Fengshan. Instead, she dreamed of working in a large mission hospital, like the Methodist Hospital in Sian. That's where her appendix had been removed during her last year of high school, the year after her brother Alfred came back to live and work with their parents.

Abigail looked up from her chemistry textbook and gazed out the large window of the library where she was studying for a test. But she didn't see Chesterton College campus with its lovely spring trees and students strolling or hurrying about.

Instead, like a vision, she saw the familiar compound of the boarding school in Sian, and the afternoon she had been rushed to the hospital with a ruptured appendix. She remembered Mother Ruth's loving face looking down at her on the ground where she had collapsed, doubled over with excruciating pain.

"What is it Abigail, dear? Where do you hurt?" Mother Ruth had asked, concern cracking her voice.

Abigail could only moan. She remembered how the moans seemed to be coming from someone else far away. How she had felt her body crushed by huge claws of jagged pain.

"Quick," Mother Ruth said to Abigail's frightened girlfriend. "Get the headmaster!" And to another student, "Get the cart driver. Tell him to hitch up two mules instead of one. It's an emergency."

Abigail had jerked in and out of consciousness on the short ride to the hospital. She still vaguely remembered jolts of pain that made her retch and vomit and black out again and again. Days passed before her memory became clear. By then, Mama, Papa and Alfred were at her bedside with Mother Ruth.

One of her first questions had been, "How did you – how did you get here so fast?"

Alfred answered with a short laugh."Fast? To us it seemed to take forever. But then, we weren't unconscious like you. Do you know how long you've been in this bed?"

"About – about two days?"

Mama leaned over and stroked her cheeks. "No my dear, it's been ten days since your operation. Ten days since the doctor took out your appendix."

Then Papa took her hand and said, "We're so thankful Almighty God decided not to take you to heaven just yet." He was smiling, but Abigail remembered the tears running down from his eyes and onto his mustache.

Abigail had been in the hospital for a month. The last week she was often out of bed and walking around. She was curious to see everything the nurses allowed her to see. She had never before seen so much of a hospital. She liked it, and wanted to be part of it some day.

One evening when a nurse was helping her get ready for bed, Abigail realized she wanted to be like the nurse. She didn't actually hear God's voice calling her, though her heart felt like she had. She felt God wanted her to be a nurse in a hospital in China because a hospital could do so much more for patients than a clinic could.

Now three years later, she still felt God guiding her in the same direction.

*   *   *

Several days before Easter break, Abigail had special company. She knew Alfred was coming to see her, just not the exact day. His ship from Shanghai had arrived weeks ago in Seattle. Some days she could hardly bear the suspense of wondering when he would get to Windridge and she could be with him, and hear about dear Mama and Papa and the others back home in China.

Then suddenly he was there, standing at the dining hall door during the evening meal, waiting for her to notice him.

"Alfred," she cried out, stunned for a moment. The next moment, she jumped up from her table, forgetting to excuse herself as she rushed to greet him. To her great surprise, his former fiancee was hiding behind him.

"Meggie," Abigail screamed with delight and burst into tears.

Arms around each other, the three of them moved away from the understanding smiles of the other diners and into the student lounge.

After a few minutes of non-stop questions and answers, laughter and tears, Alfred said, "Guess what, little sis, we don't have to talk about everything right this minute. We're taking you with us tomorrow to Meggie's for Easter weekend. I already have the dean's permission."

He patted his pocket and paper rustled.

"Meggie and I haven't eaten since morning, so let's go back and have dinner before they shut down the dining hall."

That night, Alfred stayed with one of his classmates who was now the men's dorm head. Meggie slept with Abigail, thanks to an obliging roommate who spent the night with friends in the room across the hall.

After breakfast the next morning, Abigail and Meggie were ready to go before Alfred. As they waited for him, Abigail begged Meggie to let her sit behind Alfred on his motorcycle. Meggie laughingly gave up her spot, and agreed to ride instead in the sidecar.

Then Meggie whispered, "I can't wait any longer to

tell you. Your brother and I have a surprise for everyone this weekend."

Abigail's face lit up. "Oh Meggie, you're getting engaged again!"

"Better than that, we're getting married. Shh – let me finish. Last night while I listened to you talking so eagerly about going back to China as a nurse, I felt I should be willing to go too since I'm already a nurse. I don't think I have a special call from God. But Alfred does, so maybe that's enough. After so many years apart, I know I want to marry him – even if it means going to China and so far from home."

"Have you told Alfred?" Abigail stammered.

"Yes, of course, right before breakfast this morning. Then we asked ourselves, why not get married this weekend? So we are."

"Whatever will your parents say?"

"Shh, here comes Alfred. Let's talk about it later, after he's told you."

*   *   *

The couple made their surprise announcement that first evening home with Meggie's parents. They had just finished a delicious fried chicken dinner. Too full to eat their apple pie quickly, they were enjoying small, lingering bites and discussing who to invite for Easter Sunday dinner. Beyond the lace curtains of the dining room window, the sun was dropping behind the newly leafed elm trees.

Alfred stared at the trees while the others talked. When there was a pause, he blurted out, "I don't know if Meggie and I will be here on Sunday. We'll probably be on our honeymoon."

"What? Are you married?" her father said, tightly grasping the edge of the table.

"Not yet," Meggie said. "We want to marry this weekend. Here, of course."

She and Alfred nodded in unison, leaning forward tensely, their bodies touching.

"How many years now since you first talked about marriage?" Meggie's mother asked, dabbing her eyes with her napkin.

"We counted this morning," Meggie said. "It's been six years, six very long years."

Alfred nodded and put his arm around her.

Meggie's father cleared his throat. "I think we should pray." He reached out his hands and they all held hands.

Still seated at the table and with bowed heads, they held hands in a circle as if they were asking God's blessing on the meal again. When Meggie opened her eyes, her mother and Abigail were smiling at her. Both had glistening tear-spots on their cheeks.

"Yes, my dears, I too think it's about time you wed," Meggie's mother said. "I don't like the China part, but God will help me with that."

She took a deep breath and went on in a voice that quavered a bit. "So how about having the wedding on Saturday morning? That gives us two days to prepare. One day to shop for a dress for Meggie and a suit for Alfred and invite family. The second day to decorate the house with flowers from the garden and prepare a suitable wedding lunch. I just hope we can beg enough eggs from the neighbors to bake a proper wedding cake."

When she was quiet, they all looked at Meggie's father.

"Well, why not," he said slowly. "Money may be tight these days, but not too tight for a nice home wedding. I don't like the idea of my daughter in China, but I guess there are worse places."

After a flurry of phone calls and telegrams, Johann was one of a dozen or so relatives who made it to the wedding. He drove all the way from Iowa in a car borrowed from Uncle Oliver. Meggie's only sister couldn't make it because she was pregnant, so Abigail stood with Meggie, and Johann with Alfred before the Methodist minister. The young women were lovely in their new white dresses with bouquets of fresh garden flowers in their arms, and the brothers so handsome in their new gray striped suits.

Years later, they still had fun telling stories about Alfred and Meggie's family honeymoon. How they rode back to Iowa with Johann, their motorcycle on a trailer behind Uncle Oliver's Model T. How Abigail went too, after calling the college dean to tell him, not ask him for permission. They enjoyed laughing about that as they drove to Iowa. They all knew the dean, how strict and unbending he was, how he probably would have said "no" if given the chance.

"He couldn't threaten to flunk me," Abigail said. "I'm making all A's." And again they laughed.

As a honeymoon gift, Meggie's parents gave them money to stay in a hotel so they wouldn't have to drive through the night. The money was enough for two rooms, one for Alfred and Meggie and one for Abigail. Johann slept in the car.

The day after the honeymooners and their best man and maid of honor arrived at Uncle Oliver's farm, his daughter Dottie and her husband honored them with a picnic. Their friends and relatives came, including their brother Oliver and his wife and children. All brought hastily prepared wedding gifts along with their favorite dishes of food to share.

But the best treat, they all agreed, was homemade ice-cream. In fact, they enjoyed it so much, they splurged and made ice-cream every evening for the honeymooners, even though the weather was still chilly enough for sweaters.

"What delicious extravagance!" they exclaimed. Laughing and talking, they ate together on the front porch after the day's chores were done. And they never tired of playing the game of seeing who could make their bowl of ice-cream last the longest.

Too soon it was time to say goodbye. Uncle Oliver reminded them as he often did that he wasn't their real uncle. And one of them answered as always, "No, you're even better. You're Mama's special friend and she named our Oliver after you."

"*Ja!* We were best friends growing up," Uncle Oliver said. "I wanted to marry her, as you know. But look what a great Papa you have, and what extraordinary lives for God your parents have lived. I will write your parents tomorrow and tell them about these wonderful, wonderful days together."

He added, "Have they told you? In a few years, when it's time for them to retire and leave China, I've invited them to live here in this big house with me."

Then he looked at Meggie and said, "I know you're afraid to go to China, my dear. Don't be. I wish I had been brave enough to go when Lizzie went. Back then, I made myself think God needed me here more. When you're old like I am, sometimes you wonder if you chose right. Go happily to China with Alfred, Meggie. Go with God's blessing, and mine."

He placed his strong, warm hand on her shoulder to reassure her.

*   *   *

Fengshan

"Something good is happening to our children this Easter weekend," Lizzie said. "I feel it!"

She pressed her crossed hands over her heart and smiled at Nils across the breakfast table.

"*Ja*, maybe," Nils said. "But we know for sure something good is happening here."

"But of course! Let's get going. I hear people waiting for us at the gate."

In the front room, they picked up several large cloth bags and Lizzie's accordion, then walked through their courtyard to the gate.

"You know, Nils, this might be our last one here."

Nils nodded. "I've been thinking that. And it's only the third."

"Thank God there'll be many more now. It's much easier for the second generation of believers."

Outside the gate, they greeted the villagers waiting for them.

"*Ping-an!* Peace!"

"The Lord is risen!"

"He is risen indeed!"

"Peace! *Ping-an!*"

They walked together to the River. Hundreds more villagers joined them along the way. And hundreds more were already at the River when they got there.

Under the huge old weeping willow standing guard over the ancient stone wharf, Lizzie put on her accordion to lead the singing. She smiled and bowed to her many friends. She noted that most of the women there were without canes. They were walking and standing on unbound feet that were normal, or nearly normal. All the young girls had normal feet and pain-free faces. Probably not many others had noticed. But she had, and she knew Chu Sister had too.

Ja, it's been worth it, Lizzie thought. *Oh Lord God, today I can say it's been worth everything, even all the heartaches. Thank you, thank you for the fragrance of your grace in our lives.*

For months now, the entire village of Fengshan had been anticipating the sacrament of baptism on this Easter morning. The believers being baptized were a bit fearful, for death was never far from those who claimed the name of Christian. Although the unbelievers in the crowd didn't fully understand baptism, they knew it was a special event, especially this time.

For this time, Yang Magistrate and some others from Shinli had bravely given up being secret Christians, and were coming all the way to Fengshan to be baptized. The magistrate was even providing a feast afterwards for everyone. Cooks and other servants from the magistrate's palatial home had been in Fengshan preparing for days. This day's celebration promised to be as important as a New Year's or Dragon festival, and the villagers proudly wore their newest clothes.

I wish Wu Headman were here today, Lizzie thought, as she started to play a hymn on her accordion.

Soon the villagers were a great, joyous choir singing along with her in Chinese:

> Amazing grace how sweet the sound,
> that saved a wretch like me.
> I once was blind, but now can see,
> was lost but now am found. . .

After a couple of hours of singing, preaching and testimonies, it was time for Nils to baptize the new believers in the River. Bible men and women from Fengshan's Good News Hall assisted. They put white choir robes on those being baptized, and helped each one down the worn stone steps and into the water where Nils waited, wearing a white Mandarin long-gown.

After the new believers gave testimonies of faith,

they were immersed in the River in the name of *Zhen Shen* True God. Then the Christian helpers wrapped white blankets from the clinic around those newly baptized and guided them back up the wet, slippery steps.

A storm had passed through the Great Long River gorge the night before. The waters were still rough, and at times sprayed high in white dazzling shapes behind Nils.

"*Wah!* See!" a woman said to Chu Sister, and pointed towards Nils. "Today angels are in the River. Today the river gods are silent."

Chu Sister looked at Lizzie standing beside her. They nodded and smiled at each other and at the woman.

*   *   *

Abbie
May 30, 2002

. . . from time to time during my childhood, Dad lamented his mother's sudden death when he told me stories about her. He said he thought she died from a heart broken too many times. I remembered that today as I read again his translation of Grampa Nils's letter to his children in America. Grampa sent a brief telegram first, then the letter which arrived much later. Dad saved them both in a gold colored envelope, though most of the gold's worn off now. Grampa's words about Gramma make me grieve too – and I didn't know her or experience her family's sorrows. I think of the anguish her children and other loved ones must have felt, especially since they couldn't comfort each other or attend her burial. . .

. . .Grampa's letter says she died unexpectedly the evening of a special Easter baptism, probably from heart failure. He and her close Chinese friends filled her hastily made camphor-wood coffin with fragrant spices, then escorted her all the way to Sian to be buried beside Hilda and Oscar

and other Christians. During her last voyage on the Gospel Boat down the Yangtze, thousands of river people lined the shores, waving white cloths in grief and farewell, many singing hymns they had learned from her...

... after they reached Sian, Grampa writes he was stricken with remorse because he had not helped her more in her search for the Stone Ten Keepers. Now it was too late for him. So he hoped one of the children would do it for her – and for him. He longed for at least one of them to return to China soon. He was old and tired and ready to pass on the work to those younger and stronger...

... in the last part of Grampa's letter, he tells that when he returned home to Fengshan, the villagers had already placed a stone monument in Gramma's memory beneath the ancient sacred weeping willow by the River. Later, under the Chinese characters honoring Fengshan's Foreign Angel, Grampa chiseled the words she had chipped onto a bluff boulder beside the Des Moines River so long ago...

JESUS SAVES

Fear not, even in the RIVER,
I will be with you. Isa. 43

Epilog

Abbie's Journal
July 23, 2002
. . . three years now since our visit to China that made me start sorting through my parents' China boxes. It's taken longer than I expected, and I'm not finished yet because I can only bear to do a tiny bit at a time. All the looking and reading have been fascinating and – to my surprise – healing as well. Though I sometimes shed tears for hours after I read, I no longer look at my China family and see mostly tragedy, but instead mostly privilege and God's grace. . .
. . . to help record my discoveries, I've joined a memoir group at the library. We write our family's stories, then read them aloud to the group. Wow – it's great! I love hearing the stories of the others, and they are responsive to my China ones – especially my new writing pal Da-lin. The newspaper has even run a couple of my stories and an article about me. While my stories are different, they still appeal to others – like this story from my childhood. . .

"Go," my father Alfred said to Young Chu, our cook, who had insisted on accompanying us as we fled from the bombings and devastations of war.

"Go home, my brother. The time has come for you to leave us. Take your wife and your precious daughter and go to our home beside the Great Long River to live. I have heard the fighting is over there. Should anyone question you, here, here is the deed to Great House with the magistrate's chop. Hide it in your inner clothes. Please go, Young Chu – go now before they take you away because you are our friend."

Soon after I heard my father say those words, Cook and his wife and their little daughter left.

Now fifty years later, I see them again with memory's eyes. Cook was carrying all their belongings in two woven baskets that hung heavily from the ends of a stout bamboo pole balanced across his shoulders. Behind him, his wife carried a smaller bamboo pole loaded with food, their young daughter tied to her back. Her name was Heavenly Gift, but we always called her Mei-mei, Little Sister.

Looking down at us, Mei-mei laughed and waved to my brother Philly and me. Mei-mei had lived all her short life with us and didn't understand she was leaving. I wonder if she missed us as much as we missed her. I wonder if she grew up, married and had children who still live beside the Great Long River. I wonder if she is a believer.

"Never forget True God loves you. Always trust Him," my father said in farewell to the man who had been his loyal friend since their boyhood days together in Fengshan.

I felt pangs of fear when I saw tears running down my father's cheeks and onto his shirt. My mother tried to say something, but only choked sobs came out as she bowed to Cook's wife, our housemaid, who was like my mother's dear younger sister.

"Shieh shieh. Thank you, thank you, thank you," Cook and his wife murmured, bowing and backing away from us. "You have been too generous with us, much more than we deserve. We will never forget you, our foreign family. We will pray to True God of Heaven to bring us together again when the war is over."

I ran alongside them for a ways, calling out in Chinese to travel in peace and return safely to us soon. When Dad whistled to me from the gate where he was watching, I waved a last goodbye, then ran back to our compound, where we would soon be under compound arrest.

Cook was one of my special friends, and for a long time I felt a huge sadness inside me for him and his family. Back then, I didn't know they were gone from our lives forever.

I remember how Cook boiled our sugar to remove bugs and dirt. When it was clean and cool, he gave me sweet brown lumps to suck. Often he took me with him to the street market to shop for the vegetables and meat he cooked for our rice meals. In the evenings after the outside lanterns were lit, I liked to sit with him and his family beside our cool stone water cistern. Sometimes my parents and others joined us.

Cook liked me too. For his wedding, I remember wearing a new red silk Mandarin jacket and pants embroidered with lotus flowers. I felt so proud to stand with my father beside my friend and his shy, pretty bride.

We never again heard from Cook and his family.

A few years later when we were settled in Taiwan and no longer refugees, my father said he thought our hearing nothing from Young Chu had been a good sign. What did Mom and I think? Me? I didn't know. I said softly I hoped the Red Army hadn't shot them just because they were our friends. I hoped they were safe and happy and living in Gramma and Grampa's house above the river – that fierce hungry dragon river of so many of my family's China stories.

. . . one thing I do know – Cook and his family are among my thousand fragrant memories of China. And someday, True God of Heaven will bring our families together again – if not here on earth, then in eternity. . .

Acknowledgments

~ **To my wonderful family with love forever** – without God's hand of grace upholding us during the past century, our "Nilsson Stories" would have been very different. And without your tremendous support and help, our stories would not have become novels. So – *a thousand fragrant thanks to all you with Nelson ties, especially*: Dave; Marla, Peter, Eva and Else; Peter and Hilda; Rodney, Sharon and Joseph; Doug and JoJo, Millie and Chris, Kristie and Lindey; Canden and Katie, Aunt Bernice, Darlene and Warren, JoAnne; Uncle Hugo, Ruth, Helen, and Gus; Pauline and Merle; Beth and Bill; "Aunt" Angie. . . *with extra thanks* to my husband Dave for his ever-present support, and to my son Peter and my cousin Canden for their extraordinary editing and publishing assistance. . .

~ **To awesome friends and groups with great gratitude** – without your interest, information and enthusiasm touching my writing life, this word journey would have been very lonely. *So thanks forever*: Linda Wells, Melissa Rees, Jan Plummer, Terry Rhine, Sue Keiser, Katie Rizer, Joy Valek, Marcie Owens, four Valparaiso University scholar friends from China; Westchester Writers, Chesterton and Porter and Michigan City Library Book Clubs, Wild Women of Windridge, Chesterton United Methodist Church and Book Club, JOY CIRCLE, Bible 'n Life Class, Edward Jones friends, St. John's United Church Women's Guild, Portage United Methodist Women, Chesterton-Porter Rotary Club; Write-to-Publish Conference, Midwest Writers Workshop, Earlham School of Religion Writers Colloquium, University of Wisconsin Writers Institute; Central College dear colleagues and students, BYKOTA Sunday School Class, McPherson Pen-Inktons; Morrison Academy Alumni

Silver Chapter; Chesterton Tribune, Senior Life, The Beacher, Post-Tribune, The News Dispatch; and the Amy Foundation. **With a special second thanks to author buddy** Melissa Rees for the awesome gift of a framed painting print of the Yangtze River to keep me inspired on my trilogy writing journey. . .

~ **To my daily companion with lots of pats and hugs** – without you patiently beside me as I wrote every page and on hundreds of thinking walks, hey BT buddy, I couldn't have done it. *So duo shi*, Black Tongue, you gorgeous Chow-Rott! No doubt you dreamed of your China ancestors even as I wrote of mine. I hope someone is reading this story to you in heaven. . .

~ **To various agents and publishing editors – I** *greatly appreciate* that you've enhanced this novel with some excellent suggestions. But until there's a "real" publisher, you'd probably prefer to remain anonymous. . .

~ **To many marvelous authors** – who have immeasurably enriched and directed my life with their works**, *with special thanks to:*** John Wesley, Emily Bronte, Nathaniel Hawthorne, Louisa May Alcott, L.M. Montgomery, Oswald Chambers, Willa Cather, Pearl Buck, Frank Slaughter, Peter Marshall, C.S. Lewis, Harper Lee, Miss Read, D.E. Stevenson, Rosamunde Pilcher, Mary Stewart, Alex Haley, Calvin Miller, Frank Peretti, Amy Tan, Tony Hillerman, Lisa Huang Fleischman, Gail Tsukiyama, John Grisham, Gus Lee, Jan Karon, Charles Frazier, David McCullough, Adeline Yen Mah, Harry Petrakas, and so many others. . . *but above all, thanks to the Greatest Author ever, Almighty True God. . .*

~ *Millie Nelson Samuelson, 2005, 2011, 2015*

Author's Comments

The wonderful adventure of writing historical novels began for me, the real Abbie, on the eve of a new millennium – thanks to early retirement and a library memoir writing group in Chesterton, Indiana.

Until then, I had never completed a story in writing, though I told many during the decades I was a busy educator and homemaker. Those were the years I lived overseas or in Kansas – and completed instead hundreds of pages of college classroom lectures, academic documents, press releases, feature articles, and oh-so many letters, emails and novel notes.

To my amazement, my memoir stories have become novels, almost like three heirloom patchwork quilts – **Hungry River** (1889 to 1931), **Dragon Wall** (1933 to 1959), and **Jade Cross** (1962 to 2008). Inspired by my family's extraordinary lives in China, these story-quilts are pieced together with fictional borders. Though in truth, even the borders differ little from real life – they're just rearranged or borrowed from someone else's experience.

Some of the pieces in the story-quilts come from the journals and memoirs of my "Nilsson" grandparents who traveled up and down the Great Yangtze River during the late 1800s and early 1900s. Some pieces are from my own memory, such as our family's traumatic escape from China in 1950 down the Yangtze.

Other colorful pieces come from family letters and manuscripts – both published and unpublished. One of these is my mother's devoted portrayal of a special missionary woman. Lovingly known as Mother Ruth, this woman gave up a life of Swedish nobility and used her inheritance to serve God beside her husband in China, where their only children are buried.

The stories I've quilted together come from a

century of memories of my Anglo-American family who lived and traveled in China. Like my son who smuggled Bibles into China in the 1990s, we thought of ourselves as adventurers for God, although the Chinese often called us "foreign devils." Occasionally, however, we received the honor of being called "white Chinese" or *bai-zhong-ren.*

Centering on characters with mostly fictional names, my novels are told mainly in third person, and I'm the narrator. I chose for my aunt and myself the name disguise of Abigail and Abbie, after my favorite Old Testament character. (You can read her amazing story in I Samuel 25.) Most of what happens to Abbie in the novels, really happened to me. And as I am in real life to my dear Aunt Mildred, Abbie is the namesake of her Aunt Abigail, Alfred's sister and my real father Fred's younger sister.

Some of my characters are scarcely disguised – for example, my paternal grandparents who are the main characters in **Hungry River**. I like Gramma's nickname of Lizzie from Elizabeth too much to change it. Instead of his first name Philip, I call Grampa by his last name Nils, from Nilsson in Sweden or Nelson in America. I have given them the surname of Newquist, Gramma's actual maiden name, to honor maternal surnames.

Another whose name I didn't change was that of my grandparents' first child, Hilda. At age fifteen, she was brutally killed in a 1911 uprising in Sian – martyred, my family always said. How could I change her name! One of my cousins was named after her, and now I have a grand-darling also named after her.

My father was the seventh of nine Nelson children. In addition to Hilda, two brothers died as babies in China. Like most of his siblings, Dad was born in China and the one perhaps most often identified as white Chinese. Dad's Swedish-American name was Albin Fridolf Nelson. In time, he changed it to A. Fred Nelson. His Chinese name was always *Nieh Fu De*. In my novels, the character Dad inspires is Alfred Newquist, and his character blends traits and experiences from his real brother Oscar. His other brothers – Theodore, Arthur and Edward – inspire the characters of Oliver and Johann. Alfred and his granddaughter Jeanne, who is Abbie's daughter, are both intrigued by their Swedish roots, as is my own daughter Marla Jean.

I use other slight name disguises as well. For example, my maternal grandmother was Cynthia Nettie (Clark) Ivers. In life, she was called Nettie – in my stories, Cynthia McIvers. Her daughter, my mother, was Blanche Lucretia (Ivers) Nelson. I renamed her Omega or Meggie for *alpha and omega* symbolism. Alfred and Meggie are two of the main characters in Book Two, **Dragon Wall**. Abigail is the third main character. She is Nils and Lizzie's youngest child and Alfred's sister. All three are introduced in **Hungry River**.

Some of my story people are combinations from real life – such as my three older brothers who died in China during wartime conditions around 1940. In the retelling, Abbie has two older brothers who died, similar to my surviving brother and me. My younger brother Doug inspires the trilogy character named Philip – in memory of our Grampa Philip and our brothers Philip, Daniel and Donald who were buried in China.

In addition to combining my uncles and brothers, I also combine my sons Peter and Rodney into Abbie's one son. His name is Marlan, a combination of my sons' middle names Mark and Allan. In real life, their father and my husband is David Samuelson. Of course in the Bible story, King David became the original Abigail's husband and so would be a fitting name for my character's husband. However, I rename him Daniel Samson – two more name disguises provided by unforgettable Biblical characters. He and Abbie are introduced as a couple in **Dragon Wall**, and featured in **Jade Cross**.

Just as my Anglo characters are named for special people and reasons, so are my Chinese characters. For obvious reasons, I think, you need to ask me about them in private.

Besides characters' names, I have also chosen place names with purpose and care. Most are real places – with two main exceptions. Fengshan along the Great Long River is not a real place (at least according to my research). However, as I've imagined it, Fengshan is very like places my parents and grandparents lived in China. The name means Wind Mountain, and is the name of a town in Taiwan where my family did once live. Interestingly, the street address in America where I wrote about Fengshan is Windridge Drive. . . wind ridge, wind mountain. Hmm. . . I didn't notice the connection until long after I'd chosen the name Fengshan and my first novel was mostly written.

For many decades, I was deprived of even visiting my birthland because of the Communists. In 1950 when my family fled from China to Taiwan, we left behind our home and friends, as well as many graves of relatives and close friends. I still feel that separation sorrow. So even though several places in America are dear to my heart, I'm never sure how to answer the question, "Where are you from?"

These places dear to my heart I have combined into the fictional Windridge, Indiana, in my novels. Like Fengshan in China, Windridge is reminiscent of the wonderful places my family has lived in America – especially the towns of Boone, Mt. Carmel, Rockford, Janesville, McPherson, and Chesterton.

Since the people and places in my story-quilts are very real – or in some instances, close representations. So I make no similarity coincidence disclaimer. I just hope my loved ones enjoy recognizing themselves and the places they've lived, while remembering that individual perceptions may differ (especially from a long-distance view), and that occasionally my novels are truly fiction.

Fashioning a trilogy of heirloom story-quilt novels has been personally rewarding beyond all expectations! As I examined my family's records and mementoes long stored in my China and Taiwan boxes, I was deeply touched by the meaningful pattern in story that emerged from the memories – memories daring, tragic, and joyous.

But most importantly, my family's stories affirm the blessings of faith in God through Jesus Christ – a faith available to every person, in every country, of every millennium!

~ *Millie Nelson Samuelson*

Author's Notes

Photos in My Trilogy:
The photos in my trilogy are from my Nelson/Samuelson family's collection. My father, missionary Fred Nelson, took many of them. He often included himself in photos by using a tripod, or by handing his camera to someone else. Why am I including photos in my novels? About fifteen years ago I read *Cane River*, Lalita Tademy's fascinating novel based on her Louisiana family. Her historical novel included a number of her family's photos and clippings. I thought at the time: *What a great way to enrich and authenticate a story. I want to do that with my novels.* And so I have! Someday maybe I'll caption all the photos, but those I haven't I think are described by the storyline.

Chinese Astrology:
The Holy Bible does not say astrology is false, but God's people (believers) are warned NOT to follow astrology (I Samuel 15:23 is one example passage). I believe as I have been taught – we are warned so we won't let astrology take dominance in our lives instead of God. While the Newquists (Nelsons in real life) certainly did not follow Chinese astrology, they knew it was highly important to the Chinese and therefore information they needed to know. That's why I've noted the Chinese astrological year for each chapter along with the Western year.

Chinese Romanization:
I have used the Chinese Romanization (phonetic spelling) of Wade-Giles that I grew up with, not the more recent one of Pinyin decreed by the People's Republic of China.

Sanpan vs. Sampan

I've chosen to use the Mandarin *sanpan*, meaning "three boards boat," instead of the more familiar Cantonese *sampan*.

Scripture quotations are from The Wesley Bible, a New King James Version:

Newquist Family Timeline
for *Hungry River*

(Many of these dates are similar to my/Millie's own family's dates.)

1864 – Nils William Newquist is born in Sweden.
1869 – Elizabeth/Lizzie Abigail Beckman is born in Sweden.
1873 – Lizzie's family emigrates from Sweden to America and settles in Iowa.
1889 – *Hungry River* begins in Fengshan, China, with a tragic drowning in the Lin family.
1891 – Lizzie arrives in Shanghai with Bertil and Ruth Carlson, all early scouts for the Salvation Army.
1892 – Nils arrives in Shanghai, a crewman with the *Sverige Ericsson* merchant ship. When he is severely injured by a mob, Lizzie takes care of him and their romance begins.
1895 – Nils and Lizzie marry in September in Shanghai. Nils becomes an American citizen.
1896 – Nils and Lizzie travel up the Yangtze to Fengshan for the first time with Wang Sister and Chu Boatman.
1897 – Hilda Cecilia Newquist is born in Shanghai.
1900 – Twins Alfred Nils and Adolph Nils Newquist are born in Fengshan.
1900 – Baby Adolph dies as the Newquists escape from the Boxers down the Yangtze. They flee tumultuous China and arrive in Des Moines, Iowa.
1901 – Oscar Charles Newquist is born in Des Moines.
1903 – Nils and Charlie Beckman, Lizzie's brother, travel to Sweden to visit Nils's family.
1904 – Oliver Nils Newquist is born in Des Moines while his father Nils is still in Sweden. Nils, Charlie, and Ruth Carlson return from Sweden to Des Moines. Nils, Lizzie,

their children and Ruth return to Shanghai.

1905 – They all move to Fengshan. Johann Adolph Newquist is born in Fengshan.

1907 – Great House is finished and they move in.

1909 – Hilda goes to Sian to boarding school for the first time.

1911 – Alfred and Oscar go to Sian to boarding school for the first time. Hilda, Oscar and other children and teachers in the school die at the hands of rioting rebels, and are buried in the Sian Christian cemetery. Lizzie, Alfred, Oliver and Johann flee to Sweden with Ruth, while Nils remains in China.

1912 – Abigail Hilda Newquist is born in Sweden while her father Nils is still in China.

1913 – Lizzie and her children travel to Iowa with Ruth.

1914 – Nils reunites with Lizzie and their children in Iowa.

1915 – Nils, Lizzie, Johann, and Abigail return to China along with Ruth, while Alfred and Oliver remain with "Uncle" Oliver Bergstrom in Iowa.

1922 – Johann returns to America to live with "Uncle" Oliver Bergstrom and finish high school. Abigail goes to Sian to boarding school for the first time.

1926 – Alfred returns to China alone to work with his parents.

1929 – Abigail goes to America to attend college.

1931 – Alfred returns to America and marries Meggie (Omega McIvers). Lizzie dies unexpectedly in Fengshan, and Nils buries her in Sian beside Hilda and Oscar. The Stone Keepers are still a mystery. ***Hungry River*** ends.

*   *   *

1933 – ***Dragon Wall*** begins, and ends in 1959.

1962 – ***Jade Cross*** begins, and ends in 2008.

Key to the Journal Dates
in *Hungry River*

In love and tribute to my family, each of Abbie's Journal month dates is the same as an important event in our lives (but not the year). Probably these are mainly of interest to relatives. . .

Prolog: July 4, 1999 (1776 – US Independence Day)
Chapter 1: Feb 17, 2000 (1942, Millie's birth, China; 1967, Millie Jo's birth, USA); Feb 24, 2000 (1909, Mom Blanche's birth, USA)
Chapter 2: Mar 20, 2000 (1933, Gramma Lizzie's death, USA); Apr 13, 2000 (1869, Gramma Lizzie's birth, Sweden)
Chapter 3: Apr 20, 2000 (1974, Doug and JoJo's marriage, USA); May 6, 2000 (1864, Grampa Philip's birth, Sweden)
Chapter 4: May 20, 2000 (2003, Rodney and Sharon's marriage, USA); May 26, 2000 (1933, Dad Fred and Mom Blanche's marriage, USA)
Chapter 5: Aug 1, 2000 (1986, Peter and Marla's marriage, USA); Aug 18, 2000 (1964, Marla's birth, USA)
Chapter 6: Sep 1, 2000 (1962, Dave and Millie's marriage, USA); Sep 16, 2000 (1946, JoJo's birth, USA)
Chapter 7: Dec 20, 2000 (1972, Rodney's birth, USA); Dec 28, 2000 (1998, Hilda's parents' marriage)
Chapter 8: Feb 6, 2001 (1991, Eva's birth, USA); Feb 12, 2001 (1904, Dad Fred's birth, China)
Chapter 9: Feb 26, 2001 (1946, Doug's birth, USA); Mar 15, 2001 (1937, Dannie's birth, China)
Chapter 10: Mar 29, 2001 (1935, Philip's birth, China); July 16, 2001 (1940, Donnie's birth, China)
Chapter 11: July 26, 2001 (1938, Dannie's death, China); Oct 7, 2001 (1994, Else's birth, Navajo Nation, USA)

Chapter 12: <u>Oct 10</u>, 2001 (1913, Double Tenth Day, China becomes a Republic); <u>Nov 22</u>, 2001 (Thanksgiving Day)
Chapter 13: <u>Nov 27</u>, 2001 (1984, Lindey's birth, USA); <u>Dec 25</u>, 2001 (Christmas, Christ's Birth, God's Greatest Gift of all to all!)
Chapter 14: <u>Jan 9</u>, 2002 (1981, Kristie's birth, USA); <u>Jan 31</u>, 2002 (2003, Hilda's birth, USA)
Chapter 15: <u>Feb 9</u>, 2002 (1962, Peter's birth, USA); <u>Feb 14</u>, 2002 (1968, Peter's birth, Taiwan)
Chapter 16: <u>Mar 6</u>, 2002 (1942, Philip's death, China; Mar ? 1949, Grampa Philip's death, USA); <u>Mar 9</u>, 2002 (1980, Sharon's birth, USA); <u>Mar 10</u>, 2002 (1941, Dave's birth, USA)
Chapter 17: <u>Mar 17</u>, 2002 (1992, Dad Fred's death, USA); <u>Mar 27</u>, 2002 (1895, Grampa Philip and Gramma Lizzie's marriage, China)
Chapter 18: <u>May 17</u>, 2002 (1969, Chris's birth, USA); <u>May 30</u>, 2002 (1941, Donnie's death, China)
Epilog: <u>July 23</u>, 2002 (1991, Mom Blanche's death, USA)

An Excerpt from

Dragon Wall:
A Great Wall Novel

Millie Nelson Samuelson
Yesterday's Stories for Today's Inspiration

Book Two
Yangtze Dragon Trilogy

Dragon Wall
Prolog

Abbie's Journal
September 11, 2002
. . . OH GOD, OH DEAR GOD – how well I remember Mom moaning that prayer over and over when her anguish in war-ravaged China was too great to bear. On today's unforgettable anniversary, I too moan the terrors of war. At the same time, I'm so proud of America, so grateful for the heroism of Americans here and overseas. This evening, some news clips from Hussein's Iraq were shown on CNN, declaring Americans live in fear since 9-11 last year, and our leaders too. Those poor, deluded people – they just have no concept of our vast freedoms and power and fearlessness, nor of our lack of ambition to conquer for the sake of conquering. . .

. . . on my desk, I have a daily reminder from my China boxes of the dreadful cost of conquest. It's a piece of the ancient Great Wall – one of Grampa Nils's precious mementos, passed on to Dad and now to me. Whenever I hold it in my hand, I ponder its history. Not long ago, I read online many Chinese can't understand the fascination of foreigners for the Great Wall. Sure, they're glad for the tourism money it brings. But to them the Wall is a symbol of unimaginable oppression and conquest. Let it crumble and fall away – they say – it's a reminder of millions and millions of tragic deaths. Living my childhood in the shadow of the Wall, I often heard its dreadful stories. Like my young Chinese playmates, I thought of it as a huge dragon, a twin to our family's dragon Yangtze River – as both could be fearsome and mysterious, and not to be slighted for fear of what might happen. . .

. . . *several months ago, I read a touching Wall story by Jim Clayton. His story went something like this:*

Centuries ago, one of China's emperors spent his entire reign expanding the Great Wall to keep barbarians out and his subjects in. Millions of men and lads were conscripted and sent north to the Wall as laborers. Few returned home, and the wailing of wives and mothers could be heard throughout the land. Laborers daily witnessed horrible deaths, then were forced to pound the bodies into the Wall along with stones and clay. No one had friends for long, as few survived the torturous conditions.

One day a man noticed the friend who slaved beside him was shivering and staggering. Ai yah – he mourned – I am so sorry. He took off his tattered outer garment and put it on his friend. And he worked harder so the guards wouldn't notice his friend was scarcely working.

That evening, his friend was too weak to stand in line for the small portion of rice gruel and tea allotted to each, so the man brought his own portion to his friend, and went hungry and thirsty. Though exhausted, the man stayed awake during the night to comfort his dying friend. In the darkness before dawn, he struggled to bury his friend's body in secret and thus appease their pagan gods. But alas, he was discovered and brutally killed by the guards.

Meanwhile, on the other side of the world, an Irish Christian monk who spent his days in a monastery fervently praying for the heathen and carefully copying the Holy Scriptures to save them for future generations, wrote these words of Christ – I was thirsty and you gave me water to drink. I was hungry and you fed me. I was cold and you gave me your garment. You did all these for me. Now welcome home, my deeply loved and worthy friend. You will share in my Kingdom forever and ever.

. . . wow, what a story – as the Chinese say, one to ponder for a thousand fragrant years. It's no wonder the Great Wall, like the Great River, is one of China's dragons. . .

Dragon Wall
Chapter 1

Abbie's journal
Oct 10, 2002
. . . today is the Double Tenth National Day – like a Chinese Fourth of July. And I understand better than many what it stands for. I remember all those decades of bloody revolutions and riots and wars my family lived through. I've been thinking I should do something meaningful with what's in my family's China boxes. Maybe even write a book. Scary thought, to be sure! But why just stash away my journals on top of those of my parents and grandparents. . . if I don't do something with our China stories, who will? And in time, some descendant or stranger will throw away our boxes of aging papers – like I almost did before my amazing trip back to China two years ago. . .

Shanghai, 1933
Year of Rooster

Every few minutes, the young female mourner paused from her loud wailing. She wiped her face with a grimy cloth, and peeked curiously at the people crowded along the street watching the funeral procession pass. This was Li-ming's first experience as a paid mourner in Shanghai.

She was hot and sticky in the stiff white mourning robe and hood covering her patched, dirty clothes. But she barely noticed her discomfort as she gazed at the amazing city where she had arrived just yesterday by ox cart.

Several weeks ago, she and her cousin had disguised themselves as boys and run away from their ancestral home in the remote village of Twentieth Tower

Gate of China's Great Wall. Soon to be married to old widowers, they both agreed in secret they would rather die escaping than live forever miserable. And so one moonless night, they fled from the serpentine shadow of the Great Dragon Wall, with their stolen cash dowries securely hidden in their underwear.

After weeks of perilous travel, they had arrived at Shanghai's East Gate, dust-covered, hungry, and their dowries mostly spent. There the plump manager of the Shanghai Sang-fu Mourning Company, with a leering smile, offered them food, work and housing. Li-ming and her cousin had looked at each other and accepted without any deliberation. Each desperately hoped their work as paid mourners would soon erase their impoverished past, and in time, even repay their families.

The two had rejoiced at this good fortune bestowed by the gods, and stopped to burn incense at the first shrine they passed on their way to the Mourning Company. However, the idols were silent, and neglected to tell them that paid wailing by day would soon be accompanied by far more unpleasant duties at night. And that their chances of living past age twenty were now few.

As the newest mourners, Li-ming and her cousin walked last in the long funeral procession. They followed dozens of other paid mourners, a sign of the deceased's family's wealth and status. Ahead of the mourners, Li-ming could see the musicians, whose flutes and strings sounded a dismal, off-key dirge, with occasional pauses for piercing clangs from cymbals.

In front of the instruments, the family idols paraded along on the shoulders of coolies. These fierce-faced statues, clothed in soot-darkened silk brocades, rode haughtily on black and gold sedan platforms. The smoke from rows of pungent incense burning before each idol wafted upwards. Shaven-headed priests and monks in their best robes and sandals escorted the idols, along with idols on loan from the city's largest temple.

Mixed in with the idols and priests were numerous ox-drawn carts loaded with extravagant food offerings. Li-ming had heard other mourners comment that Fan Merchant was making sure the funeral of his number-one wife made up for his well-known neglect during her life. He obviously had no intention of being avenged by her unhappy ghost.

I would not mind being neglected, Li-ming thought, *if my husband had money. Besides, if I did not like him, I would want him to have others and not bother me.*

In front of the idols, the lacquered wooden coffin swung heavily from a stout wooden pole, balanced on the shoulders of coolies. Six in front, six behind, all wore identical white mourning robes and headbands. From time to time, the coolies staggered from the weight of the load. Then they paused, and chanted together as they resumed their swaying march.

Accompanying the coffin were coolie-carts carrying elaborate paper houses, paper servants, and other paper effects to be burned at the deceased woman's tomb for her use in the after-life. These were lavish works of art, and onlookers gasped at the splendor soon to be Mistress Fan's. When Li-ming viewed these earlier, she had whispered to her cousin that maybe they could become second wives or concubines of rich men. Her cousin had glumly replied they were not pretty enough. And besides, they had ugly, large peasant feet.

"With beautiful clothes and styled hair, we could be pretty. And I have heard large feet are becoming fashionable," Li-ming had whispered back, trying to smooth her coarse black braid.

When she heard the young man leading the procession was the departed woman's only surviving child and unmarried, Li-ming stared openly at him. Dressed in expensive clothes under his mourning robe, he carried his mother's gold-framed portrait with dignity as he strode down the street. He cried out and struck his chest in grief at appropriate intervals. His father followed, seated in one of the family's gleaming black and chrome private rickshaws, pulled by a uniformed servant.

Behind Fan Merchant and the idols came dozens of other family members, relatives and friends. The strong, younger ones walked. Older men, women with bound feet, and middle-aged women with half-bound feet rode in sedan chairs carried by servants or in hired rickshaws.

*   *   *

Unknown to Li-Ming and her cousin, they were observed by two young women staring at the procession from the doorway of a cloth shop on Nan Ching Dong Lu Street.

"*Wah!*" the first young woman said to her companion. "See those last two? They are the newest ones, are they not? They look like ignorant country girls, the same as we were. We must tell Lin Teacher about them as soon as we get back to the shop. Maybe she will find a way to rescue them in time like she did us."

A few minutes later, the two young women were startled to see someone else of interest in the crowded street. A large, elderly foreigner with eyes closed sped past them in a rickshaw that nearly bumped into them.

"*Hai,* clumsy coolie! Watch where you are going!" the second young woman shouted.

The foreigner jerked his shoulders, but didn't open his eyes to look at them. If he had, he would have seen the startled look on their faces.

An Excerpt from

Jade Cross:

A Stone Ten Novel

Millie Nelson Samuelson
Yesterday's Stories for Today's Inspiration

Book Three
Yangtze Dragon Trilogy

Jade Cross
Prolog

Centuries ago near the end of the Tang Dynasty, an ancient scroll was inscribed with these Chinese characters and secreted in a monastery in near the Great Wall:

When I, an aged and nameless Buddhist monk, opened the courtyard gate late yesterday afternoon, a woman stood before me whose face and body were masked by heavy cloth, and whose feet were as large as a man's. In one hand, she held more imperial gold pieces than I had seen in a long time. With the other, she directed a sword at my heart. I quickly led her to a private area. There in a low voice, harsh and trance-like, she narrated this extraordinary occurrence for me to record.

It happened, she said, on a night with no moonlight or starlight – a black night, one to beware of wandering spirits. She paused when a serving boy brought us tea, which she sipped briefly beneath her face covering.

Continuing her account, she explained how she was the woman the others had chosen to hide and watch and make this secret report of what she witnessed. She had hidden where her husband instructed her to, far outside the safety of their city's wall, but within the Great Wall. The terrain was rocky, with scattered bushes and trees, but no dwellings or people. In a nearby valley, she knew with sorrow that jagged ruins still smoldered. They were the remains of her people's temple destroyed by order of China's new imperial dynasty.

The woman was weary and stiff by the time a column of men staggered into view. They were bent over, their faces nearly touching the earth as they pulled and heaved what she soon realized was her people's holy stele. The men were disguised as imperial executioners, and not one of them did she recognize. So she did not know if her husband was one of them, and she has not asked him.

The men stopped near her hiding place, gasping for breath and rubbing their sweating bodies with rags. Then with frenzied motions they took turns digging a deep pit several times larger than a burial hole. While most of the men dug, a few stood guard or paced around, peering into the darkness with their spears drawn. She thought she heard footsteps and whispers from the blackness beyond the pit, but she saw no one, nor did she know what to expect since had she not been told the full plan in case she was captured.

When the pit was finished, the men knelt awkwardly beside their holy stone. The woman praised their courage for doing what the emperor had forbidden and threatened with death by a thousand cuts. While they knelt, she counted twelve men.

Rising from their brief obeisance, with great effort and muffled groans, the men lowered the stone that was twice the height of a man into the pit. As they did so, she could faintly see its engraved symbols and characters, once reverenced but now disgraced, slide from view.

With amazing speed, the men refilled the pit with earth, and planted a partially grown tree on the spot. They stomped down the surface before covering the area with rocks and twigs. While she was admiring how cleverly the task had been completed, suddenly one of the men rushed to her hiding place and thrust a heavy bundle into her hands. Do as you will be instructed tomorrow, he whispered, bowing and stepping backwards away from her. A moment later, he and the other men disappeared into the darkness. In fear and awe, she fell to her knees. She could not remember what happened during the next hours until she found herself entering her home, wondering where to hide the heavy bundle straining her arms.

That is all you need to write, were the woman's final words to me. We sat in silence while she sipped more tea, and my brush strokes dried. When I handed her the scroll, rolled and tied, she rose and bowed. I escorted her to the gate.

She knows I will keep her secret, for I do not want to risk losing my coming nirvana. Ai-yah! Indeed I will keep her secret. But I also feel compelled to make this second scroll, and that she does not know. My heart tells me although I do not understand the significance of what I have recorded here, someday someone will find this scroll who understands. Peace. Peace. Peace.

Jade Cross
Chapter 18

A Yangzi River Town, 2006
Year of Canine

Far up the Great River in an ancient town on its banks, a mysterious relic had been lacquered and treated centuries ago to look like worthless wood. At some point in time, old cloths and straw rope were wrapped around it for further disguise.

The sacred relic was the secret possession of the Chen family – a secret passed down from mother to daughter generation after generation since the tenth century. Chen family members, both female and male, had died guarding the secret. But for years now, no one even whispered about it.

To the dismay of Chen Lee-mei, the secret itself might soon be dead. Her mother had told her the relic was a ten shape – a priceless, sacred jade ten. But to discover its secret, she needed to find the ancient scroll that explained it and why it was in her family. And time was running out.

Ai yah, ai yah, Lee-mei moaned as she stood in her dismantled home, folding her hands tightly and frantically looking around one last time. *What indeed is the meaning of this relic? And why has my family protected it with our lives and hidden it for hundreds of years in our ancestral homes?*

She shuddered, remembering from years earlier the shouting Red Guards viciously grabbing her mother who was clutching her and saying softly into her ear, "Lee-mei, older daughter, you are too young, but today you must become the keeper of our family's precious secret. Remember all I have taught you. Late last night I rehid the Scroll of the Stone Ten in. . . ."

Savagely silenced by a teeth-shattering blow from a guard, her mother hadn't finished before she sank to the ground and was dragged away. Nor did Lee-mei ever see her again or hear what happened to her. Nor could Lee-mei remember being taught much about her family's secret, except she was never ever to speak of it.

In the decades since then and sometimes for years at a time, she forgot about the relic and its scroll, and she blocked out the memory of her bleeding, unconscious mother. But now that her ancestral home and lands were soon to be covered by waters from the great new dam on the River, she needed desperately to find them. For what would happen if she lost the secret of her family's ancient, sacred treasure?

Lee-mei sighed, and another shudder of fear spread over her. *I guess it is time to tell my sister and my daughter. It is time to ask for their help in my search. Maybe tomorrow, while we are working at the new town and no one else is around, I can talk with them. Maybe they have kept secrets from me, too. . .*

Yangtze Dragon Trilogy
Millie Nelson Samuelson

Millie Nelson Samuelson's books are available from Amazon.com in paperback and Kindle, and autographed from her website (below):

Yangtze Dragon Trilogy
  Hungry River: A Yangtze Novel
  Dragon Wall: A Great Wall Novel
  Jade Cross: A Stone Ten Novel

Women of the Last Supper: Fourth Edition

A Missionary Memoir by A. Fred Nelson

Nathaniel Hawthorne: Lessons from an Early American Homeschooler, 2016

Yesterday's Stories for Today's Inspiration

 **Stone Light Books**

www.milliesbooks.org